**Introducing a deliciously sinful
and witty new trilogy from**

Bronwyn Scott

Rakes Beyond Redemption

Too wicked for polite society…

They're the men society mamas warn their daughters
about…and the men that innocent debutantes
find scandalously irresistible!

The notorious Merrick St Magnus knows just
HOW TO DISGRACE A LADY
September 2012

The untameable Ashe Bevedere needs no lessons in
HOW TO RUIN A REPUTATION
October 2012

The shameless Riordan Barrett
is an unequalled master in
HOW TO SIN SUCCESSFULLY
November 2012

Be sure not to miss any of these sexy men!

AUTHOR NOTE

Welcome to *Rakes Beyond Redemption*. If this is your first look at the series or your last because you've been with us the whole way it doesn't matter! Each of the three books stands alone quite well. But why miss one when the series features *three* sexy men? If you're just joining us, let me catch you up.

The premise of the series is to explore how three second sons are transformed by family or personal crisis from their fast-living, hard-loving lifestyles to being men who take pride in their families and position in society. Really, the ultimate Regency make-over.

In Book One, HOW TO DISGRACE A LADY, Merrick finds himself at the heart of a wager that compromises the honour of a lady. In Book Two, HOW TO RUIN A REPUTATION, Ashe must rise to the challenge of meeting the conditions of his father's will in order to save the earldom. In Book Three, HOW TO SIN SUCCESSFULLY, Riordan has instant fatherhood thrust upon him when he inherits two young wards.

Enter Maura, governess number six. She enchants both the children…and Riordan! But in order to hold true to her principles Maura knows she'll have to resist the charming Earl—unless he can convince her one can sin successfully…

Happy reading!

Bronwyn

PS It's the gentlemen who get all the action in *Rakes Beyond Redemption*, but it's the ladies who set the *ton* on its ear next, in my forthcoming duet. Stay tuned for more about two women who redefine what it means to be a lady.

HOW TO SIN
SUCCESSFULLY

Bronwyn Scott

First published in Great Britain 2012
by Mills & Boon, an imprint of Harlequin (UK) Limited.
Harlequin (UK) Limited, Eton House, 18-24 Paradise Road,
Richmond, Surrey TW9 1SR

© Nikki Poppen 2012

ISBN: 978 0 263 89276 5

Harlequin (UK) policy is to use papers that are natural, renewable
and recyclable products and made from wood grown in sustainable
forests. The logging and manufacturing process conform to the
legal environmental regulations of the country of origin.

Printed and bound in Spain
by Blackprint CPI, Barcelona

Previous novels from Bronwyn Scott:

PICKPOCKET COUNTESS
NOTORIOUS RAKE, INNOCENT LADY
THE VISCOUNT CLAIMS HIS BRIDE
THE EARL'S FORBIDDEN WARD
UNTAMED ROGUE, SCANDALOUS MISTRESS
A THOROUGHLY COMPROMISED LADY
SECRET LIFE OF A SCANDALOUS DEBUTANTE
UNBEFITTING A LADY†
HOW TO DISGRACE A LADY*
HOW TO RUIN A REPUTATION *

†*Castonbury Park* Regency mini-series
**Rakes Beyond Redemption* trilogy

And in Mills & Boon® Historical *Undone!* eBooks:

LIBERTINE LORD, PICKPOCKET MISS
PLEASURED BY THE ENGLISH SPY
WICKED EARL, WANTON WIDOW
ARABIAN NIGHTS WITH A RAKE
AN ILLICIT INDISCRETION

And in M&B:

PRINCE CHARMING IN DISGUISE
(part of *Royal Weddings Through the Ages*)

For my extraordinary husband and my awesome kids,
who all are so patient with my writing schedule,
and the puppy, Apollo, who isn't. I love you all.

Prologue

May 1835, London—the official opening of the Season

Rumour held that Riordan Barrett could bring a woman to climax at fifteen feet using only his eyes. At close range, the possibilities were endless, just like the lush curves of Lady Meacham's delectable body. Riordan rested a light hand on the small of said lady's back, contemplating those possibilities as he ushered her through the throng gathered at Somerset House to mark the beginning of the Season with the annual Royal Academy art exhibition.

Lady Meacham tossed him a coy glance that left no doubt she was thinking the same. He knew what she wanted, what they all wanted; she wanted the rumours to be true. She wanted to experience the pleasure he was reputed to offer. He wanted it, too, wanted to lose himself in it for a little while. He was good at that— losing himself in pleasures. Cards, wagering, racing, drinking, the usual vices of a gentle- man—he knew them all. He was no stranger to the debauches of the *demi-monde* or the bed- chambers of other men's wives. He and the Lady Meachams of the world both knew why. 'Plea- sure' was just another word for 'escape', a less- desperate word.

Desperate already and the Season had only just begun. When had the glitter of a London spring full of balls and beautiful women lost its shine? Riordan shook off the thought and ma- noeuvred Lady Meacham in front of Turner's latest: a depiction of the burning of the House of Lords and Commons which had taken place last October. If this went well, he'd spend the afternoon immersed in Lady Meacham's volup- tuous charms, sprawled in his bed, forgetting.

Riordan bent to Lady Meacham's ear and began the game in earnest. 'Note how Turner's brush conveys the energy of the flames, how the use of yellows and reds depicts the molten temperatures of the inferno.' The light sweep of his fingers against her arm suggested he was stoking a different fire. Lady Meacham's perfume filled his nostrils with its expensive, heavy scent. He preferred something sweeter, fresher.

'You're quite the expert on, ah, stroke technique,' Lady Meacham murmured, her body angling subtly so that her breasts brushed the sleeve of his coat in discreet invitation.

'I'm an expert at a great many things, Lady Meacham,' Riordan replied in private tones.

'Perhaps you should call me Sarah.' She tapped his sleeve playfully with her furled fan. 'You're so well informed. I must ask, do you paint, yourself?'

'I dabble a bit.' He'd painted with more aspiration than dabbling once upon a time. But somewhere between then and now, painting had stopped occupying a central place in his life, much to his regret and to his surprise. He couldn't recall how it had happened, only that he no longer painted.

Lady Meacham, *Sarah*, looked up at him from beneath long lashes, a smug smile playing on her lips. 'And what is it that you paint?'

This conversation was going precisely where they both intended it. Riordan had his response ready.

'Nudes, Sarah. I paint nudes. They tell me it tickles.' Lady Meacham gave a throaty laugh at his naughty innuendo, the final confirmation she was willing to forgo Somerset House's over-heated Great Room for a more comfortable address off Piccadilly and his brushes.

Her hand lingered overlong on his sleeve in a communication of familiarity. 'There really is no speck of decency in you, is there?'

Riordan covered her gloved hand with his, his voice a low leonine rumble for her alone. 'Not a scrap, I'm afraid.'

Her eyes lit at the possibilities the phrase invoked, a coy, knowing smile on her kissable mouth. 'I find that quality positively delicious in a man.'

She was more than willing and less than a challenge. It was somewhat disappointing she'd been caught so easily. Still, he should feel more excitement over the conquest, *more desire*. Sarah Meacham was a prize indeed. Her husband was out of town with his mistress and gossip at White's had it she was looking to take her first lover since the birth of the 'spare' last autumn. There'd been bets laid as to who that lover would be.

He'd come up to town specifically to win that wager, in case anyone doubted there wasn't a redeemable bone in his body. He couldn't have it be said Riordan Barrett was losing his touch, that his brother, Elliott, had finally talked some sense into him. The fates had decreed that Elliott, the heir, was to be good, so very good, and Riordan, the spare, was to be bad, so very bad, a natural juxtaposition to his beloved brother's goodness. So here he was, up to town early, cutting short a visit with his brother in Sussex, to swive another man's wife and prove to everyone Riordan Barrett was as wicked as rumour reported.

It was all very sordid if one dwelled on the details long enough or if one didn't have enough to drink. Over the last year, Riordan had discovered it was taking more and more of the latter to keep himself from doing the former. His silver flask was ever-present in his coat pocket and, right now, he was too sober for his preference.

Riordan reached for the flask, only to be interrupted by the approach of a footman bearing a silver salver and a sealed letter. 'Milord, pardon the intrusion. This arrived for you with the utmost urgency.'

Riordan studied the letter with curiosity. He didn't have an interest in politics or any business investments that required his attention. In short, he was definitely not the sort of man people sought out with any of the urgency implied by the footman. He broke the seal and scanned the four short lines scribed in inky precision by Browning, the family solicitor, then re-read them in the hope that repetition would make the note any less fantastical, any less horrifying.

'Not bad news, I hope?' Lady Meacham enquired, her hazel eyes wide with concern, proving he looked as pale as he felt.

Not bad news—the *worst* news. The news would be all over London within a day, but London wouldn't hear it from him. He wasn't ready to dissemble to his latest *affaire* in the midst of the Academy art show. Riordan gathered his remaining senses and fixed Lady Meacham with a rakish smile to mask his roiling, rising emotions. 'My dear, I regret my plans have changed.' He gave a short, sardonic bow. 'If you'll excuse me? It seems I have become a father.'

He'd reach for his flask, but there seemed little point. There wasn't enough brandy in the world to ease this. He was going to need help. He'd take any he could get.

Chapter One

'I'll take anything you have.' Maura Harding sat ramrod straight with her gloved hands folded demurely in her lap. She strove to sound affable instead of desperate. She *wasn't* desperate. Maura forced herself to believe the near-fiction. If she didn't believe it, no one else would. Desperation would make her an easy target. People could sense desperation like dogs smelled fear.

According to the small watch pinned to her bodice, it was half past ten in the morning. She'd come straight from the mail coach to Mrs Pendergast's Referral Service for Young Ladies of Good Breeding and she needed a position by nightfall. She'd been right on schedule up to this point—the point where Mrs Pendergast peered over the rims of her spectacles and hesitated.

'I don't see any references.' Mrs Pendergast's impressive bosom heaved in disapproval as she made her pronouncement.

Maura drew a deep breath, silently repeating the mantra that had sustained her on the long journey from Exeter: *In London there would be help.* She would not give up now simply because she had no references. After all, she'd known this would be a likely obstacle. 'It's my first time seeking a position, ma'am.' *First time using an assumed name, first time travelling outside of Devonshire, first time on my own...quite a lot of firsts, Mrs Pendergast, if you only knew.*

Mrs Pendergast's brows went up in an expression of doubt. She set down Maura's carefully written paper and fixed Maura with an uncompromising stare. 'I do not have time to play games, Miss Caulfield.' The false name sounded, well, *false* to Maura, who had spent her whole life being Miss Harding. Could Mrs Pendergast tell? Did it sound as false to her? Did she suspect?

Mrs Pendergast rose to indicate the interview was over. 'I am very busy. I'm sure you did not fail to notice the crowded waiting room full of young ladies *with* references, all eager to be placed in households. I suggest you try your luck elsewhere.'

This was a disaster. She could not leave here without a position. Where else would she go? She knew of no other referral agencies. She knew of this one only because one of her own governesses had mentioned it once. Maura thought quickly. 'I have something better than references, ma'am. I have skills.' Maura gestured towards the discarded paper. 'I can do fine needlework, I can sing, I can dance, I can speak French. I can even paint watercolours.' Maura paused. Her accomplishments did not seem to impress Mrs Pendergast.

When reasoning failed, there was always begging. 'Please, ma'am, I have nowhere else to go. You must have something? I can be a companion to an elderly lady, a governess to a young girl. I can be anything. Surely, there's one family in London that needs me.'

It wasn't supposed to be this hard. London was a big city with far more opportunities than those offered in the remote Devonshire countryside outside Exeter where everyone knew everyone, a situation Maura was trying very hard to avoid. She didn't want to be known, although she was fast discovering that choice came with its own consequences. She was now officially a stranger in a strange place and her carefully concocted plan was in jeopardy.

It worked. Mrs Pendergast sat back down and opened a desk drawer. 'I might have something.'

She rifled through the drawer and pulled out a folder. 'It's not exactly a "family" situation. None of those girls out there will take it. I've already sent five governesses in the last three weeks. *All* have left.'

With those ominous words, Mrs Pendergast pushed the file towards her. 'The gentleman is a bachelor with two young wards he's inherited from his brother.' Maura was only half-listening. Elation poured through her, drowning out her other sensibilities.

The large woman made a tsking sound. 'It's a bad business all around. The new earl is a dissolute rake. He's out cavorting at all hours of the night, getting up to who knows what debaucheries while the children run wild. Then there's the business with the earl's brother.' She made another tsking noise and peered meaningfully

at Maura over her glasses again. 'The manner
of his death was highly shocking and sudden.
As I said, it's a bad business all around, but if
you want it, the position is yours.'

If? Of course she'd take it. She couldn't afford to be choosy at this juncture. Maura was
starting to see how precipitous her flight had
been, even if it had been necessary. 'It will be
fine. Thank you. You won't be sorry.' She would
have gone on gushing her gratitude, but Mrs
Pendergast held up a hand.

'*I* won't be sorry, but *you* might. Did you hear
a word I said, Miss Caulfield?'

'Yes, ma'am.' It wasn't exactly a lie. She'd
heard *most* of the words. She'd heard 'new earl'
and 'two wards' and something about the suspect nature of the former earl's death. The situation didn't sound as bad as Mrs Pendergast
was making it out. She had a position, that was
all that mattered. Life could now proceed according to plan.

Mrs Pendergast communicated her doubt
with a hard stare. 'Very well then, I wish you
luck, but either way, I don't want to see you back
here. This is the only position you'll get without

references. I suggest you find a way to make this work where the other five have failed.'

Maura rose, hiding her surprise. Clearly, she'd missed a little something while she'd carried on her mental celebration. 'The other five?'

'The other five governesses. I did mention them, Miss Caulfield. Did you miss the dissolute-rake part, too?'

Maura's chin went up, determined not to show her surprise. She hadn't listened as well as she'd thought. 'You've been very clear, ma'am. Thank you again.' The 'dissolute' part was unfortunate. She might have launched herself from the frying pan and into the fire, exchanging one dissolute male for another. But she doubted anyone could be as dissolute as Wildeham, the man her uncle had chosen for her to marry. Besides, she doubted she'd see much of this roguish Earl of Chatham. Dissolute rakes weren't exactly the stay-at-home types when surrounded by the entertainments of London. It was difficult indeed to be rakish at all by staying home.

An hour later, a hired hackney deposited her in front of the Earl of Chatham's Portland Square town house and departed with the last of her coins. In her estimation, it was money well spent. On her own, she would have walked for hours and never found the place. To put it mildly, London was daunting! Never had she seen so many people crammed together in one place. The traffic, the smells and the noises were enough to intimidate even the heartiest of country souls. Maura shaded her eyes and looked up at the town house.

It fit in perfectly. It was daunting, too, all four soaring storeys of it. There was nothing for it. The only way ahead was forwards. She picked up her things and walked up the steps to face her future. Forewarned was forearmed. She would focus on the positives. One positive was that her plan was proceeding according to schedule. Another was the address.

When she'd set out from Exeter, she'd imagined being placed in the comfortable home of a well-to-do family, possibly one hoping to launch a daughter on to the bottom rungs of society. Never had she thought to find a position in an *earl's* home. Of course, she'd also never thought to have to *find* a position in the first place. For that matter, she'd never thought to leave Exeter.

She'd faced a lot of 'nevers' in the past month she'd not expected to encounter.

As a gentleman's daughter, the granddaughter of an earl, she'd been raised to expect more, although those assumptions had been misplaced. She could have kept those assumptions intact. Her uncle had made it clear she could live in comfortable luxury and marry a title, but for a price she'd been unwilling to pay. Even now, with Exeter a week and miles behind her, that price made her shudder in the noon sun.

Her lack of co-operation had made it impossible to stay so here she was, a stranger alone, ready to start her life afresh, which was a nice way of saying she'd cut all ties to her uncle's family. It had either been cutting ties with them or cutting ties with her true self and in the end she'd hadn't been able to bring herself to that ultimate sacrifice. So, they'd been left to their own devices and she was now left to hers. There could be no going back, although she was certain her uncle would try. She wouldn't let him discover her. She'd disappear into the earl's household and her uncle would eventually give up and find another way to fulfil his obligations to the odious Baron Wildeham.

Her resolve firm, Maura raised the carved lion-head knocker and let it fall with a heavy clack against the door. Inside, she could hear the undignified running of feet and a yelp, followed by a giggle, followed by a crash. Maura winced at the sound of something shattering. There was a shrill scream. 'I'll get it! It's my turn to get the door!' Then chaos spilled out on to the front step.

Maura saw it all happen in slow motion. The door flew open, answered by a man in stockinged feet and dishabille, dark hair ruffled in disarray, shirt-tails flying. He looked like no butler she'd ever seen. But Maura hadn't the time to appreciate the odd sight. Behind him, two children came barrelling into the corridor. They skidded to a tardy and incomplete halt behind him and...oomph!

Their momentum set off a chain reaction, sending them all down in a heap, Maura at the bottom, looking up over the tangle of arms and legs into the bluest eyes she'd ever seen. Even with two children heaped higgledy-piggledy on them, she was not immune to the fact that those blue eyes went with an entirely masculine body of hard ridges and muscled planes which, at present, had landed on her in a most indelicate manner.

'Hello.' He grinned down at her, walnut-dark hair falling in his face with casual negligence.

'I'm here about the position,' Maura managed to get out, but she immediately regretted it. 'Position' wasn't quite the best word to use, although given the situation, she was fortunate to formulate *any* coherent thoughts with all that well-muscled maleness pressing down on her.

'I can see that.' Mischief twinkled in those blue eyes, suggesting he wasn't oblivious to their unorthodox circumstances, circumstances, she noted, he didn't seem to mind. Whoever he was, he *should* be chagrined. No tutor or footman worth his salt would be caught in such raucous behaviour if he valued his post. But it was clear this attractive mess of a man wasn't the least bit worried. He was laughing, quite possibly *at* her, as he rose and helped the children up.

Everyone apparently thought the accident a great lark. The children were both talking at once. 'Did you see the way I came around the corner?'

'I grabbed hold of the banister post and slingshotted myself into the hall!'

Slingshotted? Great heavens, was that even a word?

'You were amazing, William. It was like you were a cannon ball!' the blue-eyed man put in with an inordinate amount of enthusiasm.

'We broke Aunt Cressida's vase!' The little girl giggled nervously.

The man ruffled her hair. 'Don't worry, it was ugly anyway.'

Unbelievable! Had they forgotten about her? Maura was halfway to her feet, struggling with the tangle of her skirts and luggage when a large hand reached down for her. 'Are you all right?' The rich baritones of his voice were easy and friendly, further sign he was a man who took nothing too seriously.

'I shall recover.' Maura tugged at the fitted jacket of her travelling costume and smoothed her skirts, trying to restore some proper order to the encounter. 'I am the new governess. Mrs Pendergast assigned me just this morning. I should like to speak with Lord Chatham, please.' That should get some results.

His eyes twinkled with more mischief, if that was possible. 'You *are* speaking with him.' He gave her a gallant half-bow at odds with his dishabille. 'The Earl of Chatham at your service.'

'You're the earl?' Maura tried not to gape. Dissolute earls weren't supposed to be handsome, hard-bodied males who flirted with their eyes.

The corners of his eyes crinkled in amusement. 'I believe we've established that. Now, what shall we call you?' He fixed her with a white-toothed smile that probably made most women go weak at the knees. Maura liked to think her knees were weak from having been ploughed over on the doorstep instead. He turned to the children, who were staring up at him with wide eyes full of obvious hero worship. 'We can't very well call her "new governess". That's no sort of name at all.' They started to giggle again.

The little girl smiled up at him and clapped her hands. 'I know! I know! We'll call her Six.' The little girl curtsied very prettily. 'Hello, Six, I'm Cecilia and I'm seven. This is my brother, William. He's eight.' She laughed again. 'Six, seven, eight, we're all numbers in a row. That's funny. Uncle Ree, did you get my joke? Six, seven, eight?'

'I most certainly did, my dear. It was the funniest one yet.' The earl smiled down at her indulgently and wrapped his hand around her considerably smaller one. The gesture was endearing and it succeeded in doing queer things to Maura's stomach.

'Perhaps we should step inside,' Maura suggested, well aware, even if they weren't, that their little coterie on the porch was drawing stares from the street.

'Oh, yes, do forgive me.' The earl jumped into action and ushered them all indoors to the hall where the remnants of Aunt Cressida's vase were being swept up by a maid. 'Now we can have proper introductions and...' He paused, his brow furrowing as he groped for the right words. 'And a pot of tea. That will be just the thing. You'll have to excuse me; I seem to have left my manners on the floor with the vase.' He pushed a hand through his dark hair, looking entirely likeable.

She'd not been ready for that. She hadn't planned on liking him, Maura realised as they settled for tea in the drawing room, children included. What she *had* expected was a middle-aged man with greying side-whiskers, lecherous eyes and wandering hands, a man like her uncle's crony Baron Wildeham.

Tea came and Maura discreetly looked towards the doorway. 'Are your wards going to join us?' There were four tea cups on the tray. Surely the children weren't staying for tea?

The earl looked at her queerly, gesturing to the children. 'They're already here.' Then he laughed, his mouth breaking into his easy smile. 'Mrs Pendergast didn't tell you, did she? That tricky old woman, no wonder she got someone here so quickly.'

Maura sat up straight, feeling defensive. 'She mentioned the wards were young.'

'She'd be correct. It's William and Cecilia I need a governess for,' the earl explained, motioning that she should pour out.

Maura was glad for something to do, something to occupy her hands while her mind restored order. There'd be no young girls to shepherd into society as she was expecting. Instead, there were two slightly precocious children who slid through the hallways in stockinged feet. She told herself she could manage. She'd helped her aunt with her young cousins, after all. She just needed to readjust her thinking.

'How do you take your tea, milord?' Her hand hovered over the sugar and cream.

He dismissed those offerings with a wave of his hand. 'I take it plain and you can call me Riordan or Mr Barrett if you wish.' There was a tinge of bitterness in his voice. What had Mrs Pendergast said about the death of his brother? The new earl seemed a reluctant heir. Maura wished she'd listened more closely.

'Neither is appropriate, as you well know.' Maura passed his tea cup and tendered a smile, hoping to ease the disagreement. Arguing with one's employer on the first day was no way to start. 'I should call you Lord Chatham.' She smiled again, looking for a better subject of conversation. What had her governesses done on the first day? She sipped her tea and racked her brain for an appropriate next step.

'Lord Chatham?' He arched a dark eyebrow in query. The expression drew attention to his eyes, twin-blue flames flickering with life and mischief.

'I think that would be best, under the circumstances.' She *knew* that would be best. He was a dangerous sort of man when it came to a woman's sensibilities with his good looks and penchant for informality. A half-hour in his company had proven it. He hadn't even bothered to put his coat on or tuck in his shirt-tails.

To her surprise, he laughed and leaned forwards, smiling wickedly over his tea cup. 'You weren't *under* any circumstances on the porch, you were under *me*.'

'Lord Chatham! There are children in the room.' But the children didn't seem to mind. They were laughing. They did that a lot, she noticed, no doubt encouraged by the irrepressible audacity of their guardian. Laughter was well and good, but they would have to learn to control it just a bit.

'So there are.' He rubbed at his chin in thought for a moment, although she had the distinct impression he was teasing her. 'If we are to be formal, I'll need to call you something more than Six.' He was smiling again, flirting outrageously with his blue, blue eyes while saying nothing technically objectionable at all.

From her perch on a chair, Cecilia looked crestfallen. 'I want to call her Six. It will ruin the joke if we don't.'

Lord Chatham quirked another eyebrow in Maura's direction, a little smile hovering about his lips while he waited for her response. Good heavens, the man was a handsome devil. Cecilia's lip began to quiver. Maura felt a moment's panic. She didn't want to be the governess who made her charge cry within the first half-hour. Her next words came rushing out to forestall any tears. 'Sex is fine.'

Sex is fine? Maura clapped a hand over her mouth, but it was far too late.

'Is it? That's good to know.' Lord Chatham's smile widened in good humour.

Maura blushed hotly in mortification. What had happened to her tongue? It had done nothing right since her arrival. 'Six,' she stammered. She turned towards Cecilia. Anything was better than looking at *him*. 'You may call me Six if you like, Cecilia. It can be our special name.'

Cecilia beamed at her and Maura knew the sweet taste of victory, a taste she'd barely swallowed before Lord Chatham said, 'And me? Perhaps I should have a special name for you, too. Shall I call you…?' He let the question hover provocatively, forcing her to interrupt if she didn't want him to provide an answer. He would say it, too. If the last half-hour had shown her anything of his character, it was that.

'Miss Caulfield. You should call me Miss Caulfield,' Maura supplied hastily. The situation was fast spiralling out of control. She should establish her authority before it slid away entirely. She didn't want Chatham thinking she could be swayed by a simple smile. 'Cecilia, why don't you and William go upstairs to play while I settle in? Then we can spend the afternoon getting acquainted over a walk in the park.'

Maura recognised her error immediately. Sending away the children meant she was left on her own with the outrageous Lord Chatham. 'I must apologise for my slip of tongue.'

'No need to apologise, Miss Caulfield.' Lord Chatham leaned back in his chair, his eyes studying her with amusement. 'In my experience, slipping tongues can be quite entertaining.'

His remark was the final straw. She tried an arched eyebrow of her own. 'You forget yourself, Lord Chatham. In the past hour I've been landed on, flirted with and flustered out of my usually solid wits. I'm starting to see why the other five governesses left.'

'No, you're not. You've barely scratched the proverbial surface.' The good humour that floated in his eyes disappeared instantly at her remark. He rose, suddenly an icier, more distant version of himself. 'The housekeeper will show you your rooms.'

A crash and squeal sounded overhead, followed by a child's cry of despair. Voices were raised as maids scurried to clean up the latest disaster in what was clearly a long string of disasters of which Aunt Cressida's vase was only a recent victim. Maura turned her eyes towards the ceiling. 'It seems, Lord Chatham, you don't need a governess, you need a miracle.'

He gave a cold chuckle. 'And Mrs Pendergast sent me you. Welcome to Chatham House, Miss Caulfield.'

Chapter Two

She was late. Riordan glanced towards the mantel clock. The hands showed only a minute had passed since the last time he'd checked. He wished Miss Caulfield would hurry up. He was hungry and he was regretting his harshness with her that afternoon. She couldn't possibly know what she'd walked into. Still, late was late. He'd been very clear when he'd sent up the invitation that he'd wished to dine at seven o'clock sharp. It was now five minutes past.

Not that he was in the habit of dining with governesses. He wasn't. He hadn't dined with the first five. But they hadn't been young and pretty. Nor had they dominated his thoughts for the duration of the afternoon. They'd been dried-up old sticks who thought far too much about propriety and far too little about living. It was no wonder they hadn't lasted. If there was one thing he knew, it was how to have fun. He was determined the children would have that, if nothing else, after all they'd been through. On those grounds, he was doing quite well in his new role as a father figure.

He'd be the first to admit he liked children. He just didn't have a clue about how to bring them up. His brother, Elliott, had been the mature one there. It had been Elliott who'd taken on Cecilia and William four years ago after the children's father died of a sudden fever. Now Elliott was gone, too. No one had ever imagined the children would be stuck with him and whatever help he could cobble together.

The rustle of skirts at the door told him his latest attempt at acquiring such help had arrived. 'I apologise for being tardy. I'd expected to dine with the children. The summons was a surprise.' This last was said with the faintest hint of frost, to suggest he wasn't quite forgiven for his earlier harshness.

'The *invitation*,' Riordan corrected with a smile in an attempt at melting her glacial greeting. He'd expected as much, especially after his rather cold dismissal this afternoon. He hoped to make it up to her with dinner. He couldn't afford to have another governess leave. He knew what he meant by offering dinner, but it was clear from her choice of dress she didn't know what to make of his request. Was this work? Was this a get-to-know-you welcome sort of dinner? She'd clearly opted for the former.

She'd chosen a modestly cut gown of deep-green poplin trimmed in white lace. It was prettily done, nicely suited for tea at the squire's or an afternoon of shopping in the village, but nowhere near fashionable enough for dinner in London with the town's leading rogue. The simplicity of the gown and the practicality of its fabric created a stark contrast against his formal evening attire.

'Are you going out this evening?' Her eyes swept him briefly, likely trying to gauge the gravity of her mistake. Her mind was easy to read, not because she was transparent, but because she was not afraid to be straightforward. He'd enjoyed her boldness this afternoon even if it had ended on a sour note.

'Yes, but nothing that demands my attendance with any scheduled rigour. I am free to arrive when I choose.' Going out had lost much of its allure in the month since his brother's death. Three months of mourning was the standard for a sibling if the sibling had managed to die conventionally. Elliott had not. As a result, London was happy to let Riordan proceed as usual with his customary social routine after a two-week hiatus to fetch the children from Chatham Court.

Riordan suspected such benevolence had more to do with society's greed for gossip. If he was left rusticating for three months in grief, there'd be considerably fewer rumours for the scandalmongers to spread regarding his brother's demise and the Season would be that much duller for it.

The butler announced dinner and he offered Miss Caulfield his arm, secretly pleased she was as discomfited with his show of propriety as she'd been with his earlier impropriety.

'Such formality,' she commented, taking the chair Riordan held out for her at the table. 'I apologise for being under-dressed. I wasn't sure...' Her voice trailed off and Riordan imagined her upstairs in her room debating the merits of the green poplin or the one good silk gown she owned. 'You were right to save the silk for a better occasion,' he said lightly, taking his own seat.

'How did you know?' She shot him a sharp look, her thoughts evident. He'd bet odds of two to three she was imagining peepholes secreted in the walls of her room. It was a fairly worldly thought for a governess, or any young lady, and it did make him wonder.

Riordan dismissed her fears with a laugh. 'Have no worries, Miss Caulfield. It's all very simple. To understand women, a man must understand their clothes.' He'd learned that particular skill a long time ago and it had served him well in the intervening years.

She settled the linen napkin on her lap and gave him a doubtful look that said she didn't believe him. Riordan leaned back in his chair, letting the footmen serve the soup while he studied the effects of candlelight on Miss Caulfield's features. This morning, much of her hair had been hidden under her bonnet, but this evening it was pinned up in a pretty twist that hinted at its thickness and length while it exposed the delicate arch of her neck. The effect was enough to make him imagine what it would be like to take all that hair down and sift it through his fingers. 'The light turns your hair into red-gold; very lovely,' he commented as the footmen moved away.

'And what does *that* tell you about me?' She shot him another sharp look with her green eyes.

'You don't believe me about the clothes, do you?' Riordan set down his soup spoon, starting to enjoy himself. He was good at this. Observation and subsequent conjecturing had always come easy for him. Most women loved his little 'fortune telling' game. 'Allow me to demonstrate. You wear shades of green often. With your colouring, all that red hair and those emerald-green eyes, it makes sense. Greens would be your best palate. I'm right, am I not?'

'Yes.' Even discomfited, her manners were impeccable. She sipped from her soup spoon without spilling a drop. His governess was very well bred indeed.

'You're intrigued now. I can see it in the way you've subtly leaned forwards.' Riordan lowered his voice, giving the conversation a private allure.

Her eyes sparked, a good sign. She was

warming. 'All right, if you're so good, tell me why a governess has a silk gown.' But any further conversation had to wait a moment while the fish was served.

'You have more than one,' Riordan said when the footmen had retreated. He wasn't sure how he knew *that*, but it seemed right. She was born for fine fabrics and delicate trimmings. Riordan reached for her hand and traced a lazy circle in the palm. 'Tell me I'm right.' A woman who wore silk gowns and imagined peepholes in her room was an exciting mystery. 'You're not the usual governess.'

She stiffened and withdrew her hand. 'You're not the usual earl.' All her attention went straight to her neglected fish. He'd touched a nerve there. Intriguing, but not surprising. Her clothes were too well made. He'd seen it instantly. Pretty and young with well-made clothes and a bold demeanour with a man she should view as her superior suggested there was more to Miss Caulfield than she let on.

'I don't hold it against you, Miss Caulfield. The "usual" has never held much of my attention.' He would leave it at that. No sense frightening her off. If she thought he guessed at more, she might be compelled to run and that was the last thing he needed. He needed a governess to stay and he was willing to overlook any secrets said governess thought she had.

Miss Caulfield finished her fish without a single *faux pas*. He always watched women during the fish course at dinner parties. It was the perfect chance to see if they were all they claimed. Miss Caufield was definitely more. Unlike many a pretender, *she'd* kept a piece of bread in her left hand and the fork in her right, never once reaching for the very taboo knife. Anyone of any true social refinement knew fish juice stained knives if they weren't silver. It confirmed what he'd noted earlier: she had *excellent* table manners, as if she ate at candlelit tables complete with china, crystal and the requisite earl every day.

By the time the beef was served, his thoughts had taken a more erotic turn. He found he could not contemplate her manners without also contemplating her delectable mouth with its kissable lower lip, or the column of her throat as she swallowed. This led his eyes lower to her bosom, which the cut of her gown showed to advantage, which gave way to a bevy of illicit thoughts, most of them involving all the ways he could get her out of that gown and on to the table.

'Is everything to your liking?' he asked in low tones that were more seductive than solicitous. 'Would you like some more wine?' He was flirting deliberately now, his hand provocatively caressing the stem of his own empty wine glass, and wondering if she'd call him on it. She did. It was bravely and boldly done of her. Not every employee would dare. Good for her. He had little use for people without spines.

'Tell me, Lord Chatham, do you flirt with every woman you meet or just the governesses?'

Riordan reached for the wine and refilled her glass as an excuse to lean close and make some more mischief. 'I assure you, this is not flirting. If I were flirting with you, Miss Caulfield, you'd know it.' But of course he *was* flirting with her, just a little by his standards, and they both knew it.

Riordan laughed and filled his glass. 'A toast, Miss Caulfield, to our, ah, relationship. Cheers.'

Maura clinked her glass gently against his. It was impossible not to get swept up in Lord

Chatham's bonhomie. He couldn't help it, she realised. But she could. She could have enough sense for the both of them. He might not be flirting with her by his standards, but society would see it otherwise. No wonder Mrs Pendergast had called him a dissolute rake. Women probably swooned in his wake and he likely didn't lack for female attention. Handsome, charming and personable, he could have any woman he wanted and not have to work that hard at it.

Well, he couldn't have her if that's what he was intending with all this light flirtation. She would make that clear over cheese and fruit as their dinner came to a close. It would be just the right note to end the evening on. Two bites into a sharp cheddar, she began her campaign. 'I thought the purpose of dinner was to discuss the children. Here we are, at the end, and the children haven't even been mentioned.' She couldn't be more direct than that.

'What would you like to know about the children?' He filled his glass again and Maura began to wonder if that was his third or fourth. Wine disappeared from his glass like water.

'We could start with their schedule and perhaps move on to their education,' Maura prompted. This was the most extraordinary discussion she'd ever had. She wasn't supposed to be the one asking the questions. She'd expected to be told.

'Their schedule?' Lord Chatham stabbed at his cheese as if the question irritated him. His tone became frosty, as it had been that afternoon. 'They don't have a schedule, Miss Caulfield. Their lives have been turned upside down, they've lost their trusted guardian, they've been through five governesses in as many weeks. They've had no stability in their lives since my brother's death.'

Maura refused to be intimidated. 'They've had you. Surely you have imposed *some* order on their lives in the absence of a governess.' Her own parents had been active participants in her life.

'Some, but I wouldn't go as far as to call it a schedule.' Lord Chatham sat back in his chair, wine glass empty again and dangling negligently in his hand. 'I can see you're disappointed in me. Perhaps your standards are too high.' He wasn't flirting now. His tone had taken on a self-deprecating note. 'Don't forget,

I'm a bachelor with bachelor ways. If I knew how to raise children, you wouldn't be here.'

He set down the wine glass and rose. 'If you'll excuse me, the hour is later than I anticipated and my presence is required elsewhere, as tardy as it is. Feel free to partake of the cheese and fruit without me.' He offered a short bow and left. It was quite possibly the most expedient exit she'd ever witnessed and most definitely one of the rudest.

His bachelor ways indeed! Maura fumed up in her room afterwards. Everything he did, everything he said, reminded her of his 'bachelor ways'. Even his departure from the dinner table had reeked of them. Apparently he was expected at the Rutherfords' ball and the Duke of Rutland's fête before meeting up with some fellows at a gambling hell on St James's. He wouldn't be back until early morning.

It had been on the tip of her tongue to reprimand him for his less-than-fatherly behaviour, but she'd already angered him once today and she knew he wasn't the only man who habitually spent the night on the town while leaving his children in the hands of others. That didn't make it right. Maura didn't hold with the *laissez-faire* parenting of the aristocracy. Her own upbringing had run quite counter to the norm and for that she would always be grateful.

She'd also be grateful for her bed. Maura began taking down her hair and stowing the pins carefully in a little trifle box on her bureau. It had been an eventful day and she was beyond tired. She smiled to herself as she went through her evening *toilette*. Maura pulled a white nightgown over her head and surveyed her room. It was smaller than what she was used to, but it was a nice room on the third floor. There was a window overlooking the garden and it was hung with fresh curtains. The walls were papered with a tiny pink-floral print and the bed was covered in a pink-and-white counterpane. A clothes-press stood in one corner and a small chest of drawers in another. It would do, and after three days on the mail coach it seemed like heaven.

She might not be living the life she'd been born to, but she'd done well today. She'd got a position, navigated the streets of London and met the intriguing Earl of Chatham. Not bad for a gently bred girl from Devonshire. But she would need to tread carefully. The earl might flirt, he might raise his wards with the same benign insouciance with which he lived his life, but that didn't mean he didn't see far more than he let on.

The perceptive Lord Chatham had implied correctly that she wasn't the usual governess. She hadn't meant to give herself away and yet she had in ways she couldn't control. Hopefully he had guessed nothing more and was not interested in guessing anything more. As long as she did her job with his wards, she hoped he would look no further. The last thing she needed was for someone to get too curious about her origins.

Maura hopped into bed, revelling in the cool sheets and the fluffy pillow at her head. That was one thing Lord Chatham might have in common with her; she wasn't the only one with secrets. That was all right with her. He could have his secrets as long as she could have hers.

It had not escaped her notice when she'd stepped down from the mail coach that morning that it was to have been her wedding day. If she'd stayed in Devonshire, she'd have been married to Wildeham by now and subjected to a lifetime of his obscene attentions, a fate certainly worse than throwing in her lot with the Earl of Chatham.

Maura blew out the candle beside her bed and whispered in the darkness, 'A toast, Lord Chatham. Here's to our, ah, relationship. Cheers.'

Chapter Three

Acton Humphries, known to most in that part of Devonshire as Baron Wildeham, watched the scene unfold from his favourite position, recumbent on Lucas Harding's divan, post-dinner brandy in hand. Across the room, Harding fiddled distractedly with the heavy paperweight on his desk. Harding could split the messenger's head with the leaded-crystal ornament and he was mad enough to do it. The man's colour was high and it wouldn't be the first time rage had driven his actions. 'You mean to tell me that my niece has managed to elude you and disappear entirely?' Harding ground out when the messenger finished his report.

Acton sat up to join the proceedings. 'Surely

you must understand how improbable it seems. Miss Caulfield is a gently bred young lady who hasn't been beyond Exeter in her entire life and you gentlemen are trained professionals,' he drawled lazily, but only a stupid man would be drawn in by his apparent nonchalance. Acton was as angry over this latest development as Harding was. His long-standing relationship with Lucas Harding had developed a certain tension in the last week, ever since it became obvious Harding's ungrateful niece had simply disappeared a coincidental four days before she was due to become his wife and Baroness Wildeham to boot.

'I am sorry we don't have better news.' The messenger shifted uncomfortably from foot to foot, sensing that anger was indeed boiling just beneath the surface in a barely disguised simmer.

'*Better* news? You don't have *any* news!' Harding exploded. The explosion was justified, Acton mused. Maura's disappearance had put her uncle in dire straits and she'd made him look the fool. She was contracted to marry him in exchange for erasing a gambling debt her uncle had rather rashly acquired. Harding had never believed his stallion, Captain, would lose to Acton's Jupiter. Most fortunately, Acton was willing to take payment in the form of a bride as opposed to cash, especially when that bride was the delectable Maura Harding.

When he'd struck the deal, Harding had had a bride to offer. Now, he had neither bride nor money and the deadline was looming. If Harding didn't retrieve Maura soon, he'd be destitute. Acton knew very well Harding was a mere knight and his property wasn't entailed. If he took the house, Harding's family would be left unsettled: his wife, the young twins and the two older sons. Maura was a fair trade for her uncle's continued stability. The man had cared for Maura since she was sixteen and this was how she repaid him? Acton would never tolerate such disobedience. It was a woman's lot in life to serve her family. Marrying him had become Maura's duty, her service for the four years of living under her uncle's roof.

'Find her,' Harding ground out, his temper cooling a bit. 'Expand your search. Try the coaching inns again in case anyone remembers her.' Acton privately disagreed. If she'd gone to a coaching inn, chances of finding her became slimmer. Hundreds of travellers passed through those inns and people's memories could be dulled as time went on. The Runners could end up chasing false leads. But Acton knew Harding had honestly thought they'd find her in a nearby village or attempting to get work in Exeter. Harding had guessed wrong on that score and her trail was growing cold. Now it was time to do things his way.

'What about London?' Wildeham offered. 'It seems a logical choice if someone wanted to hide and we haven't tried there yet.' It had only been a handful of days. By his calculations she would only just have arrived. A trail in London, if there was one, would still be very warm.

Harding shook his head in disagreement. 'Unlikely, Wildeham. Maura has little to no money that I know of and no skills. Even if she could have afforded coach fare or begged a ride, she's got nothing to live on once she reaches the city. She's a gentleman's daughter. She's been raised to marry, not to labor.'

Wildeham saw the logic in Harding's argument. If a girl like Maura thought to find employment in London, she'd be quickly disappointed. The town would devour a girl like her, and that worried him very much. He didn't want Maura dead. He wanted her alive and penitent, *very* penitent.

Wildeham shifted in his seat to accommodate the early stirrings of arousal. Penitence conjured up all sorts of images of Maura on her knees before him. If anyone was doing any devouring, it was going to be him. He'd spent quite a few hours imagining the fantasies he'd play out with her once she was his. She would be sorry she'd run. There was nothing like the thrill of laying a rod across the smooth white expanse of un-touched buttocks… But he digressed. Wildeham pulled his thoughts back to the situation at hand.

Maura Harding had run and he was more cer-tain with each passing day she'd gone to Lon-don. Her uncle only saw a pretty, well-mannered girl. But he'd had the occasion to see much more. Harding and the Runner could talk all they wanted about searching the larger towns of Devonshire, but they'd never seen Maura with her temper up. They'd never seen her try to slap a man after he cornered her in the pantry for a little bit of slap and tickle. They'd never been on the receiving end of her tongue, and not in the French way he preferred. The little vixen had

bit him when he'd tried to kiss her, nearly sev-
ering his tongue in two. That was all right with
him. He liked it rough and he always hit them
back. Nothing too hard, mind you, but enough
to make his position on the matter clear. The
more Maura fought, the more he wanted her,
and he was going to have her. It was time to do
things his way.

'Are you two still debating a local search?'
He interrupted Harding and the Runner. He
was growing impatient with their theorising,
although this 'treasure hunt of sorts' could be
fun in a tantalising, torture-pleasure scheme
of things.

'It's what makes the most sense.' Harding
sighed. 'She can't have gone far.'

Acton warmed to the game. 'By all means,
continue with your efforts. It's your coin, after
all. I've got my own man for odd jobs like this.
I'll send him to London at my expense and see
what he turns up. We'll make it a wager, fifty
pounds on the side to whoever finds her first.'

Harding smiled tolerantly as if he wasn't the
one faced with losing something more substantial than fifty pounds if the girl wasn't retrieved.
'All right, fifty pounds it is.'

Acton rose from the divan. 'I will call it an early night, then. I have plans to make. Do give my regards to your wife, Harding.' It was still early enough to summon Paul Digby, a sturdy ox of a man. Acton had used Digby before for all sorts of dirty work. Digby was a thinker, an unusual quality for a man his size. Digby could find anyone when he set his mind to it. If Maura was in London, she was about to be found.

Maura embraced the morning with a positive attitude and a plan. She'd not expected to be working with children when she'd made her application, but she would adjust. Childhood wasn't so far behind her that she'd forgotten what it was like to be seven or eight. With that in mind, she'd risen early, arranged for breakfast to be delivered to the nursery and written out an orderly schedule for the day. She ran through that schedule in her mind on the way to the nursery; there would be breakfast, morning lessons, an afternoon walk, she would review manners over tea, there would be play time before dinner. It was all very efficient.

And entirely inappropriate. At the sight of the nursery, all her plans went out the window.

The place was a mess. Toys of every sort lay spread on the floor or tucked haphazardly into any available nook. Clothes lay draped over furniture, wrinkled. Maura picked up a discarded shirt and shook it out. She'd not expected this.

Yesterday afternoon, there'd been no time to see the children's quarters. The children had been ready for her, neatly dressed and pressed. They'd gone walking in the park across the street. The 'invitation' to her most unusual dinner with Lord Chatham had been waiting on her return. But she hadn't worried. She should have. Nothing had prepared her for this. *This* would demand a re-routing of her carefully laid plans.

'Six!' Cecilia poked her head out of her little bedchamber off the nursery's main room. 'You're here early!' She ran across the hall to William's room. 'Will, Will, Six is here!'

'I thought I'd come up for breakfast and we could continue getting acquainted.' Maura smiled. She and the children had got off to a decent start yesterday, even if William had been less enthusiastic than Cecilia. William had been very quiet, very reserved on the walk.

'What are we going to do today?' Cecilia

asked, slipping a hand through hers and swinging her arm.

'We are going to eat and then we're going to play a game,' Maura said cheerily. She tugged on William's blanket. 'Now, out of bed, sleepyhead. Breakfast will be here any minute.'

'Up here?' William questioned. 'Uncle Ree just lets us eat in the breakfast room downstairs whenever we want. Breakfast is served until eleven o'clock.'

That was interesting and potentially full of problems. 'Does your uncle eat with you?'

'No,' William said dejectedly. '*He's* usually in bed until noon.'

'You eat alone?' Maura busied herself in the little chamber, straightening here and there so her questions didn't seem like an interrogation. This was something she needed to know. She didn't want to upset a family ritual of eating together.

'Yes,' Cecilia proclaimed proudly. 'We fill our own plates and eat as much as we want of whatever we want. The chairs are big, though, and my feet don't touch the ground.'

Children eating copious amounts of self-selected food unsupervised wasn't a family ritual; it was a recipe for disaster. The breakfast trays arrived and Maura hurried to clear the round table in the centre of the nursery.

'Mmm, it smells good.' Cecilia scampered after her and Maura noticed even William didn't have to be asked twice to the table as she set out the dishes and removed the covers.

'What's that?' William pointed to the plates arranged with strips of toast alongside an egg cup.

'These are eggs and soldiers.' Maura placed a plate in front of each of them and sat down. 'Have you ever seen it before?' She'd rather thought they would have. She'd been raised on it.

They shook their heads. 'Soldiers?' William asked curiously, poking around at the egg.

'The toast strips are the soldiers.' Maura picked up a spoon and tapped the top of the soft-boiled egg. The top broke open, revealing the runny yolk inside. 'Now, you take a soldier and dip it in the egg.' She demonstrated and took a bite. 'Yummy. Try it,' she urged them.

After the first bite, eggs and soldiers was an immediate success. 'This is better than the porridge we had with those other governesses.' Cecilia made a face reflecting her distaste of the porridge. 'But,' she proclaimed with a mouth of toast, 'this is as good as breakfasts with Papa Elliott.' She paused long enough to swallow. 'He was Uncle Ree's brother, but he's dead now, like our father. I hope Uncle Ree doesn't die.' It was said with a child's innocent carelessness of the facts, but Maura's heart went out to them. Three father figures in eight years was a lot of change.

'Why is it called eggs and soldiers?' William ate his last bite.

Maura leaned forwards. 'My mother told me eggs and soldiers was the tale of Humpty Dumpty.' She recited the nursery rhyme to them. 'The toast strips are all the king's men and the runny egg is poor old Humpty Dumpty who can't be put back together again.' They laughed and Maura gathered up the dishes. 'Who's ready for a game?'

'None of the other governesses played games,' William said sceptically.

'Well, Six does and I like her,' Cecilia put in emphatically, turning blue eyes Maura's way, a sudden concern mirrored in her eyes. 'You aren't going to leave, are you?'

'No, of course not,' Maura reassured her. She

couldn't possibly leave, no matter what. Leaving would mean being homeless. It would mean having no way to support herself. The children could put frogs in her bed and she'd have to stay. 'Who knows what lava is?'

Cecilia had no idea, but William did. 'It's the hot stuff that comes out of volcanoes. Papa Elliott told me about Mount Etna in Italy.' He grinned. 'It sounds exciting, all that noise and rumbling. I'd like to be an explorer and see one some day. Papa Elliott said the last time Mount Etna erupted a little village almost got destroyed.'

'The village was called Bronte,' Maura supplied. 'We could pretend today that our nursery is that village and we are explorers who have come to rescue the people from the volcano.' Maura bent over and swept up a rag doll. 'I got her, she's safe. Does anyone know this little girl's name?'

'That's Polly,' Cecilia supplied.

'Can you take Polly to a safe place on a shelf away from the lava?' Maura handed the doll over to her. 'In fact, the whole carpet is lava and we have to pull everyone and everything out and get them to safety. Cecilia, can you be in charge of saving all the dollies? William, you can be in charge of saving the village's things, like their games, and the soldiers. Step quickly so the lava doesn't burn your feet, too! I'll get the books.'

Off they went, all three of them hopping about, grabbing up the 'villagers' and getting them resettled. It was a noisy business. Sometimes the rescuers weren't fast enough and got burnt. Cecilia squealed the most over her imaginary close calls with the lava. Even William got involved, telling them an elaborate story about how his soldiers had come to help, but been cut off by a sudden earthquake that left them stranded on the mountain's left slope.

It took the better part of an hour, but when the last villager was rescued, the floor was empty and the nursery was tidy.

'Whew.' Maura plopped into a child-sized chair at the table. 'That was hard work. Good job, rescuers. See how nice the nursery looks.'

'You tricked us.' William sulked, suddenly suspicious. 'That wasn't a game, it was a trick to make us pick up.'

'Did you have fun?' Maura challenged good-naturedly.

'Well, yes, a little bit,' William confessed. He'd had more than a little bit of fun.

'Then it was a game,' came a male voice from the doorway.

'Uncle Ree!' The children ran to him, pelting him with hugs. Maura rose, pushing at a loose strand of hair, conscious of her appearance after an energetic game of 'Save the Villagers'. She looked rather mussed compared to Lord Chatham's immaculate *toilette*. He was turned out for driving in tan breeches and boots and a dark-blue coat that emphasised his eyes.

'I heard all the commotion and thought I'd come up to see what was going on.' Lord Chatham looked a question over the children's heads.

'I'm sorry if we were too loud,' Maura apologised hastily.

'Not too loud, just too early.' He *did* look a bit pale and there were traces of bags under his very blue eyes.

'Uncle Ree stays up late and sleeps in,' William said. 'I want to be like him. That's why *I* stay in bed,' he announced proudly. Maura could think of better behaviours to emulate. She could well imagine what had kept Lord Chatham out until all hours of the morning. After drawing circles on her hand at dinner, he'd likely moved on to actresses and courtesans.

'We were rescuing villagers from the volcano.' Cecilia hopped up and down on one foot. 'We saved Polly first. *And* we had eggs and soldiers for breakfast.'

Lord Chatham grinned at her, looking entirely irresistible. 'It sounds like a very productive morning.' He glanced out the window. 'The sun is out and since I'm up, who wants to go to the park? Will, get your boat, the new one I got you, and we'll try it out. Cecilia, get your hoops and the little kite. There should be enough of a breeze to fly it.' The children went wild with excitement and scurried about the room, gathering their things.

She was coming to hate when he did that. How dare he be *likeable* after just reminding her how *unlikeable* he should be. He'd been out carousing all night, a behaviour that boded ill, and now he was offering to play the doting father figure and take the children to the park. *With hardly a care for your own plans*, her defences reminded. *Are you going to let him walk in here and disrupt your day?*

Maura stepped forward. An outing to the park wasn't quite what she had in mind. 'Lord Chatham, the offer is most generous and I'm sure well meant. However, I must politely protest. We haven't done our lessons yet.' She kept her voice low. 'Yesterday, you and I talked of the necessity for a schedule.'

Lord Chatham shrugged, unconcerned. 'Lessons can wait. A day of good English sunshine cannot. One never knows when we'll see the sun again. We must take advantage of such days when they present themselves.' He gave her a wink. 'You should hurry along, too, Miss Caulfield. You're not ready to go.' Then added conspiratorially, 'Lessons will take care of themselves, you'll see.'

She understood implicitly there was to be no further discussion. Maura knew how to argue. Her uncle was famous for his blusters and tirades. She could stand her ground in the face of such debate. But Lord Chatham's tactics were nothing like her uncle's and she'd been ill prepared for them this first time. Unlike her uncle, Chatham was not a man who shouted to get what he wanted. He simply charmed. He might have put off discussion of the children's schedule for the moment, but discussion would have to come. Children *needed* a schedule.

There would be little she could do about it if he made a habit of impromptu excursions whenever he happened to wake up early. Having a schedule ensured her safety, too. She couldn't make a habit of being about town too much, at least for a while. If anyone was looking for her, she didn't want to be caught unawares. Today could be the exception. It was too early for anyone to have tracked her this far. She was counting on her uncle's limited thinking to keep his search rooted to the area closer to home.

It was immediately clear this was to be no usual sojourn. Maura had thought they'd go to the park in the square across the street with the other neighbours. She'd walked there yesterday with the children. But the sight of Lord Chatham's open barouche with two matched greys champing at the bit in front of the town house soon disabused her of the notion.

'William, come sit beside me,' Lord Chatham instructed, getting them all settled with his ever-present charm. 'A gentleman always sits with his back to the driver and the ladies always sit facing forwards.'

Maura experienced some relief over that arrangement. She far preferred sitting next to Cecilia. There would be no accidental jostling of thighs or other contact when the carriage hit a bump in the road. She'd feared for a moment she'd have to sit next to him. Not because he repulsed her—quite the opposite, and the attraction was unseemly for one in her position. He was her employer and a rogue of a fellow, too, if Mrs Pendergast was to be believed. His behaviour at dinner had proved as much. He was not averse to flirting with the hired governess and whatever else he could get away with.

She took her seat next to Cecilia and realised this was worse. Sitting across from him ensured she had to look at him, at his blue eyes, at his broad shoulders, at his long legs, which were booted and crossed at the ankles and dangerously close to hers when they stretched out across the carriage as they were doing now. So much for avoiding any casual contact.

'Where are we going?' The carriage pulled out into the traffic and Maura couldn't deny she wasn't just a little bit excited. This would be her first trip about London. Yesterday in the hired hackney, her mind had been too occupied to look around and the window had been too small to see much of the view even if she had been inclined.

'Regent's Park. It's open to the public today, Miss Caulfield. We couldn't waste the sunshine *and* the park, especially when it's only open two days a week. It's far too great of a treat to pass up, isn't it?' Lord Chatham's blue eyes were twinkling. He *knew*, drat him. He knew this was as big of a treat for her as it was for the children.

Chapter Four

'You're very good with a kite, Miss Caulfield,' Riordan called out from the boat pond where he and William were sailing the boy's new model schooner. Miss Caulfield and Cecilia had opted to take advantage of the breezes and it did his heart good to see the little girl running on the green, hoisting the kite into the air on command. He'd half-expected the kite to break, as much else did that Cecilia touched. Riordan supposed it was the nature of being seven and inquisitive. If it had, he'd have bought her a new one, but to his pleasant surprise, the kite had stayed up, ably piloted by Miss Caulfield.

Riordan smiled, watching Miss Caulfield manoeuvre the kite away from a grove of trees.

She'd been a pleasant surprise herself this morning, romping with the children in the nursery. She'd not assigned the task and then stood idly by, ordering the children about like governess Number Three. From the look of her, she'd joined in the game whole-heartedly. She'd been delightfully mussed with her hair coming down and the faintest of smudges on her cheek. It had made him wonder what she'd look like more thoroughly mussed and by a man who knew how—a most arousing mental exercise, to be sure.

She was certainly a lot prettier than Number Four, Old Pruneface. She was wearing green again, this time an apple-green walking dress with a wide-brimmed hat to match—a hat, he noted, that had been discarded since their arrival. *Ah, Miss Caulfield*, Riordan thought with a smile, *you are more impetuous than you let on.*

The wind changed and the kite took a dive. Cecilia squealed a warning. Miss Caulfield tugged on the twine, but the kite continued to fall. Riordan gauged its trajectory. It was headed for the boating lake. Riordan sprinted towards

Miss Caulfield, who was losing the battle. Beside her, Cecilia jumped up and down, frantic.

'Allow me, Miss Caulfield.' He took over the string and reeled it in, tugging every so often until the kite stabilised. 'There, Cecilia,' he assured the little girl, 'everything's fine now.' But he was reluctant to turn the kite over. It had been ages since he'd flown one. He and Elliott had flown plenty of kites, built plenty of kites in their childhood. Miss Caulfield was eyeing him with barely disguised impatience. Apparently she, too, was something of a secret kite *aficionado*.

Riordan couldn't resist showing off, just a little. He waited until he had the kite in a controlled stall before he let the line go slack, then he tugged, turning the kite on its belly in a flat rotation: a smooth, graceful move that mimicked the gentle glide of a bird.

Cecilia clapped and William was impressed enough to come up from the pond with his boat. 'Do it again, Uncle Ree!' He did it several more times, casually lecturing William and Cecilia on the aerodynamics of lift until their interest was satisfied and they ran back to the pond.

Riordan continued to fly the kite, aware of

Miss Caulfield's eyes on him, studying, wondering. 'How do you do that?' Miss Caulfield asked at last. 'Will you tell me how?'

Riordan grinned. 'Better than that, I'll *show* you.' He passed her the spindle of twine and sat down on the grass. 'All right, here's lesson number one. Do exactly as I tell you. The first step to an axel turn is a controlled stall. Let the kite hover in the air. Good.' He leaned back on his elbows, watching the sun turn her hair the colour of burnished copper. The faintest hints of freckles were making an appearance on the bridge of her nose, a small penance for going without her hat.

His new governess was pretty, slightly mysterious with a dash of impetuosity thrown in— three traits he appreciated in his women. The question was how far could he pursue this? She was in his employ but did that mean he couldn't flirt a little, especially if she was amenable? She might be. There'd been times at dinner when she'd forgotten she shouldn't be interested in him. Coaxing her to forget a little more could be fun.

'Now, pull at the twine to turn the nose away from you. Let the line go slack. Wait until one wing drops a little lower than the other and then tug. No.' Riordan winced as the kite dipped dangerously low in an out-of-control dive. She tried again with no better results.

Riordan levered himself up off the ground. It was time to intervene. He came up behind her, sliding his hands over hers on the spindle. 'It's more of an intuition. You have to *feel* the moment when the one wing dips.' She smelled wonderful, light and fresh like honeysuckle and lilac in the spring, but her body was tense. Such close proximity made her self-conscious, as it had in the barouche. If he had to guess, it was because it excited her. 'Relax, Miss Caulfield. I can hardly ravish you in a public park,' he whispered playfully against her ear. It wasn't entirely true. He and Mrs Lennox had proven that claim decidedly false in Green Park last summer. He and Lady Granville had confirmed those findings just a couple of weeks ago, but Miss Caulfield didn't need to know that.

Riordan steadied the kite, feeling Miss Caulfield's tension ease as the kite trick demanded more of her attention. He kept his voice low. 'Do you feel the slack? Now, wait for it—no, don't go too soon.' His hands tightened over

hers. 'Wait for the last possible moment…and…
now!' They tugged together and the kite flat-
turned effortlessly.

'It's like a bird in flight,' Miss Caulfield
breathed.

'Is that the best you can do?' Riordan teased
her. The description seemed far too tame for
such a smooth, elegant move. Surely the woman
who recklessly took off her hat in the park and
imagined a nursery to be the burning town of
Bronte just to get it tidied up could do better
than that?

'It's apt,' Miss Caulfield replied, taking um-
brage. 'What do *you* think it's like?'

He stepped closer to her, his hands tightening gently over hers as he guided the kite into
another graceful flat turn. 'I think it's like making love to a woman.' He put his mouth close
to her ear, breathing in the freshness of her.
'A good lover cultivates patience; a good lover
knows how to wait until the most final of moments to…'

'Lord Chatham, that is quite enough.' Miss
Caulfield dipped and slipped under the circle
of his arms. 'You are really a most audacious

man.' Her face was flushed, but it wasn't all from embarrassment.

Riordan laughed good-naturedly at the return of her self-consciousness. 'Maybe I am, a little.' He executed a few more tricks he remembered from childhood while Miss Caulfield watched, one hand shading her eyes as she looked into the sky, a very convenient alternative to looking at him.

'Growing up, my brother and I would spend winters in the attics building kites.' Riordan did a back spin with the kite. 'Come spring, we'd fly them every chance we got. We had fabulous competitions.' He hadn't thought of those days for a long time. 'We started when we weren't much older than William.' Their fascination with kites had lasted quite a while. Even when Elliott had gone away to school, they'd flown kites when he came home on holiday.

'You miss your brother,' Miss Caulfield said softly. 'You were close. His death must be a terrible blow for you.'

'Yes, Miss Caulfield. It is,' he said tersely, thankful she wasn't looking at him. He gave all his attention and then some to the kite, willing the moment of vulnerability to pass. He had not missed the present-tense reference. Everyone said his brother's death *had been* a terrible blow, as if it was something he'd got over and relegated to the past. But it wasn't like that. He missed Elliott every day. He missed knowing that Elliott was out there, somewhere, keeping order and doing good.

Miss Caufield allowed him to fly in silence, standing quietly beside him. It was a smart woman who knew when to give a man his space. After a while, Riordan began reeling the kite in. 'Why don't you get the children and we'll go to Gunter's for ices?' He watched her pick up her hat and head down to the boat pond. He wasn't sure why he'd told that story about building kites. She was a virtual stranger. Maybe he'd told her in apology for his inappropriate comment about making love to a woman. Maybe he'd told her because he didn't want her to think he was an entirely graceless cad.

'Is it always this busy?' Maura looked about her in delighted amazement from the barouche. They were parked across the street from Gunter's Confectionary with other carriages of the fashionable who'd come to take advantage of the good weather. Busy waiters ran from the store to the carriages, delivering ices and other treats. She marvelled at the waiters managed to stay clear of horses. Any moment, Maura expected there to be an accident.

'It's always this busy. Do you know why?' Lord Chatham leaned forwards with a smile. He was going to tease her. Maura was fast coming to recognise that smile. She braced herself.

'It's the one place a young woman may be seen alone with a man without the presence of a chaperon.'

'Of course. It has nothing to do with the quality of the merchandise,' Maura replied drily, but she did look around to test his hypothesis. Young men lounged against carriage doors sharing ices with young ladies. 'It looks fairly harmless.' Not nearly as wicked as Lord Chatham's low tones had implied.

Lord Chatham shrugged as if he found her comment debatable. 'I suppose it depends on who you're eating ices with.'

A waiter came to take their orders and Maura knew a second's panic. What to choose? There'd been ices occasionally at her uncle's home, but never this array of flavours to pick from. The children chose strawberry. Lord Chatham chose burnt filbert. Maura hesitated a fraction too long.

'Chocolate crème, if you please, for the lady,' Lord Chatham supplied with a wink. 'It's positively decadent.'

Maura flushed. A gentleman had ordered for her, had treated her like a real lady for the first time. She understood it meant nothing beyond good manners—she was a practical girl, after all. He'd been doing his duty. Still, it had felt nice. No one had ever felt compelled to his duty on her behalf before.

The chocolate crème *was* decadent, Maura decided after the first bite. She let the cool richness slide down her throat, taking care to savour it, aware that Lord Chatham was watching her.

'Do you like it?' he asked, although he must have known the answer already. 'We can set up an order for the house. You can have ice cream delivered every day.'

'Every day?' Maura raised an eyebrow. 'That sounds like the height of luxurious living.'

Lord Chatham took a bite of his ice cream. 'The Italians eat it every day. Florence is full of *gelaterias*. Their ice cream is *gelati*,' he explained to the children who were hanging on his every word. 'The flavours would astound you; all types of chocolates, vanilla, strawberry, almonds—almost any flavor you can think of.'

'I want to live there,' Cecilia put in. 'I would eat ice cream every day.'

Lord Chatham waggled his dark brows and gave Cecilia a mock-serious look. 'I did live there and I did eat ice cream every day. It was one of the best parts of being in Italy.'

'What were the other best parts?' William ventured, taking a break from his ice cream. 'The volcanoes? Mount Etna is in Italy.'

'As is Mount Vesuvius. One day, I climbed that mountain…'

The rest of the afternoon, Lord Chatham regaled the children with tales of his time abroad. They listened enrapt. Maura listened, too. It was easy to get caught up in the stories. The earl was an excellent storyteller and the topic was captivating. She'd never known anyone who'd travelled as extensively as Lord Chatham. How wonderful it must be to travel like that. Lord Chatham had clearly enjoyed his time abroad. His face took on a softness, his eyes were far away as he recalled narrow streets and hill towns, rich wines and foods eaten in villas that caught the afternoon breezes. Her own world seemed very small. The furthest she'd ever travelled had been her flight from Exeter to London. That hardly counted as a trip. It had been an escape.

Cecilia's head lolled against her and Maura moved an arm about the sleepy child. 'Perhaps we should go home.' The ice creams were eaten and both children were pleasantly drowsy from their exciting day.

The drive home was slow and the noise of late-afternoon traffic made conversation difficult. Maura stayed busy with her own thoughts, most of them occupied by the man sitting across from her. He was proving to be quite the conundrum: fun-loving and stern by turn; easy-going and yet vulnerable; handsome and flirtatious by nature. Her employer presented a most tempting attraction, an attraction that must be resisted. Her post depended on it. She must not even think it, no matter how much the temptation beckoned, no matter how often he lured her with his smiles and bold words designed to spark her passions and curiosities.

Maura scolded herself for the momentary lapse. He would flirt with anything, that much was clear. But she couldn't afford to be his next conquest. It boded ill that she was thinking such thoughts after only a day in his employ. Perhaps this was why the other governesses had left. Perhaps they had been made of sterner stuff.

'A penny for your thoughts.' Lord Chatham stretched his legs. The traffic noise had died down the closer they got to Portland Square and the quieter, elite streets. 'Or are they worth more than that?'

'I was wondering why the other governesses left.' It made little sense. The children were decent children, even if they were a bit unruly at times from a lack of structure. The home was in a good neighborhood, the work no more onerous than any other a governess might expect. In short, there was nothing wrong with the posting, technically. But Mrs Pendergast had made it clear the situation was intolerable.

'I suspect, Miss Caulfield, they didn't like me.' The hint of a mischievous grin hovered on his lips.

'I find that hard to believe.' They probably had liked him too much.

'Is there a compliment in that somewhere?' He laughed it off and then sobered. 'I assure you, Old Pruneface—that was Number Four—didn't like me one bit. I interrupted her lessons far too often. She told me if I interrupted one more time she was leaving. So I did and she left.'

'Maybe it was calling her Old Pruneface.' But Maura did not miss the secondary message. Was there a warning for her in it? He would continue to interrupt as he had done today when and where he pleased? 'About the schedule, Lord Chatham—' Maura began.

'Didn't you like our lessons?' he broke in with a soft, melting smile.

'Lessons?'

'I told you the lessons would take care of themselves and they did. We had etiquette about how to ride in a carriage, we had science about wind and lift and some about the water, too, when William and I were at the pond. We had history and geography, Italy and volcanoes.'

'So we did,' Maura conceded with a modicum of surprise. He'd been thoughtful and in-

ventive about the day's interruption. She'd not
known many men like that. Indeed, she'd not
known any until today.

He gave her one of his playful winks. 'You
are not the only one, Miss Caulfield, who can
turn fun into more noble ends.'

'Today was lovely, but there is also merit in
structure.' Maura stood her ground. 'We can
plan outings. We can set aside a certain day
of the week for them,' Maura cajoled. 'I'm not
saying we can't have outings. I believe in them
wholeheartedly.'

The carriage pulled up to the town house, ef-
fectively curbing further conversation. All she
managed to wring from Lord Chatham by way
of closure was a lukewarm 'we'll see' before
they began the process of getting the children
inside. She helped William into the house while
Lord Chatham carried a sleeping Cecilia up the
steps, looking more like a father than an earl.
It was a heart-warming sight that would have
made it all too easy to forgive him his myriad
sins: the indifference that led to children eating
breakfast alone, a messy nursery, the anarchy
by which he ran his town house and the rakish-
ness that led him to flirt unashamedly.

Surely a man who was so good with children wasn't all bad, which made it that much worse for her. It would be better if he were an irredeemable dissolute like Wildeham. Then she'd know what to make of him, how to manage him.

The butler, Fielding, met them in the foyer with a stern look. 'Milord, your solicitor is waiting to see you. He's been here since two o'clock.' Maura sensed it was as close to a reprimand as the butler would dare. Except for a slight tightening of his jaw, Chatham looked unperturbed over the development.

'Miss Caulfield, if you could take Cecilia?' Lord Chatham deposited the child in her arms. 'It seems I have forgotten the appointment. Fielding, show Mr Browning to my study. I will see him immediately.'

Maura climbed the stairs with her bundle, William trailing beside her. She was starting to see reasons for the earl's indifference. No wonder he wasn't interested in the children's schedule and ignored the importance of structure. Lord Chatham couldn't even keep his own.

Chapter Five

'Well?' Riordan took his seat behind the large walnut desk and fixed the solicitor with a stare he hoped would qualify as 'imperious'.

'It's not good news,' Mr Browning began, giving the glasses on his nose a push with his middle finger, a gesture Riordan found singularly annoying.

'Of course it isn't.' Mr Browning never managed to bring good news.

'Lady Cressida Vale and her husband, the viscount, want custody of the children.' At least Mr Browning wasn't sugar-coating anything but that didn't stop a cold stab of fear from settling in Riordan's stomach.

'You mean they want custody of the trust

funds.' Riordan held his temper, but just barely. He'd expected this. Lady Vale had intimated as much at the funeral.

Mr Browning gave Riordan a censorious look over the rims of his glasses for speaking so baldly. 'There is no proof of such motivation.'

'She is a maternal cousin of their father and I am a paternal cousin. When it comes to next of kin, we are equal, except that my family stepped forwards to care for the children when her side had the chance and did not.' Riordan remembered very well Elliott swooping in to save the day four years ago when the children had become penniless orphans.

'Things are different now.' Mr Browning was prevaricating this time. It could only mean there was more bad news.

Riordan leaned back in the chair and steepled his hands. 'Naturally things are different. Elliott left the children well provided for. Ishmael, their father, left them nothing but a mouldering estate.' No one had wanted to take on the burden of two young children with no prospects.

'The guardianship is different now, too,' Mr Browning pressed on uncomfortably. He pushed a paper forwards in explanation. 'The former earl was deemed a proper guardian.'

'Are you suggesting I am not?' Anger started to simmer.

'I'm not. They are.' Browning nodded towards the paper, urging him to read it.

Riordan scanned it, his anger boiling at the list of sins enumerated against him: an improper lifestyle of womanising and gambling, no structure for the children, an incoherent education—the list went on. All of which could be remedied by the presence of a motherly figure in the household, presumably Lady Vale. The thought was laughable. Lady Vale was about as maternal as…well, no *apt* comparison came to mind, to borrow Miss Caulfield's word from earlier in the day.

'The children will have their structure. Tell the Vales that.' Riordan pushed the paper back across the desk with a sense of satisfaction. 'I have a governess.' Ha, the Vales could try to trump that. The Vales argued for structure—well, he had it. Miss Caulfield and her appreciation for such structure would feel vindicated.

Browning coughed and fidgeted. 'With all

due respect, milord, you've had *five* govern-esses.'

'I haven't exactly "had" five governesses.'

Browning coughed at the vulgarity. '*Hired.* You've hired five governesses in an unseemly short period of time.'

'And the point is?' If that skinny ferret of a solicitor was going to agree with the opposition, Riordan would make damn sure he had to come out and do it blatantly.

'Well, *five*, milord, seems to undermine your case rather than help it.'

'That's your opinion.' Riordan skewered Browning with a hard look. 'My brother left those children to me. He did not leave them to the Vales and for good reason. The Vales can disagree with me all they like, but Elliott's will is uncontested.' He was relying on the immov-able bulwark of English law to hold firm.

Mr Browning was silent and Riordan felt the weight of unspoken words hanging between them. 'Mr Browning, say something,' Riordan said quietly.

'I am sorry for the loss, milord. I liked the earl a great deal.' Meaning that he didn't care for the current earl nearly as much. Riordan was used to it. It wasn't the first time he had been measured against the perfect standard of Elliott and come up lacking. 'The nature of the earl's death does call into question the sanctity of his will.'

'Put that in plain English for the rest of us.'

'The Vales could argue the earl was mentally unstable.'

Riordan studied his hands. 'Would they win?'

'I don't know. Does it matter?' Mr Browning offered astutely.

It wouldn't. It was the scandal of it all coming out that mattered. Elliott's memory would be besmirched. Riordan would put a stop to that if he could. His brother had been an upstanding saint of a man who'd met with a mysterious end. He didn't deserve to have his life publicly examined and criticised.

Riordan reached for the paper again. He stared hard at the words itemising his fall: womaniser, no home structure, lack of a motherly presence for the children. Browning was most regrettably right. A governess would not plug the dyke. He tapped a finger on the polished surface of the desk, thinking. A governess might not, but a wife most certainly would.

He looked up at Browning, a plan unfolding that would preserve Elliott's memory and save the children. 'What if I married?' He'd have to do it quickly and to a worthy candidate. His wife would need to be without blemish. It would be difficult indeed for the Vales to argue his home was without a maternal presence with a wife at his side. Yes, that might just work.

'And the other issue?' Riordan asked. There was nothing more to be done about the Vales today, but perhaps Browning had better news on other fronts.

Browning disappointed him immediately with a shake of his head. 'The investigation regarding your brother's death has turned up nothing. We've spoken with the house staff in Sussex. They noted nothing unusual in the days leading up to the incident.'

Riordan frowned. Browning couldn't even bring himself to say the word. 'What about mail? Had there been any letters or news that might have upset him?' It was hard to believe anything so disturbing would have arrived by mail. Elliott was unflappable, not easily alarmed.

'Nothing that anyone was aware of. We did conduct a search of his rooms and the house.'

'Relationships?' Riordan hardly dared to voice the thought. It seemed somehow dishonourable to his brother's memory. But at this point, all the usual rocks had been turned and nothing had been found beneath them. The finances and debts were all in good standing. But something was not right. Elliott was dead without cause.

'I hardly know what you mean.' Browning furrowed his brow in puzzlement. Riordan had hoped Browning for once might use his imagination and save him the effort of explaining in painfully explicit terms. Apparently, he was going to have to be a bit more plainspoken.

'Was my brother a molly? Did he have a male lover?' Riordan ground out the words. He knew of men who'd killed themselves either to prevent exposure or because of it, the shame too great. Last year, the Duke of Amherst's fifth son had been found out and three days later had been discovered floating in the Thames. Elliott was thirty-three, after all, and to Riordan's knowledge his brother had never been in love, never seriously courted a lady although he was well aware of his duty to procreate and continue the earldom. But certainly, as close as they were, he would have known, wouldn't he?

Browning's face was crimson. He'd discomfited the poor man beyond the usual. 'There is nothing to indicate that.' The words came out in a hoarse wheeze of offence over the subject.

'There has to be something. Keep looking, keep asking questions,' Riordan encouraged. 'Someone, somewhere, knows something and we will find them.' It was his dismissal. Browning had delivered enough bad news. It had been a good day up until now. As soon as the solicitor left he could get back to life as usual: women, wine and forgetting.

He started with the wine and forgetting the moment Browning had been shown out. Riordan poured himself a healthy tumbler of brandy and settled into his favourite chair by the fire. Maybe he'd follow it up with a woman later. Lady Hatfield had indicated interest at the Rutherfords' last night, but it wasn't Lady Hatfield who came to mind. Instead it was a woman with cinnamon tresses and green eyes, who was bold and cautious, impetuous and reserved, hungry for a taste of life, of passion if she dared. If *he* dared. He was aware that *that* particular woman was the only thing giving his home a whiff of decency at the moment. Conventional wisdom suggested he couldn't afford to run her off until he could put his plan in motion.

Too bad. She'd been delightful in his arms today while they'd flown the kite. The gentle curve of her hip, the slenderness of her waist, the tempting pout of breasts that were just full enough to fill a man's hands beneath the muslin bodice of her gown had not gone unnoticed. She would be a pleasure to undress, a pleasure to reveal.

Riordan rose to fill his glass again and moved the decanter to the little table next to his chair. There was no sense in having to keep getting up to fill his glass, not as many times as he planned on filling it tonight. He wanted to banish the doubts that had haunted him since Elliott's death. Hell, who was he kidding? There'd been doubts and ghosts long before Elliott's death. He wanted to banish those, too, wanted to prove the Vales were wrong about him.

He would marry. They wouldn't expect him to do such an honourable deed and sacrifice himself for the good of others. But they didn't understand his love for Elliott. He'd do anything for Elliott, he'd make up for all the ways he'd disappointed him in life. Riordan settled in his chair and drank deeply. It was easier to keep the memories chained during the daylight. He could busy himself like he had today with an outing for the children. But at night, without the benefit of moving from one entertainment to another, the memories were free of their chains. He let them come, let the doubts rise with the night, all the better to drive them back with brandy...

He would never forget the horror, the sinking feeling of that day at the art show when he'd scanned the message. In four brief lines on parchment, for which Riordan irrationally would never forgive Browning for writing, he'd become an earl and a substitute father. All thanks to what was politely referred to as a self-inflicted gunshot wound to the head. The words were a courteous euphemism for suicide, as if couching the act in terms that implied a hunting accident made any difference. Social sensibilities aside, the outcome was the same: at the august age of three and thirty, Elliott Randolph Fitzsimmons Barrett, Earl of Chatham, was dead and he, Riordan Christopher Barrett of the much shorter name and fewer socially acceptable accomplishments, second son and heir to nothing in particular, was most regretfully still alive, a generally held poor substitute for his brother. It should have been him in that box, not Elliott. That was perhaps the biggest mystery of all.

The manner of his brother's death had been most shocking and unexpected. Elliott had been the perfect heir and the earldom was a well-run gem set amidst the green-field bounty of Sussex. As earl, Elliott had had no financial worries. Elliott's social record was without blemish. He'd held his seat in the House of Lords with admirable attendance and was every hostess's dream. There was no reason to make such an abrupt and scandalous end to his pristine life.

The lack of reason had been on everyone's mind at the funeral. During the reception, the guests had approached him one by one and whispered their questions in quiet tones as if they were the first to ask. Had he known of anything that would have disturbed his brother? Why hadn't the earl gone up to London as he usually did? Beneath the questions was the unspoken accusation: if Riordan had been there, he could have stopped it.

Riordan wondered the same. If he'd waited to come up to town with Elliott he'd have been there with him. He'd seen Elliott in late March, just four weeks prior. Everything had seemed fine. *Elliott* had seemed fine. He had a good relationship with his brother. They'd always been close, though not as close in adulthood as they'd been in childhood. Such distance was to be expected. Elliott was the heir and Riordan wasn't. He had to create a life away from the house. But there was no animosity between them and Riordan saw Elliott often throughout the year. What had he missed on this last visit?

No matter how much brandy he drank, Riordan would never forgive himself for coming up to town early. Still, there might be enough brandy to forget. He had to try. He was doing pretty well until a bright shaft of light penetrated his dark, fire-lit domain.

Riordan shielded his eyes from the intrusion, mumbling a curse. 'Fielding, get out. I don't need a butler at the moment.'

Maura stifled a groan. She'd made a double error. The room wasn't the library and it wasn't empty. She had a witness to her mistake. To make it worse, she'd also miscalculated. 'I'm sorry. I thought you had gone out.'

When there'd been no dinner summons or an appearance in the nursery to wish the children goodnight, she'd assumed he'd left. She'd assumed incorrectly and now here she was in what appeared to be Lord Chatham's office, garbed in a dressing gown and night shift at a most inappropriate hour.

'As you can see, I am most assuredly quite "in".' Lord Chatham rose from his chair and held his arms wide in an expansive gesture, a glass in his hand.

Maura shot a disapproving look at the glass, taking note of the near-empty decanter beside the chair. 'In your cups is more like it.' Although it was hard to tell just how far in he was. He walked remarkably straight as he moved towards her, but his clothes were rumpled, his cravat undone, his jacket discarded, leaving him in shirt sleeves and waistcoat, the very same one he'd worn to the park. He'd not left this room since he'd disappeared with the solicitor.

'I should go. I was looking for the library.' Past experience had taught her a man in any state of inebriation ought to be avoided. Wildeham was a mean man when drunk. She backed towards the door in a reluctant retreat, but Lord Chatham didn't strike her as particularly dangerous, only particularly handsome, and the curious side of her wasn't ready to abdicate the room yet.

He looked utterly rakish in the firelight, his hair falling forwards over his face as it had on the porch when they'd collided. 'Don't go, stay and have a drink with me. There's enough left in the decanter for a delicate swallow or two.'

'You've had enough to drink.' She should have been out the door by now, but it was hard to leave him.

'I'm not so very drunk, Maura.' The sound of her given name on his lips sent a bolt of white heat to her stomach. Who knew a single word could be uttered so seductively? He gave her a crooked grin. 'If I was, I wouldn't be able to do this.' He placed his feet, one in front of the other, on a line running through the carpet pattern and held out his hands on either side like a tightrope walker. He began to move: one step, two, three, four, jump. He leapt up into the air in a ball, clasping his knees to him and landing with perfect balance back on his line.

In spite of herself, Maura laughed. 'Most likely it proves the opposite.'

He stopped his high-wire act in mid-stride and said with strict seriousness, 'No, it doesn't. Everyone knows a drunken man can't walk a straight line. A drunk *definitely* couldn't jump in the air and land in perfect position.'

'And a sober man definitely wouldn't try it,' Maura answered. The response seemed to carry some weight with him. Lord Chatham paused in contemplation, studying the carpet.

'All right, how about this: Do you see the medallion in the centre of the carpet? A drunken man couldn't do this.' Lord Chatham put his toe in the centre of the medallion and began to dance—a series of pointed steps and sharp pivots, the occasional tight spin. It was unlike any dance Maura had seen. The dance was athletic and masculine.

'It's called *zebekikos*. It's from Greece,' Lord Chatham said over his shoulder, executing a final turn. 'Now, do you think a drunken man could do *that*?'

'You're impossible,' Maura conceded.

'Your hair is down.' He was close to her again, close enough to reach his hand out and take her hair between his fingers. 'It's beautiful. I thought so today at the park. You should always wear it down.' His voice was quiet. Maura was aware of the mood changing between them, shifting from the humour of his little tests to something more potent, something flammable waiting to ignite, something very different from the lewd advances of Wildeham. Now it was time to leave before she gave in to the temptation of her curiosities.

'Lord Chatham, this is hardly seemly,' Maura began, aware that her pulse had begun to race in direct contradiction. It might not be seemly but it was definitely exciting. She'd never been so close to a handsome gentleman before. Part of her argued quite convincingly she might not have such a chance again. It would be worth the risk to see where this led, to see if all kisses were wet and harsh like Wildeham's.

He pressed a finger to her lips and shook his head. 'Call me Riordan and I shall call you Maura. No more Lord Chatham and Miss Caulfield.'

'I don't think that's a good idea.' Too much

familiarity would breed all nature of problems, not the least of which would be the assumption their relationship as employer and employee was more than it should be. It was much the same logic that governed why farmers didn't name cows they slaughtered.

'Well, I do,' Riordan pressed, his hands most indecently placed at her hips in an intimate, possessive fashion.

'You *have* been drinking,' Maura persisted, but without any real chagrin. That something she'd sensed earlier was about to ignite.

'I have been a great many things tonight, *Maura*.' He drawled her name, purposely defiant. She could feel the heat of his hands warm and welcoming at her hips as they drew her closer until their bodies met. His blue eyes held hers. 'I've been dancing and jumping, and most of all, I've been in a room with a beautiful woman far too long without kissing her.'

He claimed her mouth in a move that left her breathless, the taste of him like smooth brandy-flavoured warmth, the hard planes of him pressed against her. She gave herself over to his touch, her body cognisant of his, of the caress of his hands low on her hips, the scent of his soap, the feel of evening stubble where it rubbed against her cheek. This was a heady intimacy indeed. She nipped gently at his lower lip, experimenting with the sensuality rising between them, secretly pleased when he groaned in approval.

'Lucifer's balls, Maura, you'd tempt the very devil himself.'

That was when she knew she had to stop, no matter how much she wanted the kiss to go on. There would only be trouble at the other end of it, if there wasn't already. She pulled away and did the only thing she could do—she ran like Cinderella at midnight.

Chapter Six

Slam! Riordan bolted into awareness with a jarring start, the type that left one instantly awake and confused. There was a loud squeal and a crash. Good heavens, what were *four* children doing in his bedroom? Riordan shook his head. Just two children, thank goodness, and wait… this wasn't his bedroom. This was the study. Riordan pushed a hand through his hair and fell back on the sofa.

The evening came back in vivid detail—mostly. Unfortunately, he remembered the bad news with absolute clarity. The Vales wanted the children…well, wanted control of their fortunes. He'd been drinking, a fact prompted by the empty decanter beside his abdicated chair.

Cecilia danced in front of him dressed in a gown of aquamarine silk several sizes too big for her, her feet dwarfed in matching slippers and a filmy shawl draped about her shoulders. 'We're playing dress-up!' she announced in a loud voice that hurt his head. 'You can wear my shawl. It will look pretty with your eyes. We're going to a ball.'

'We're playing hide and seek!' William corrected in an insistent whisper, making it clear he'd *never* be caught pretending to go to a ball. He crouched down behind the chair. 'Hide, Six will be here any second.'

Six. The governess. Miss Caulfield. *Maura*. His employee. The woman he'd kissed last night. After last night, he doubted he'd ever be able to call her Miss Caulfield again. Riordan groaned. He was in no shape to face her. He'd have to apologise just as soon as he could figure out what to apologise for. Exactly how far things had gone was a bit blurry at the moment. Perhaps he should hide, too. But there was no question of getting off the sofa, not with his head throbbing this much. Cecilia squatted down behind him.

The door opened and Riordan sent up a quiet

prayer she wouldn't slam it—either one of her. He blinked hard to clear his vision. The children might be playing hide and seek but Maura didn't look as if she were.

'Children, I know you're in here. The game is up,' she said sternly. 'Children…' She stopped, spotting him on the sofa. 'Oh, my lord, I didn't see you.' That was rather humbling. She hadn't seen him last night either.

'How do you mean that, I wonder? "Oh, my lord", as in using my title to address me, or "oh, my lord", as in abject surprise at finding the room occupied?' He shouldn't have done that. It ached tremendously to use his wit so soon in the day.

'Both, I suppose.' She smoothed her hands on an apron she wore over her dress. If he didn't know better she was trying to suppress a smile. It wasn't the reaction he'd anticipated. He'd thought she'd be uncomfortable. He certainly was. Riordan tempted the fates and sat up *very* slowly. The world stayed in place. That was *very* good.

'I must apologise.' Maura bobbed a short curtsy that reminded him how guilty he should feel over last night, whatever it was he'd done.

He would smile, but it hurt his head too much. The irony of the moment was not lost on him. He was worried he had to apologise for something he didn't quite remember and she was worried he'd dismiss her. She could oversleep every day and he couldn't dismiss her, not now that the Vales had laid down their gauntlet. They'd be over the moon about him losing a sixth governess.

'The children got away from me. I overslept. It won't happen again.' She was clearly anxious to be away. Her words rushed out, giving him the distinct impression she'd break into laughter if she slowed down. He couldn't imagine what was so funny.

'Children, come on out. Maura has found you fair and square,' Riordan called. William and Cecilia emerged slowly from their hiding places, penitent looks on their faces. 'Where did you get that dress, Cecilia?' Riordan looked, really looked, at the gown for the first time. It was expensive and well made, far too fine a garment to be found in a child's dress-up box.

Cecilia pouted and tears started to well in her blue eyes. 'It's Miss Caulfield's.' The answer came out in a near-whisper. 'It was just so pretty, I wanted to try it on.'

Riordan cast a pleading glance Maura's way. He was helpless against Cecilia's tears, always had been, hangover notwithstanding. Maura stepped forwards and took the little girl by the hand. 'A lady never goes through another person's things without their permission. I would have been happy to show the dress to you if you'd asked.'

Maura was strict, but not unkind. Number Three, Old Ironsides, would have rapped Cecilia's knuckles—had done so, in fact, which explained why she was no longer there. Riordan had nearly tossed her bodily into the street. Maura held out her other hand to William. 'There's nothing that can't be cured with a good breakfast. I suspect breakfast is what drove you downstairs in the first place. We've got toad in the hole waiting for us upstairs.'

William looked at his feet sheepishly and Riordan knew she'd diagnosed William's adventure perfectly. Used to eating downstairs, he'd come looking for food. 'Do you know what toad in the hole is, Will?' Maura went on. 'It's sausage and toast, only the toast has a hole in it and the hole is filled with the sausage.' Will perked up at that, looking more excited about returning to the nursery.

Riordan wasn't going to let her get away that easily. He let her make it to the door, chatting to the children, before he interrupted. 'Maura, when the children are settled and fed, I'd like to see you in the library.' Goodness knew he didn't want to have the impending interview here in the study, the scene of last night's débâcle.

The door shut behind them, leaving him alone. It was time to face the day and put his plans in motion. He'd have to shave. Riordan scrubbed at his face. 'What the hell?' He leapt up, forgetting the world would spin if he moved too quickly. He clutched at the back of a chair and inched his way towards the mirror on the wall. Riordan groaned. Lucifer's balls! A dark smear of rose blush adorned each cheek, dark kohl outlined the circle of his eyes all the way from his eyebrows to his cheek bones and red rouge coloured the area nominally referred to as his mouth. Now he knew why Maura had been on the brink of a laughing jag. Cecilia had made up his face with enough cosmetics to rival a circus clown.

* * *

Half an hour later, Maura stood outside the library door, gathering her courage. He was going to dismiss her, she just knew it. She wanted to play a little hide and seek herself, anything to avoid facing Riordan Barrett and his bad news. This morning had gone poorly. She'd overslept and as a result the children had decorated their uncle's face in a month's worth of cosmetics. That wasn't even counting the kissing incident from last night.

One didn't have to live in London to know how the world worked when it came to this sort of thing—this sort of thing being kissing one's employer. Even in Devonshire one knew that when this sort of thing happened, it was *always* the woman's fault. It had been her fault Baron Wildeham had pawed her in the pantry of her uncle's home. She'd refused his advances and he'd called her a tease. It would be her fault the Earl of Chatham had kissed her while under the influence of quite a lot of brandy and very few of his senses.

Where would she go? What would she do? Mrs Pendergast had made it clear she could not go back to the agency. Perhaps the earl would give her a reference. But that seemed hopelessly optimistic. She'd been here a scant three days. She could imagine how that reference might read: 'To those concerned, in reference to Miss Maura Caulfield, she enjoys kites in the afternoon and kisses at midnight.' That wouldn't do at all.

Maura tried not to panic. She wasn't dismissed. To give up already was putting the cart before the horse. To be sure, the horse was in harness but it wasn't over yet. She had to think positively, she had to…

'Are you going to come in?' Lord Chatham lounged in the open doorway of the library, dressed for the day in tan breeches and a dark-green coat, his face cleanly shaven and thankfully free of cosmetics. 'I saw your skirts sweep past a few minutes ago. I expected you'd come in, but when you didn't I thought I'd come looking for you.' He ushered her inside with a sweep of his hand, drawing the door to a partial close behind them. Whatever he wanted to say to her, he wanted to say it in relative privacy.

The library was an imposing room with its heavy wood paneling and floor-to-ceiling shelves filled with books. A fireplace with a carved mantel dominated one wall surrounded by a formal grouping of sofa and chairs. A long table filled the centre of the room for reading and research. Formal and masculine, the room seemed at odds with the earl's character. She doubted he spent much time in this room. Not that he wasn't masculine—there was no doubt of that—but he certainly wasn't formal.

He gestured to the sofa, indicating that she should sit, a confirmation of his inherent informality. Employees didn't sit when their employers reprimanded them. They stood in front of big desks, wringing their hands. 'You might have at least told me.' He gestured to his rouge-free cheek.

Maura blushed. 'Some things are best discovered in private.'

'Well, next time, tell me.' He grinned and she took hope.

'Next time, milord?'

'I'm sure there will be a next time, there always is with children. You can relax, Maura. I'm not going to dismiss you.' Lord Chatham laughed, his own posture at ease compared to her rigid bearings.

'You're not?' she repeated, wanting to make

sure she heard him aright. Relief swept her. She was safe.

'No, I'm not. However, I do find myself in the awkward position of needing to apologise while also needing to ask a favour.' He leaned forwards, hands on his knees. 'I am sorry if anything that happened between us last night was upsetting to you.' It had hardly been upsetting—titillating, arousing, yes, but not upsetting, not that she'd ever say that out loud to him. He didn't need any further encouragement.

Maura summoned her best professional tone. 'It was just a kiss, Lord Chatham.' *With hands, and bodies, and tongues, a most thorough and comprehensive kiss that far exceeded any previous experience she'd ever had in that venue.* Relief flickered in Lord Chatham's blue eyes and Maura wondered for a moment if he even remembered all they'd done. Ouch. A lady liked to be remembered.

Lord Chatham cleared his throat. 'I was not myself, as you so aptly pointed out. I can only say I was driven to that state by grief and I must humbly beg your forgiveness.'

Double ouch. *Grief* had driven him to kissing her? It wasn't exactly the romantic apology one hoped for; something along the lines of 'intoxicated by your beauty, swept away by your charms' would have been preferable. But apparently the 'intoxicated' part was the best she was going to get. What was the appropriate response to such a disclosure? Maura decided there wasn't one. 'Apology accepted, Lord Chatham.'

'That's the third time you've called me Lord Chatham in the last five minutes. I thought we'd dispensed with that last night.' He fixed her with an inquisitive stare, daring her to contradict him.

'As I recall, it was undecided. You thought it a good idea while I thought it a poor one. So, we're at an impasse.' First names were an informality she could not allow for her own defences. It was bad enough to think of *Lord Chatham's* kiss, of his hands on her hips, when she looked at him. But to think of those hands, those lips as belonging to *Riordan* was an invitation to let it happen again, or worse, to *want* it to happen again.

'You had a favour you wanted to ask?' Maura changed the subject, hoping he'd let the matter of names drop.

'Yes. It's a rather large favour, but I could not help noticing at dinner the other night how very fine your manners were and it seemed to me that you would be the perfect person to help me with a little project.' He paused here. Maura had the distinct impression he was searching for the right words, the right persuasion. 'I would like you to help me plan a dinner, a small gathering, nothing too grand on account of my brother's passing.'

The attempt to minimise the enormity of the task was obvious and the request odd. Yesterday, he'd been upset over his brother's death. She'd heard the pain in his voice when he'd talked of his brother at the park. He made a habit of wearing an armband on his coats. It seemed strange he'd want to entertain at all. However, she knew he'd kept his social schedule. The first night she'd been here, he'd been all too eager to get to the round of entertainments. 'If you're in mourning, Lord Chatham, why entertain at all? Surely everyone will understand?'

Lord Chatham looked down at his hands laced together on his thighs. 'It has come to my attention that I must marry and quickly. I do not have the luxury of waiting until next year. I must take advantage of this Season.' He gave her a wry grin. 'In this case, my reputation is something of an asset. No one expected me to really mourn in isolation for six months. As long as I am tasteful, society will condone my transgression on this, especially if it means one of their darlings gets to marry an earl. Young, available earls aren't exactly thick on the ground.'

Something unnameable plummeted to the bottom of her stomach. He was going to marry! He'd been kissing her while he'd been planning to marry another. It seemed somehow wrong, although she couldn't quite explain the error to herself. All she said was, 'I see. Who?' Perhaps he already had a young lady in mind, which made the unnameable something all that much worse.

'One of them.' He made one of his airy dismissive gestures. 'It hardly matters who as long as I marry. I have it on good authority I must put a maternal presence in this home.'

'I see,' she said again.

'Do you? I wonder.' He leaned back in his chair. 'So you'll do it? You'll plan me a tasteful dinner party filled with tasteful young women?'

Did she have a choice? One could hardly refuse one's employer when he looked at her with those blue eyes. But that didn't mean she liked the idea. It meant people coming to the house. The fewer people who came to the house, the fewer people she'd meet. She would have preferred all the anonymity she could garner. Traditional mourning would have suited her, but it was only planning the party, she reminded herself. She didn't have to go to it. 'When is the party to be?'

'The end of the month.'

'That's a nice way of saying two weeks!' Maura exclaimed. 'That's hardly enough time. There are invitations to write, there are menus to plan. I don't even know who should be on the guest list.' She'd helped her aunt plan dinners—actually, more than helped since her aunt wasn't all that capable and easily overcome by details. Maura knew exactly the amount of work required for a successful dinner and it was substantial.

'I will give you a list and my Aunt Sophie will assist,' Lord Chatham said as if that solved all her problems. 'How hard can it be, truly? Invite a few people, put some food on the table.'

Maura drew herself up into her best posture. 'I assure you, Lord Chatham, there is more to a dinner party than—how did you put it?— "putting some food on the table".'

He smiled, his eyes twinkling in satisfaction. 'Then thank goodness you're planning it and not me. I wouldn't know where to begin and clearly you do.'

William and Cecilia exchanged wide-eyed glances and stepped quietly away from the door. Married. Uncle Ree wanted to get married! William pulled Cecilia into a small room off the hall and shut the door.

'I don't want Uncle Ree to get married.' Cecilia pouted.

'Not to someone we don't like anyway,' William said slowly. 'Remember all those ladies who'd come to visit Papa Elliott and drink tea? They were awful. They didn't like us much.' Papa Elliott had explained to them it was an earl's duty to get married. But that hadn't made the ladies any nicer. The richer they were, the snobbier they were. Now Uncle Ree was the earl and he'd have to get married, too.

Cecilia made a loud 'hmmph'. 'The ladies

that came to see Papa Elliott didn't want to play with us. We definitely want Uncle Ree to marry someone who wants to play with us or there won't be any more sliding on the floors.'

'That's it, Cee-Cee!' William exclaimed. 'We should make a list of what Uncle Ree's wife should be like. It would be different if he married someone *we* liked.'

Cecilia perked up at the thought. 'She should be pretty and she should smell good.'

William nodded. 'She should want to play with us. She should take us to the park.'

Cecilia shook her head. 'Where are we going to find a lady like that?'

William's shoulders sagged. 'I don't know.' He scrunched his brow, running through all the ladies he knew, an admittedly short list. Eight-year-old boys didn't know many ladies. But he did know one. Maybe... He brightened. 'Cee-Cee, what about Miss Caulfield?'

Cecilia cocked her head in contemplation. 'Six is pretty, she smells nice, she plays with us.'

'She makes us do our lessons,' William put in, 'so she's strict enough.'

'We could have toad in the hole and soldiers every morning!' Cecilia bounced excitedly, starting to see the brilliance of such a match. 'What do we have to do?'

'Well…' William gave it some serious thought. 'I think the first thing we should do is make them fall in love.'

'Is that all?' Cecilia grinned. 'That will be easy. We'll tell her everything Uncle Riordan does with us.'

Chapter Seven

That had gone well. Stunningly well. Riordan helped himself to a celebratory drink in the library. Maura was still here after their rather intimate but ill-advised kiss. She hadn't brained him for importuning her even if he had been tap-hackled on brandy *and* she'd said yes to his request. Amazing.

So amazing, in fact, that Riordan felt compelled to send a note to Mrs Pendergast enquiring as to where the agency had found this paragon of a governess who could not only fly kites but who planned dinner parties for earls, came with silk dresses and kissed like a siren. Riordan opted to leave that last bit out. He might find it a desirable qualification, but he doubted

Mrs Pendergast would. Truth was, he found it more than a desirable quality. He found it a most *remarkable* quality.

Riordan had kissed plenty of women, most of them jaded practitioners of the art, like himself. Maura had been different, a bold *ingénue* in his arms with her untried passion. What had started as a game, a dare he'd laid before his slightly inebriated self, had quickly transmuted into something else labelled desire. Once he'd started kissing her, he hadn't wanted to stop. But cooler heads, more sober heads, than his had prevailed. Logically it had been for the best. The only problem was that it left him wanting more; wanting those sweet, consuming kisses again, wanting her rousing to him again out of pure desire instead of some tired game of seduction.

Kissing wasn't the only quality he found desirable about Maura Caulfield. He'd not missed her reaction this morning at seeing Cecilia in the aquamarine ball gown. There'd been *no* reaction at all, not the kind of reaction a woman of limited means would make over seeing a cherished gown being used for dress-up on a sticky-fingered seven-year-old who'd just painted her uncle's face. But Maura had not panicked, or scolded. Perhaps because she had other silk gowns? Perhaps because silk was as commonplace for her as he'd guessed?

Riordan laughed out loud to the empty room. Now he was spinning fantasies from whole cloth, giving his governess a secret life where she wore silk. Still, thinking about Maura Caulfield was more pleasant than writing a note to his aunt, informing her that she would be hosting a dinner party for him in two weeks' time. The news was likely to give her the vapors.

Aunt Sophie was a silly little bird of a woman and Uncle Hamish a thin fribble of a man whose only redeeming quality was the high-perch phaeton he occasionally let Riordan drive around town. They were practically the only relatives he had left. They would have to do. The party would be here at Chatham House, of course, but he couldn't very well ask young women to dinner without a hostess, and Aunt Sophie, for all her ridiculous airs, would know exactly who to invite. Maura would have to do the rest.

He was back to the source of his distraction. It seemed all thoughts led to Maura. He would get nothing done at this rate. Riordan knew from experience distraction was a powerful tool in the art of forgetting. Usually he courted such distraction, but Maura Caulfield was an amusement he could ill afford to cultivate. He needed all his faculties for a meeting with Vale's lawyers this afternoon, which would inevitably spawn more meetings.

Riordan pushed back from the desk. The letter to Aunt Sophie could wait. Right now, he needed a walk. It was just as well the week would keep him busy with whatever legal devices he could come up with to deter the Vales. Those tasks would keep him far from the nursery and far from Maura.

Acton Humphries tossed a heavy bag of coins on the desk. There'd been a glimmer of hope at last. Paul Digby had gone back to the coaching inn and asked for *descriptions* of the female passengers parting around the date Maura had gone missing. Originally, Lucas Harding's Runners had limited their enquiries to the names signed in the coaching manifest. But Digby had reshaped the question. Names could be faked. Digby had looked past that and this time there'd been success. The barkeep at one of the inns had remembered a red-haired woman meeting the description. She'd taken the London coach under the name Ellen Treywick. The news was both good and ominous. It was the first sure lead, but it also confirmed Acton's fears. Maura was in London at the mercy of a city she knew nothing about.

The big man in front of his desk eyed the bag of coins the baron had put down, weighing his words against the chances of the bag disappearing. 'To be fair, sir, it might not be her. Miss Harding's name wasn't in the ledger and there are plenty of red-haired women in the world.'

'But it might be and this part of the world isn't that large.' Acton rose and began to pace behind his chair, looking out the wide, paned window to the garden beyond. He was willing to take a chance on the description. 'She might have been smart enough to use a false name. At this point, with no other leads, we have to assume this "Ellen Treywick" is her. Perhaps we can use the name to track her in London.' Acton dismissed the man's worries with a nonchalance he didn't feel. Maura in London! This was exciting. His blood heated at the thought of it.

The next question was where in London? He

put it to Digby. 'Where would she go? What would she do?' There were possibilities he could rule out. Maura wasn't likely to be looking for a sponsor to take her on for the Season and Harding didn't have those sorts of connections even if Maura was stupid enough to use them. Seeking out any of her uncle's few city friends would be tantamount to writing a letter home announcing her presence.

This line of reasoning also assumed she was safe and had the freedom to choose her next step. He hoped for his own selfish sake that Maura had not been swallowed up by the slums, or, worse, a brothel. Efficiency and speed were of the essence. He wanted her pure and untouched, tamed to and by his own hand.

'If it were me, sir,' Digby began after giving the answer some thought, 'I'd go to ground. I'd hide so I couldn't be found.'

'Yes, but how? You're a man, Digby, you could re-invent yourself in numerous ways. How could a woman?'

'Work, sir. I'd have to find work.'

'Check the dress shops, then. She can stitch so it's not out of the realm of possibility she's found work in a shop.' He liked the idea of shops. It made sense. 'Pack your bags, Digby, we're going to London.'

'We, sir?'

'Yes, I am going with you.' It was a rather impromptu decision on his part, but the more he thought about it, the more he didn't want to wait for Digby to bring Maura home. He wanted to be there when Digby caught up to her, wanted to see her face the moment she knew the game was up. His pleasures had been deferred long enough. They could be in London in three days.

It had been a week and they still hadn't discussed the schedule. As a result, the children were eating her alive, patience first. Each day they awoke, anticipating some timely interruption by Uncle Ree, and each day they went to bed disappointed. Today was turning out no differently. Maura couldn't recall how many times she'd had to redirect William's attention away from the nursery window and back towards his arithmetic lesson. Fuelled by a week of good weather, and the hopes Uncle Ree would pop in, the children were overly exuberant, and today they'd been an especial handful. After a week on the job, Maura was exhausted.

'We'd better try that again,' Maura scolded gently when William missed his multiplication tables. 'Now, what's seven multiplied by four?'

'Twenty-one. No, twenty-eight,' William corrected with a frustrated pout. He was as testy as she was. He crossed his arms in defiance. 'I like doing arithmetic with Uncle Ree better than this old stupid stuff.'

'I'm sure you do,' Maura said calmly, but her patience was nearing its limit. It was on the tip of her tongue to suggest he liked arithmetic with his uncle because his uncle made him do it so seldom. But she couldn't bring herself to disparage the man. All week, they'd talked nonstop about Uncle Ree and everything they'd ever done with him: how he played hide and seek in the house with them, how he always had the best presents at Christmas, how he taught them fun games. It was clear the children adored him.

But for all his heroics, 'Uncle Ree' had made precious few appearances since the park, and the children were missing him keenly. So was she, Maura allowed privately. There was an energy when he was around, a crackling in the air because one never knew what was going to happen next.

'I don't know why I have to know multiplication,' William sulked.

'A gentleman needs mathematics to run his home and his personal finances. When you're older, you'll get an allowance and you'll want to know how to budget your money so it will last until the next allowance day.' Maura tried to explain the reasons on a practical level. It was a lesson her mother had taught her at an early age as part of learning to run a household. That gave her an idea. Maybe tomorrow, she'd set up a 'household' for William and Cecilia and let them practise managing it.

William shrugged, unimpressed. 'If I run out of money, I'll win more like Uncle Ree. Uncle Ree showed me how.' Of course he had, Maura thought uncharitably. Along with being an excellent kite-flyer, Lord Chatham was a gambler. She shouldn't be surprised at this latest revelation. Many gentlemen gambled, including her Uncle Lucas. But Lord Chatham should have exercised some discretion in passing the habit on to young children.

'I'll wager my pin money and be the richest girl in London.' Cecilia looked up from making alphabet letters on a slate. 'Uncle Ree showed me, too.' That did it. She was definitely setting up a pretend-household tomorrow.

She should also give them a strict lecture on the vices of gambling, but curiosity overrode Maura's good sense. 'Exactly what did your uncle show you?'

'Odds.' William brightened. 'If there's eight to five odds, it means you'll make eight pounds for every five pounds wagered, with a profit of three pounds each. So, if I wager ten pounds on a horse, I'll make eighty pounds. If it's six to five, and I wager fifteen pounds, I'll make seventy-five; not quite as good.' William went on for a while, spouting multiplication and ratios at rapid speed, a speed she had been unable to coax from him all afternoon.

Maura was torn between praising him for his complicated multiplication and lecturing him on the severe consequences of gambling, consequences she knew all too well on a first-hand basis. In the end, she settled for a soft scold. 'Remember, this all assumes you will win. If gamblers won all the time, everyone would be rich and the gambling halls wouldn't make any money.'

'I'd win,' William boasted, unworried about

being on the losing end of a wager. 'Uncle Ree told me what to look for in a good horse: long, thin cannon-bones in the leg.'

'I hope when the time comes, William, you will wager responsibly. One should never gamble more than one can afford to lose.' Her tone was sterner now. Did Lord Chatham have any idea at all about how impressionable children were at this age?

'I know!' Cecilia exclaimed in complete agreement. 'There was this gentleman at White's who lost a house in a card game and he didn't have anywhere to live after that.'

'White's?' Even she had heard of the elite club. 'How would you know such a thing? That's a gentleman's club.' If Lord Chatham was carrying stories of his nights out home to the children, she'd have to caution him against it. Such tales weren't suitable for children's ears.

'We were there. Uncle Ree took us.'

'You were there?' Maura echoed. Maybe she should have been happy with the idea of just bearing tales.

'After Number Four left, there was a break before Number Five came,' Cecilia supplied. 'Uncle Ree took us with him some nights. We'd stay in the kitchens and eat sugar biscuits, but cook would let us peek through the door when something good happened.'

Apparently something 'good' qualified as a man losing his house in a card game. Cecilia looked downcast for a moment. 'I hope we get to go again soon. I miss going and it will be even better this time because you'll be there, Six.'

Definitely not. But she understood the children's distraction now. They were missing their uncle. Since commissioning her to plan his dinner party, Lord Chatham had made himself scarce. There had been no further outings to the park or other interruptions. Consequently, the children were disappointed and she was tense. She'd spent the entire week waiting for him to suddenly materialise in the nursery or demand she eat with him.

When those things hadn't happened, she told herself it was for the best. She was busy with the children and planning the party. She didn't have time for any distractions and she certainly couldn't hazard another run-in like the one in the study. Still, she couldn't help but feel disappointed like the children and a little bit angry.

He couldn't haphazardly abandon the children at will. They weren't toys to be played with on a whim and then tucked away and forgotten. She feared very much that was what had happened. Lord Chatham had spent a month playing father and now he was tired of it.

That decided it. If Lord Chatham hadn't shown himself by the children's bedtime, she would track him down and demand he listen to her. The children needed a schedule, one that included organised and regular time with him. After all their upsets, they needed stability they could count on.

By seven o'clock, Lord Chatham had not made an appearance, nor was he anywhere in the house, Fielding informed her. Lord Chatham had spent the day in meetings and had not returned home. He assumed Lord Chatham had changed at his club and gone out for the evening from there.

Maura would wait. She got out her needlework and a book, ready for a long vigil in the little sitting room off the hall. She would be the first to hear his footsteps when Lord Chatham returned.

* * *

He returned shortly after eleven. Maura set aside her needlework, her pulse pounding. She'd had four hours to mentally rehearse what she wanted to say, four hours to build up her righteous indignation over his disregard this week. Maura stepped out into the darkened hall behind him. 'Lord Chatham, might I have a word?'

He paused, his shoulders sagging infinitesimally, but he did not turn. 'Could it wait until morning?' He was tired. Funny, but she never imagined him as tired. He was always so full of life.

She would not be put off. Maura put her hands on her hips. 'No, we must discuss the children's schedule. It has already been put on hold a week and, as a result, I have had a positively dreadful day and the children, too. They miss you.'

Mentioning the children did the trick. He turned to face her, his broad shoulders shown to advantage beneath the dark cloth of his attire. There was no pretending he didn't offer a formidable image even when tired. For a moment she thought he might fob her off again. Then his face broke into his customary wicked grin and his whole demeanour changed. 'That gives us something in common. I have had a dreadful day, too.'

His grin widened as he stepped nearer to her as if he were about to impart a secret. 'You're in luck. It just so happens I know the perfect cure for dreadful days. You, Maura Caulfield, need a drink.'

Chapter Eight

'I do not need a drink,' she sputtered, stepping into the sitting room with him. 'I need to talk about the children's schedule.'

He'd managed to shock her with his invitation, but she'd come. He wasn't surprised. Everything he'd seen so far about her suggested she didn't back down from a challenge. Still, her day must have been rotten indeed if she'd waited up for him long after she would usually have been abed. The night was still early by his standards, but her mornings started sooner than his.

'Yes, you need a drink. I know these things.' Riordan poured them each a tumbler of brandy from the decanter on the side table and passed her a glass, overriding her protest. 'To dreadful days, Maura.' He raised his in a toast. 'Sip it slowly or it will burn until you've become accustomed to it.'

She did, her eyes not leaving his in case he'd tricked her into something sinister. He smiled and set down his glass, taking a chair across from the little sofa where she'd set up residence. 'Now, tell me all about your day.' Anything would be better than his meeting with the Vales and their cavalcade of legal experts. Pessimistic old Browning hadn't been wrong. They were willing to challenge Elliott's will if need be. They'd suggested today that he could sign the children over to them immediately and they would drop their challenge to the will. At that point he'd gone over the table and shaken some sense into solicitor number one.

'It's the children really. They're quite spoiled with outings and more toys than they can possibly play with. They're good children, but they had trouble this week settling down.' She took another sip of brandy. He watched the slim column of her throat work as the golden liquid slid down gently.

'Sunshine will do that to a child.' Riordan nodded.

'As will well-meaning uncles. They kept waiting, hoping you would show up again this week. They were disappointed.' She gave him a sharp look over her tumbler. 'I also understand you are in the habit of taking the children to White's.'

So she'd heard about that. He should have warned the children to be more circumspect. Riordan shrugged it off. 'White's is hardly a brothel, Maura. They were in the kitchens. They'll survive.' He cocked his head to one side, studying her. Her hair was still up and she was dressed for the day in a blue muslin dress. 'The question is, will you survive?'

She looked tired. Faint lines of tell-tale dark circles were evident beneath her green eyes. He was remembering Maura dressed in a nightgown and robe with her hair down. It was late. She should have retired by now. Had she really waited up for him just to discuss the children? He poured himself a second glass. She was barely halfway through her first.

Her eyes followed his movements to the decanter. 'Do you have decanters in every room?'

He nodded with exaggerated seriousness designed to bring a smile to her lips. 'Yes, one never knows when the need for a drink will strike. I brought most of these decanters back from Venice.'

She did smile. It was warm and he felt himself start to bask in that smile.

'You like Venice very much.' He loved it when she smiled, how she laughed when she knew she shouldn't. If only she would smile at him like that more often, but that necessitated being around her more often. He wasn't sure that was wise just yet.

'I do.' He decided that would be his goal for the evening: to make Maura smile. 'Arguably, they were the best years of my life.'

He watched her carefully. She took another sip, getting accustomed to the tingle of the liquor. She kicked off her slippers and tucked her feet up under her skirts. 'Tell me. Tell me about Venice,' she said.

Once the words started, he couldn't help himself. He told her about his friends Ashe and Merrick and Jamie. How they'd set off for a grand tour, of their days in Vienna before they moved on to Italy. He told her how they'd played a prank during Carnevale by hosting a party in someone else's house. 'We even had invitations engraved with his address on them.'

'He didn't know?' she asked, her face alight with laughter and disbelief.

'Not until he came home and saw his palazzo ablaze with lights. He had a crystal chandelier, that when it was lit up, could be seen from the Grand Canal.' Riordan was laughing now, too, remembering the hilarity of it. Most of the idea had been his from the start. The count they'd played the prank on had been a good-humoured friend. They'd joked about the incident for weeks. By the end of Carnevale everyone in Venice had been laughing about the best party having been given by a host who hadn't even been there.

Maura wiped her eyes. 'I don't think I've ever done anything as outrageous as that.' She gave a little hiccup. 'Although, there was one time when my older cousins and I bought old Miss Templeton a subscription to a gossip sheet she claimed to abhor. We saved up for that subscription, but it was worth it. She was a righteous old biddy who was always morally better than everyone else and quick to say so. We knew it would mortify her to pick her mail up at the post office and see that scandal sheet in her letters. She'd know the postmaster had put it there and had seen her address.' Maura winked at him. 'The postmaster was a terrible gossip, too. It was all the over the village within hours.'

'Why, Maura Caulfield, you have a naughty streak.' Riordan laughed and refilled her glass.

She gave a pretty shrug. 'Maybe a little one. Nothing at all like yours. Were you always a handful?'

'Absolutely. I was the bane of my parents' existence.' He regaled her with stories of his youth, trees he'd climbed, silly boyish dares he'd undertaken until they were both laughing, tears running down their faces. 'Once I sneaked down to the lake and stole the squire's son's clothes. He had to walk home naked. He got back at me, though. A few days later, *I* was out swimming and he stole *my* clothes. He left me a pile of girl's clothes instead. At twelve, I was too embarrassed to walk home naked. Instead, I walked home looking like Bo-Peep. I was a big lad, too, tall and gangly for my age. The skirts barely hit my ankles.'

Riordan was laughing hard now, spurred on

by Maura's own mirth. 'It served me right, and for my part I knew how to take a joke. But, heavens, I looked ridiculous. I probably should have gone home naked with my altogether on display. Can you just imagine?'

Maura took a drink and he went on. In hindsight, he should have waited until she swallowed before he told her the rest of it. 'Anyway, all I needed were sheep so I stopped by Squire Matheson's and helped myself to three of his prize sheep, tied some pretty ribbons around their necks and brought them home with me.'

The unthinkable happened. Maura laughed so hard the brandy came out her nose. 'Oh! Oh! It burns!' Maura waved a frantic hand in front of her nose, trying at once to wipe at the spill on her dress and to fan her nostrils.

He tried to play the gentleman, he really did. Riordan pulled off his cravat and held it to her nose, but he was laughing too much to be effective. He might have held his composure and treated the situation with the gravity it deserved—brandy out of the nose *did* hurt—but Maura chose that moment to sneeze out a series of high-pitched brandy-induced 'achoos' that sounded more like squeals. *Hilarious* squeals, and he was lost.

'It's not funny!' Maura protested with no success, they both knew it was. He hadn't had this much fun in ages. Riordan made no move to return to his chair. He told her about the time he'd stood up on his horse and ridden the big hunter around in a circle. 'It went well until we ran into a low-hanging branch. "Whump!" I went down with a thud.'

'Were you hurt?'

'No, I came through it marvellously intact.' Riordan pushed his hair back from his forehead. 'I got off with a scratch. You can see it here along my hairline if you look.' He moved closer. 'Come, Maura, you can look better than that. I won't bite.' *Definitely a lie. He'd been known to bite.*

Maura leaned in towards him, the light floral scent of her intoxicating in its freshness. Her cool hand smoothed back his hair where his hand had been. 'You were lucky.' Intimacy charged the air between them, a little of the laughter replaced by something more potent, something akin to what had flamed between them in the study. She was close enough to kiss.

'What's the worst thing you've ever done, Riordan?' she whispered with a smile.

Ah, sweet victory. It had taken two glasses to get her to utter his name. She was tipsy with brandy and intoxicated with his stories. He knew what she wanted. Tonight she was in love with the bad boy, in love with his immature exploits, his laughter.

He wondered what she'd do if he said, 'Seduced my wards' governess.' Technically it would be a lie. He hadn't seduced her yet, but he would very shortly. He was rock hard with wanting her, wanting to kiss those laughing lips, wanting to caress the curves beneath the brandy-stained bodice. 'Are you sure you want to know? It's shocking.'

'More shocking than riding a horse bareback? More shocking than hosting a party in another man's house or walking home in a Bo-Peep costume? I doubt anything you could say would shock me at this point.'

It was a testament to how far they'd come in the late hours of the night. He'd never reminisced like this, had never shared these things with anyone. Hadn't ever made a woman laugh so hard that brandy had come out her nose.

He grinned. 'Would you care to bet on that? If I shock you, I get to claim a forfeit.'

The brandy had made her bold. 'All right, it's a deal.' Her eyes sparked with anticipation. 'Tell me. No, wait; let me set the glass down.'

He probably shouldn't tell her, but he wanted to win, wanted to claim that forfeit more than anything else in the world right then. He leaned close and whispered, 'When I was sixteen I lost my virginity.' He paused. She wasn't properly shocked yet. He added, 'With my father's mistress—her idea.'

'Oh, my,' Maura breathed, 'that is wicked indeed.' Her pulse leapt at the base of her neck, indicating she didn't know if she should be aroused or scandalised.

'Yes, it was.' Riordan kissed the column of her throat. He drank of her scent, the faintest of lilacs, the subtlest hints of honeysuckle and roses, a veritable English spring. Desire rode him. It was late and the day had been hard. He wanted to forget the battles he had fought for Elliott, for the children. He wanted to lose himself with Maura, to let go of his troubles while he watched her passion unfurl; it would be impetuous, like the woman herself if given free rein.

Riordan claimed her mouth in a kiss and let the pleasure come. He wooed her with mouth play, kissing her lips, the tip of her chin, feeling her willing ascension as he laid her back on the sofa. 'Let go, Maura, and be wicked with me,' he whispered.

Oh, this was madness! Maura answered his kiss with a brandy-born boldness of her own. Riordan was braced above her, all sin and temptation in the lamplight, his dark hair falling in his face. His hips moved against hers in seductive invitation. She arched towards him in intuitive response.

'That's my girl,' he murmured appreciatively, his mouth finding its way from her neck to her breast where it rose ready for his touch. His breath blew against the fabric, warm and arousing. She gave a little moan, heat gathering in her belly, hot and curious.

Riordan smiled down at her, with knowing in his eyes. His hands, his body, slid to her feet. The air crackled with anticipation. She held her breath, mesmerised by the movement of his hands moving up her legs and disappearing beneath her skirts. Those hands stopped at the tops of her stockings. They began to roll and his mouth began to kiss behind the bent curve of her knee, down her calf to the hollow at her ankle. Her stockings were most happily divested and discarded on the floor beside the sofa. Part of her knew this was wicked—more than that, it was dangerous. This would not end with stockings. Part of her no longer cared.

'Did you know that in the Far East, there are those who consider the feet to be the gateway to the body?' Riordan's voice was a soft rill in the darkness, binding her in intimacy's spell. His fingers pressed at the sole of her foot, alternately caressing and pushing as they massaged. Never had she felt anything so decadent. She hadn't known such a touch was possible.

He pressed the upper portion of her sole. 'Some healers believe this connects to the lungs. If you massage here, it will clear congestion.' He pulled ever so gently on her toe. 'This toe connects to the ear, this one to the eyes. This part of the big toe affects the throat.'

Maura listened, fascinated. 'What else?' She hardly dared to breathe for fear of breaking the spell.

Riordan's mouth turned up in a half-smile.

His hand moved to a tiny spot behind her ankle. 'By feeling here, you can tell how many children a woman has had.' He winked. 'You've had none.'

He stretched out over her and captured her arms, raising them over her head. 'How is it you're so good with them?'

'I had younger cousins, a pair of twins not much older than Cecilia and William. When I went to live with my uncle, I helped my aunt with them.' Maura silently willed him not to ask more. These moments were not for disclosure. With a boldness that surprised her, she arched up and kissed him, pleased to note she was not the only one aroused by their play. Evidence of his desire lay hard against her thigh, obvious but non-threatening, nothing at all like Wildeham's—another memory to thrust away. There was no room for her past in this night.

His free hand tangled in her skirts, pushing them back until she could feel the coolness of the room against the thin fabric of her undergarments, a contrast to the warmth of his hand where it rested at the juncture of her thighs. She knew a moment's doubt against the intimate pleasure of his contact.

'Relax, Maura,' Riordan whispered against her ear. 'The best is yet to come, I promise.' He kissed her against the curve of her jaw, his hand slipping inside her pantalettes, the audacity of his touch lost in the host of sensations that very touch invoked. So intense was her body's reaction to the intimate caress, there was no time to question, no capacity to question, only to feel the rightness of his presence at the core of her. This was magic indeed and Maura gave herself over to it, arching against his hand, moaning her delight as it grew, and expanded, encompassing the whole of her until she thought she'd shatter from the ecstasy of it all. She was not far wrong.

'Let go, Maura,' Riordan's voice coaxed hoarsely, his eyes blue and burning as they locked with hers. 'Let go, be my kite.'

She did shatter then, flying, soaring, until she spiralled safely to earth in Riordan's arms, understanding completely in those moments what it meant to be a kite in a flat turn, what it meant to be a woman in the throes of love.

'Did you like it?' Riordan pulled her close against him.

'What was that?' Maura asked, breathless. Surely something so wondrous had a name.

Riordan chuckled warmly near her ear, holding her tight. 'That, my dear, was the most fun you can have with your clothes on.'

Chapter Nine

He wanted to remember the way she looked in that moment; amazed, awed, by what had happened. Suddenly he knew what he wanted to do. 'Come upstairs with me,' Riordan whispered. 'I want to show you something.' The 'something' was a room he hadn't been in since he'd returned home from Italy. It was a hard room to face, full of memories both pleasant and unpleasant. But tonight, for the first time in five years, he wanted to paint more than he wanted to stay away.

'Where are we going?' Maura asked, a little wobbly on the stairs from brandy and fatigue. He steadied her with an arm about her waist.

'We're going to my art studio. I want to show

you my etchings.' He chuckled quietly. 'Actually, I just want to claim my forfeit.'

'I thought you already had.' Maura laughed softly in the darkness, a warm rich sound that gave him courage.

They reached the top of the stairs. The studio was at the end of the hall, past Maura's room and the nursery. Riordan opened the door. The room was unlocked after all this time. He let go of Maura's hand long enough to light the lamps, illuminating the room in a dim glow, section by section.

Time had stood still here. As always, his Venetian divan dominated the room, his favourite prop long before he'd actually gone to the Continent. Maura let out a gasp at the sight of it. 'What a wonderful sofa!' She ran her fingers along the back of it, caressing the wood frame.

'You can sit on it.' Riordan laughed at her delight. 'My father was furious with me for buying it. I spent a large chunk of my quarterly allowance on it. I found it in a second-hand shop in Cheapside and I knew I had to have it with or without parental approval.'

He moved to a stack of canvases leaning against the wall and sorted through them, plucking out a fresh one for his easel. It was easy to move about this room, assembling his equipment. Everything was in its place. One could almost believe he'd never left. His favourite brushes sat on a small table near the sofa in a glass jar, waiting for him to pick them up again. Completed canvases leaned against the far wall covered with tarps.

He knew what was beneath each of them. There was a painting of Chatham Court he'd done one summer, and a landscape of the Tower Bridge and Parliament. Nostalgia swept him. He blamed it on the brandy. That was how the brandy worked when he had enough of it. First came the euphoria of escape, then the sad nostalgia and finally the anger, the regret. He pushed it all away. Tonight was different. He thrummed with energy and purpose.

'You paint?' Maura broke into his thoughts. She studied him with her green eyes, a soft smile on her lips as if she'd just received a treasured gift. 'I think that's the first significant thing you've ever told me about yourself.' She glanced about the room, taking in the details. 'This room is important to you, isn't it? It's not just a place.'

It *was* an important room to him. This room contained his soul, all that was truly *him* was in this room. He rummaged through a drawer for paints, trying to give the thought words. How could he explain it to her? 'This room is me, the person I want to be. When I pick up a brush and put it to canvas, I'm free. I can re-create the beauty around me or create new beauty from the pictures in my head. I can imagine any-thing.' He wasn't doing a good job of explain-ing. His words sounded foolish and fanciful. He stopped to stroke a brush, its fine tip still supple. 'I haven't been in this room since I came back from Italy and yet nothing has changed. Every-thing is as I left it.'

'If you loved painting so much, why did you stop?' She was too insightful by far. He was used to being the insightful one, the one who could read people's characters. It was unnerv-ing to be on the other end.

Riordan pushed his hands through his hair, surveying his supplies one last time to make sure he had everything organised. 'My father hated it. An earl's son, second or not, should not dabble in the arts.'

'You must have done more than dabble,'

Maura insisted. 'There are plenty of noblemen with hobbies.' Her colour was high. She was nervous or excited, or perhaps both. She was not entirely distracted by the conversation. She'd not forgotten what they were here for. Neither had he. There was a forfeit to claim and he knew exactly what it was going to be.

'We fought about it. A lot.' Riordan sat beside her. 'My father died while I was in Italy.' There'd been no chance to make reparation. Much had been left unsaid and undone between them. 'I'm not proud of how I left things with him,' Riordan said quietly. 'I don't fancy myself a vicious person by nature and yet I was cruel to him in my own way.' To her credit Maura only nodded. She didn't try to make excuses for him or justify his choices.

'I'm ready to claim my forfeit, Maura.' He reached a hand up to her hair. 'May I?' Riordan gently dislodged the first pin.

'You brought me up here to take my hair down?' Maura quizzed.

'No, I brought you up here because I'm going to paint you.' He plucked out a second pin and set it aside. He shot her a sidelong glance. 'What did you think I was doing?' He knew what she'd thought. She'd thought he'd intended something more decadent. 'How wicked of you, Maura,' he murmured, unable to resist a little teasing.

He set the last of the pins aside and combed his fingers through her hair until it was loose and spread across the arm of the sofa. 'You're so beautiful, Maura, a veritable Titian. Your hair is the red-gold he favoured. He would have loved you.' He breathed. 'You look like a well-pleasured woman. I could make you famous.'

'Scandalous is what you'd make me,' Maura replied, shifting ever so slightly on the couch.

'No, don't move. Stay still, absolutely still.' Riordan backed away from the couch, moving to his easel. She *was* lovely in the shadows thrown by the lamps. Lovely and intoxicating, as if the brandy weren't enough on its own. She made him forget himself. He'd babbled on about things he'd never mentioned, weaknesses in himself he never exposed. And dark stories told in a dark room led to dark pleasures; he would make love to her with his brushes and his voice, and her pleasure would be immortalised on canvas for him to remember for ever.

Riordan selected a brush and began to paint. He'd always had the uncanny ability to paint without drafting or days of sketching and he painted that way now, letting his fingers remember the feel of a brush in them, letting those fingers convey on to canvas the image of loveliness that lay spread before him, her lips still plump from kisses, her expression still dreamy from her pleasure. Yes, that was what he wanted to capture, the essence of a woman freshly satisfied.

'Raise your arm, curve it under your head like you're using it for a pillow,' Riordan instructed softly, not wanting to break the magic of the lamps and the intimacy of their setting. These were magic moments. 'Part your lips just a little more, yes, like that, like you've just been kissed. Take your other hand and put it at the base of your neck as if you want to play with the necklace there. Now, turn your head slightly and look at me, just look at me.'

She should stop this. She shouldn't let him paint her or whatever it was he was doing with those decadent brushes on the canvas. Every stroke he took, every word he uttered, telling her to move this way and that, were a seduction all its own. He wasn't even touching her and she felt about ready to explode, to shatter as she had downstairs. There were a million reasons to stop this, but nothing as compelling as the pleasure riding her now. It was clear he had no intentions beyond this night. He was bride-hunting. There *could* be no intentions beyond this night. But she could have no intentions either. She was in hiding. Even if governesses married earls, *she* couldn't. She couldn't have anything beyond this night any more than he could. But then, they'd already sinned. It could hardly hurt to move a little further down that path. *He wasn't even touching her.* And yet, she burned.

'Don't move,' Riordan whispered, moving from the easel after a while. 'I just need to get a brush.' He stretched over her for a brush from a jar by her head, letting his body gently press against hers.

She arched her neck to see him withdraw a fan-shaped brush. 'What's that for? I've not seen a brush of that shape.' Her voice sounded dreamy, otherworldly.

He ran the soft brush along the curve of her jaw. 'It's for blending. Every brush has a purpose.' His own voice was hoarse from the brandy, the late hour or something more potent, like the heat pulsing through her at his nearness. Perhaps he felt it, too. He reached for another. 'This is a filbert. It's good for painting figures.' He swept the bristles slowly down the column of her throat, his eyes holding hers.

She knew what he saw there; he saw her arousal, her irrational want, all that he'd awakened in her. He kissed her then, a long lingering kiss that tasted of brandy and sadness, dispelling the last of her doubts, passion's logic reigning supreme in that moment. There was intensity, too, as if this kiss could drive back the darkness. This Riordan, the one she'd discovered tonight, the darker one haunted by regret, was just as heady as the Riordan full of laughter and light. He was pressed against her, hard and aroused, and it occurred to her that she might be able to pleasure him as he had her. Maura reached for him, tracing his length through his evening trousers. 'Perhaps I could paint you as well.'

'Then take me, Maura.' He growled his desire, low and deep, a most primal sound. His hand moved to help her with the fall of his trousers, his usually fluid gestures fumbling in his haste and need. 'Take me in your hand, Maura.

Please.' It was a prayer, a plea, and she was caught up in the madness of his desire, delighting in the ability to bring him closer to completion with each stroke. He felt alive in her hand, hard along the length, tender at the tip. He pulsed and she instinctively increased the speed of her strokes to match until finally Riordan groaned, bucking in her hand, stiffening one last time, spending his release.

It might well have been the most intimate moment of her life. Was there anything *more* intimate than watching a man achieve his pleasure? That it was Riordan made it more so. Riordan pulled her to him, after that, and they lay on the divan in quiet for a long while, his arm about her, caressing lightly, her head on his chest, rising and falling with each breath until she slept.

She awoke in her own bed, fully dressed, her head aching, the bright light forcing her eyes shut against the glare of morning. For once she was thankful she didn't have a maid who'd be popping a curious head in. How would she explain why she was in bed, still dressed, when she couldn't explain it to herself? How would she explain she'd got foxed with the lord of the

house and engaged in the most decadent of behaviours with him? Worse, how would she face
said lord and pretend nothing untoward had happened? Surely that was the expected reaction.

He'd invited her for a drink. They'd com-
miserated over a difficult day. One thing had
led to another, no doubt inspired by the brandy
and loneliness and poor logic that looked far
less reasonable by the light of day. Now it was
morning and the world had righted to its proper
place. Maura groaned in remembrance of those
ridiculous arguments she'd mentally designed
to justify what she'd impetuously wanted in the
moment. Now, she'd have to live with those consequences.

Worry over those consequences kept her in
her room longer than usual and all for naught.
William and Cecilia dejectedly informed her
upon her arrival in the nursery that Uncle Ree
had left. An urgent summons had come early.
He'd had to leave right away for the estate in
Sussex where a worker had been seriously in-
jured in a farming accident. He had promised
to be back for the party.

'And he promised to bring me a new dolly,'

Cecilia said, trying to be positive. 'How many days is it until the party?'

Maura smiled. 'We'll make a mathematical problem out of it, shall we? This morning we can draw up a calendar that counts the days.'

It had been a most unlooked-for reprieve. Time would temper her foolishness. There would be no morning-after awkwardness. It was quite possible they would be able to go on as if their midnight madness hadn't happened. He would come home, have his party, marry an appropriate wife and they'd never have to mention their indiscretion.

Very convenient. Very depressing.

There'd be no painting, no more talk of Titian in the dark. Of course, the whole painting proposition had been nonsense to start with. The dangers of such a suggestion had only come to her much later in the bright light of dawn. She could not risk anyone seeing such a picture. It would lead her uncle straight to her, to say nothing of what it would do to her reputation.

She was the penniless niece of a knight, her reputation was all she had to recommend her, not that there'd be much reputation left if word of this escapade ever got out. Still, the virtuous teachings of childhood had a way of clinging. In reality, she'd had no reputation left the moment she'd set foot on the Exeter coach. Such was the price for escaping Acton, Baron Wildeham.

Two heads were better than one, Acton Humphries concluded, savouring an afternoon drink in the comfort of Grillon's lobby. A week in London had proven it. Coming up to town had been an excellent decision. Even the talents of Paul Digby would have been overwhelmed by the enormity of the search they undertook. It had not helped matters that no one remembered her getting off the mail coach. Likely, she'd been smart and not gone inside or had waited to ask for directions of someone after leaving the inn yard.

The second obstacle was that there were only certain places Paul Digby could go. No one would mistake him for a gentleman and a gentleman was what might be required for the next stage of the search. After seven days of visiting dress shops and a few false hopes, Paul Digby had exhausted the scope of places he could search that might play host to a girl like

Maura. Digby had been to the brothels, too, just in case. There was no sign of her.

It was time to move on to their next option: service. A bluff, brutish man of Digby's sort could not believably make polite enquiries at referral services without raising suspicions or inadvertently sounding an alarm. Wildeham did not want Maura forewarned. If she'd run once, she would run twice, and he might not be so lucky this time.

What Digby could not do, Wildeham could. Not only could he make enquiries at referral agencies, he could talk with his fellow gentlemen at the clubs. He could also start accepting invitations to parties and chatting with hostesses, pretending to be in need of some help at his Devonshire estate. He could be downright charming when he chose. If Maura was sitting pretty in some nobleman's house, he'd personally flush her out.

Wildeham folded his paper back to the society pages. If he was going to be out and about, he should keep up on all the latest news. The players had changed. One could always tell when the social winds shifted by who wasn't listed as much as by those who were. Two names were remarkable by their absence: Merrick St Magnus and Ashe Bedevere, two of London's leading rakes over the past years. They'd married, leaving the stage to Riordan Barrett, a man more than worthy of it. He didn't know the man personally, being several years older. But he knew about Barrett. Everyone in London knew about Barrett. It couldn't be helped. But even Barrett was feeling matrimonial pressure these days by the looks of it. 'The Earl of C—, formerly Mr B—, is hosting a dinner party in hopes of starting his quest for a bride...' Inheritance had its shackles and it appeared Riordan Barrett had been caught.

Too bad, Wildeham thought dispassionately. His own marriage would have shackles, too, though of a different, more titillating kind just as soon as he found Maura. Dinner party. Wildeham snorted. Poor fellow, he was being tamed already. Since when did rakes host dinner parties for decent folk?

Chapter Ten

Riordan flipped open his pocket watch. He was going to have to face her. He could put it off not a literal minute longer. He'd reached London shortly after one and promptly hid out at White's, enjoying the comfort of their chairs rather than facing the chaos of the town house on party day. Who was he fooling? The chaos was just a convenient excuse he gave to those acquaintances that stopped by to chat. The real reason he was reluctant to go home was Maura.

It wasn't for the usual reasons a man hesitated facing a woman. He didn't regret what they'd done, but what he'd told her. He'd been vulnerable to the brandy, to her. She'd been so very encouraging, hanging on his every word, and he'd spun tale after tale for her. The early tales of his childhood were fine, designed for humour, but they'd become darker tales of his adolescence, pathetic tales. Not that they weren't true, they were, but that didn't make them less pathetic— the poor little rich boy who'd wanted to paint, who'd wanted to rival the great masters. What would Maura think of that man now? There'd been no time to explain.

It had been unfortunate Browning had summoned him so early in the morning, that the need to leave had been so very urgent. There'd been no time to wait or even to leave a note. Browning had been right to insist he make all haste. The poor man had not lasted an hour beyond his arrival and his dying words had given Riordan a key in unlocking the mystery of Elliott's death.

Now he was home and there was Vale and the blasted dinner party to contend with. And there was Maura. He'd been gone longer than he'd hoped. What would she make of his absence? He'd had to stay on for the funeral and for making appointments to replace the fallen foreman. Would she understand that? Did she think he'd left as a coward's way out? That he'd used her without a care? That she'd been a convenient companion in the dark? Had she thought of him at all during his absence? Of course she would have. He could rest easy on that account. Maura would not take their encounter casually. But were those thoughts favourable? Or had she filled his absence with castigation for herself and for him?

As for himself, she intruded on every spare thought: Maura's Titian hair vibrant in the lamplight, Maura's green eyes alight with passion, Maura's body alive beneath him. But it was more than her beauty, it was the sincerity she carried with her: her genuine concern for the children, the way she gave him all her attention when she listened. Such things had been alluring to him in this time of grief and loneliness and trial and uncertainty. His brother was gone, the Vales threatened the children. He had never felt so alone in his life except for Maura.

It was unfair to use her goodness in such a way. He would not be alone much longer. Tonight he'd take the first step towards procuring a marriage, a life partner. But the prospect did not fill him with the anticipated satisfaction. He had no idea who that woman would be and it was hard to imagine comfort in the form of a stranger. Not physical comfort. He could imagine that quite well, had plenty of experience with it actually. But it was a comfort that paled by comparison to the comfort he associated with Maura.

A footman approached, asking him if he'd like anything more. Riordan shook his head. There was no time. If he didn't leave now there'd hardly be a chance to change and see the children before guests arrived. He had Cecilia's doll in his luggage and a small boat for William's collection he'd hand whittled himself in the long days away. *And Maura*, his conscience whispered. Perhaps there would be time to see Maura, too.

In his mind, he imagined a quiet homecoming where the children hugged him. Cecilia would settle on his lap and cradle the doll gently in her arms. William would play at his feet with the boat, pretending the carpet was an ocean. Maura would smile benevolently at them for avoiding their lessons and then she would quietly scold him for spoiling them. But in the end, she would sit in the chair across from him because he'd ask her to and he would tell her of his trip and what he had learned and what it meant.

Very familial. Very domestic. A very far cry from anything he'd ever wished for in his life. He didn't question the vision. It was enough to get him out of White's, into the carriage and setting off for home.

It wasn't enough to sustain him once he set foot in the front door. The vision of a quiet family homecoming died a most precipitous death in one fell swoop of reality.

Maids and footmen were everywhere, scurrying with vases of flowers, arranging chairs, carrying trays of silver. Above them all on the staircase, William and Cecilia spied him, letting out a series of 'whoops' and launching themselves down the well-polished banister into the mêlée of footmen and crystal vases.

'No! Cecilia, watch out!' Maura sprinted out of nowhere in time to prevent a collision. Maura looked harried, her hair dishevelled, a curl here and there escaping the net snood she wore at her nape. Harried, but beautiful, Riordan thought.

Disaster avoided, the children continued their run to him and he knelt to envelop them in a hug, a more boisterous homecoming than the one in his vision but no less warming. He'd missed them. Over their heads, he met Maura's eyes. Her hands were on her hips. All the things he might have said to her fled his mind and he opted simply for, 'I'm home.'

'Just in time, too,' Maura said with business-like efficiency. '*Now* would be a good time to take them to the park.'

Riordan chuckled. She was flustered. He couldn't resist. He smiled. 'Are you sure? It is an unscheduled outing, after all.'

A small smile twitched at her lips, some of her tension ebbing. 'I'm quite sure.'

Definitely not the homecoming he'd anticipated, Riordan thought as he took the children by the hand and walked across the street to the key-garden. But a good one none the less. It had been rushed and hectic, disaster just a step away, but it had also felt familiar.

He remembered party days when his mother had been desperate to have him and Elliott out from under foot while caterers and florists thronged the house. Maura's tight tone had borne certain similarities, her phrasing not all that different from his mother's when she'd say in final exasperation, 'Someone, take the boys outdoors where they can't get into trouble.'

The only thing he regretted was that there wouldn't be time to talk to Maura.

Riordan was home and she'd survived their first encounter, brief as it was, which didn't mean she'd emerged untouched by it. The moment his eyes had held hers over the children's heads, her stomach had flipped and her mind had started conjuring up warm images of family, of the four of them together. Then reality had taken firm hold. There was no place for such fancifulness. In three hours, young women would be arriving to vie for the right to share that reality with him while she was tucked up safely away in the nursery, out of his sight, out of his mind. This was how it should be, how it had to be.

Maura gave the flowers on the long dining-room table one last small adjustment and stepped back with satisfaction. The dining room looked utterly transformed from the chaos of the day. She had begun having doubts about everything being ready.

Riordan had arrived home just in time. It had

been beyond difficult to arrange the party and look after the children. Just this morning, she'd found William and Cecilia building a fort under the dining-room table while maids and footmen had hurried about with china and crystal.

To be sure, Maura looked under the table one last time to make sure Dolly Polly had gone upstairs with Cecilia. It wouldn't do for a guest to accidently step on Cecilia's treasure. This was not the kind of party where such an oversight would be tolerated. Everything had to be perfect. Her work was nearly done. All that remained was a final check with the cook and the butler before she could vanish upstairs to the nursery.

She'd not been exaggerating when she'd told Riordan two weeks were barely enough. She'd recognised from the beginning this was no mere country dinner. This was a dinner thrown by an earl in town, and a bachelor earl to boot. The message his party was sending was unmistakable even to the most socially obtuse. He was announcing his desire to marry, to look over the eligible candidates and to settle on one. Guests would have expectations.

Riordan might not understand the importance

of each little nuance tonight, but she certainly did. There would be no mere slapping of the food on the table. There were rules that must be followed and the calibre of guests attending tonight would know them.

Maura mentally ran through the list of details. The dining room was ready, the carpet had been cleaned, the fire was laid, the fire screen in place so that those sitting nearest the heat wouldn't roast. Large pieces of the family silver gleamed their impressive message from the carved sideboard. That had been Aunt Sophie's contribution. She'd been a firm believer in showing off the Chatham estate's wealth. 'Fathers will want to see what their daughters are marrying into,' she'd said.

Maura had bowed to her wish in exchange for doing away with the silver epergne on the main table. She'd been all too happy to see it take up residence on the sideboard with its other large silver relatives. It was somewhat unorthodox to remove the standard centrepiece, but Maura insisted conversation would flow better if everyone at the table could actually see everyone else.

To draw the eye, Maura opted to fill the epergne with blue forget-me-nots and bright-yellow daffodils with a few strategically placed deep-pink tulips so that it spilled with colour, matching the smaller arrangements set periodically down the length of the table. As a result, the once heavy and squat epergne enlivened the silver display and filled one side of the room with a splash of spring colour. There wasn't a single item left to fuss over. The room was ready. Now, for the kitchens.

The kitchens were much as Maura expected— the chaos behind the scenes. With fourteen people for dinner and eight courses, it was bound to be busy. But Cook had been a blessing. The former earl had entertained often and Cook knew exactly what to do, too much in some cases.

Cook had initially pulled out one of the former earl's favourite menus, but Maura had scotched that immediately. Lord Chatham wouldn't want reminders of his brother lingering so blatantly tonight. She'd insisted on a fresh menu: a lobster turbot with Dutch sauces to start, fresh oysters, and the meat course served *à la jardinière* to take advantage of the fresh produce in the markets. There would be ices and ice creams brought in for dessert.

The food, she'd told Cook, must send a message. There was a new Earl of Chatham now and he was making his own way, without breaking too far from tradition. These were by no means exotic dishes. If Lord Chatham's reputation was as scandalous as he intimated, the food served tonight would be a good reminder he'd not forgotten what it meant to be an upstanding gentleman. He understood society's rules.

Which was why her last call was Fielding. Maura found him in the silver pantry, going over a last check of the dinnerware. She didn't envy the man his duties this evening. Like Cook, he knew his job. He'd entertained for Elliott and for Elliott's father for more than two decades. But tonight was different, it was Riordan's first night as host and there was only a nominal hostess to make it all run smoothly.

As predicted, Aunt Sophie had proven to have limited use beyond planning the guest list and invitations. Maura doubted the silly woman would know what to do if one of Society's 'crises' arose. Of course, if something did go wrong, there was little a hostess could do to address it. Maura knew very well a hostess did not get up from the table to readjust the staff or correct a serving procedure during the meal. The success of the meal lay squarely on the butler's shoulders.

'Are you ready, Fielding?' Maura enquired. 'Is there any last thing I can do for you?'

'Everything is prepared, Miss Caulfield.' Fielding was unfailingly proper at all times. If he felt any distress over the impending evening, he offered no signs of it.

'The footmen? Are they clear on the procedure of serving the meal *à la Russe*?' *À la Russe* meant the footman served a guest privately from a serving plate. 'If we need more, perhaps we can borrow a groom or the gardener.' In the country, she and her aunt had often been hard pressed to find enough men to pull it off. They'd used the occasional groom to fill out the numbers to accommodate their guests. It was always a near-run thing then, hoping the groom would remember what to do.

Fielding looked appalled at the suggestion. '*My* staff are familiar with both methods of serving.' She hadn't meant to offend him with her enquiry. The earl's staff was certainly larger than her uncle's. Fielding had no need to raid the stables or the gardens for extra footmen for a night.

Maura straightened her shoulders. 'Very well, then. I can see you have everything under control. I shall look forward to hearing about the party in the morning.'

An odd sense of sadness swept Maura as she headed for the stairs. It was nearly five o'clock. Guests would be arriving in two hours for a party she had spent two weeks planning in a whirlwind and she wouldn't be there to see it, wouldn't be there to protect it if there was a glitch. She'd not thought she'd feel so proprietary about the party or about its host. She knew it was for the best.

She should be celebrating the fact that she'd been in London for a month and there'd not been one unnerving sign that her uncle was making enquiries. If she was being hunted, she hadn't been found. It was still early in the game, though. A month didn't mean he'd given up or that she'd successfully eluded him, but it was a step closer. The longer she remained at large, the harder it would be to find her. Trails grew cold and she'd done what she could to ensure hers would cool as rapidly as possible; she'd given a false name to the coaching inn when she'd registered and another false last name to Mrs Pendergast. She hoped the deception was enough.

For now, all that mattered was that she was safe, safe to begin a new life. Marriage to Wildeham promised nothing but a life of misery and degradation. She couldn't do it, not even to save her uncle. He would find a way to settle the debt without her.

Maura popped into the nursery. Riordan and the children had returned earlier. She was surprised to see Riordan still with them, stretched out on the carpet playing...*vingt-et-un*? Couldn't the man play a simple game of jacks?

'Will, you will want to bet more here since you have an eleven and you'll get one more card,' Riordan coached, urging the boy to place a few more marbles in wager. Riordan flipped Will a card: a queen.

'*Vingt-et-un!* I win,' Will crowed, and caught sight of her. 'Six, did you see that?'

'I most certainly did.' Maura smiled.

Riordan rose and tugged at his waistcoat. '*Vingt-et-un* is good for the arithmetic skills, teaches quick addition.' He might have looked a smidge guilty. Then again she might have imagined it because she wanted to.

'As do regular flash cards,' Maura replied evenly. 'We have our own games. Cecilia, did you show Uncle Ree your countdown calendar?'

'I did, and the pictures I drew, too.' But Cecilia was too busy with her own questions to give the calendar another thought. 'Did you see the new doll Uncle Ree brought me? Her name is Heather. She has real hair. Is it beautiful downstairs? What do the flowers look like?'

Maura laughed, feeling her blue devils slip away in the wake of Cecilia's exuberance. She gathered the little girl to her and sat down on the floor, describing the decorations. William inched closer, interested, too, in the hectic comings and goings that had dominated his house for the past two days, the game of *vingt-et-un* forgotten.

'There are arrangements of blue forget-me-nots and daffodils on the table. A menu card trimmed in gilt with a little picture of the flowers all done in colour in the bottom corner is at everyone's place. It must have taken hours to draw each of them—they were hand done, you know.'

Cecilia sighed dramatically. 'I would love to see one!'

'The ladies might take them home as mementos,' Maura told her. 'But if there are any left I'll ask Fielding to save one for you. There's a favour for everyone at their place setting.' Favours were usually reserved for balls, but Aunt Sophie had thought it would be a good touch. Maura had agreed, as long as they were tasteful and small, and in this case edible. 'Gunter's sent special chocolate crèmes with different flavours inside. They came in the most elegant white boxes and tied with ribbons to match the flowers. Some of the chocolates have raspberry filling, some almond, some—'

'Miss Caulfield, there you are!' Aunt Sophie burst into the nursery, aflutter and out of breath. 'I've been looking for you everywhere.' Clearly an exaggeration since she'd been downstairs until a half-hour ago.

Maura decided to forgo pointing out the obvious—where else would she be if she wasn't in the nursery? 'Has something happened?'

'Not something, the *worst* thing! It's a disaster all around!' Maura exchanged a quick glance with Riordan. Given the source, 'the worst' could be anything from a riot in the streets to a broken plate in the kitchens.

'It's the Langleys.' Aunt Sophie wrung her handkerchief nervously. 'Their daughter, Susannah, has come down with hives from too many strawberries, if you can imagine, and now they can't come. Really, it's most inconsiderate to leave us three short for dinner at this late date. Where will I find three people?'

'What my aunt means to say is that she's a person short.' Riordan rose, all six healthy feet plus of him, a complete juxtaposition to his flighty aunt. 'We just need one to make an even dozen. We don't have to have fourteen people to dinner.'

'We might as well.' Aunt Sophie sniffed. 'It's not that simple. Not just anyone will do. It must be a female or the table won't be balanced and no decent female will come alone, which would put us at thirteen.' She threw her hands up at this. 'Thirteen! Just think of it, Chatham. It would be most unlucky.'

He was smiling again, the moment past. And he was smiling at *her*. Maura read his thoughts instantaneously and took a step back as if to ward off the words that would come next. 'No, I won't do it.' She tried to pre-empt the request. 'I can't.'

'Yes, you can,' Riordan replied with that wicked grin of his that said he knew she would, that no protest in the world would overcome his request. 'Don't tell me you have nothing to wear. We both know you do.' When he looked at her like that, she felt as if they were the only two people in the room, never mind Aunt Sophie who stood three feet away, her eyes darting between them, trying to follow a conversation that had apparently started without her.

'It will be wonderful!' Cecilia twirled a pirouette in excitement. 'I will help you get dressed, Six. It will be like Cinderella going to the ball. You have to go, that's all there is to it,' she said firmly.

'That settles it.' Riordan folded his arms across his chest and smiled in satisfaction. 'I'll send a maid up to help if you like. I think one of the girls has some experience with hair.'

'I'm the governess, it wouldn't be seemly.' Maura appealed to Aunt Sophie in a last effort to avoid the party, but Riordan swiftly overrode whatever his aunt might say.

'If grooms can be footmen, governesses can be guests.' His eyes twinkled with mischief. Drat Fielding for telling on her. 'Hoisted by

your own petard, I think the expression goes.'
A small private smile, far too intimate for employee and employer, hovered on his lips. 'You'll have to hurry if you want to be downstairs in two hours.'

Maura couldn't fight them both, although she knew she should, but with what ammunition? She could hardly say, 'I can't risk being seen in case any of my uncle's friends recognise me and send me back to a marriage I would avoid at all costs.' What would Riordan say to that? He'd probably send her back himself. Men always stuck together on such issues. There was little choice but to let Cecilia drag her off by the hand and dress for the party while butterflies of caution and excitement warred for supremacy in her stomach.

By the time the maid finished with her hair and Cecilia had clasped the pearls about her neck, excitement had won out, defeating caution with reason. Was her uncle even searching London for her? What were the odds that friends of his would be at a small dinner party for twelve? *Twelve* out of the thousands of people in town, for heaven's sake. And if they were, would they recognise her?

The young woman looking back at her in the mirror with her hair artfully arranged was far more sophisticated than the young girl who'd sat at dinners with her uncle's family. Even more remote were the odds that someone at the party tonight would know an acquaintance of her uncle and connect them together when she was going under the name Caulfield.

Odds. Perhaps she'd been under Riordan's influence too long. She was starting to sound like young William. This was a gamble of sorts no matter what logic dictated, her caution reminded her, getting in one last jab as it slunk away defeated to the back corners of her mind. But it was a gamble she would win. Chances were indeed slim that one small dinner party would see her revealed.

Cecilia and William peeked through the spindles of the balustrade, watching the guests below as they passed through the hall and drifted to the drawing room. 'We couldn't have done better if we'd planned it ourselves,' William congratulated.

Cecilia agreed, still buoyed by the excitement of helping Six dress. 'Six looks like a princess. Uncle Ree will see her and fall in love. I don't doubt it will all be settled by morning.'

Chapter Eleven

Maura's confidence grew with each course. This dinner party of twelve would not see her revealed. She could relax and enjoy the party, and she might have if it wasn't for Riordan. He was staring at her again. Maura tried not to notice. Riordan needed to be careful lest the other girls feel slighted. This party was for them, after all. It wouldn't serve for the host to spend the evening watching the governess. Maura wasn't the only one who took note. From the glacial smile on Lady Helena's face, she'd noticed, too. The daughters of marquises didn't like being upstaged by governesses.

Maura sipped from her wine glass, pinning her attention as best she could on the gentleman to her right, a Baron Hesperly, who had talked of nothing but fishing, with a passion she'd not imagined possible. But cold river trout was no match for the hot eyes that followed her every move. She was acutely aware Riordan knew every time she smiled politely or laughed softly at the baron's remarks. Just as she was aware of Riordan's charm reaching out and entangling Lady Helena in its intoxicating web.

Was Lady Helena to be the one? Envy stabbed hard at Maura's stomach. As classically lovely as a Greek statue and likely as cold, it was hard to picture Riordan's liveliness and informality next to her. Lady Helena didn't seem like the type to enjoy a picnic in the park complete with kites and boats and grass stains on skirts.

None of the girls, in fact, seemed like the type to take on Riordan's spontaneity and the exuberance of the children. Lady Audrey seemed hardly more than a child herself, Lady Marianne too compliant. Really, she had to stop. It was most uncharitable of her to sit at a table and mentally denigrate her fellow guests.

'Do you like to fish, Miss Caulfield?' the baron was asking.

Maura smiled. 'I like to *eat* fish.'

Baron Hesperly laughed a little too loudly and slapped his leg. 'Well said, Miss Caulfield.'

The outburst drew her two stares from Riordan's end of the table; one from a chilly pair of cat-green eyes belonging to Lady Helena, the other a pair of heated sapphires that made no secret of the fact he was staring. Again.

If he shot Hesperly, he'd have to shoot them all, Riordan thought rather morbidly, watching Maura charm the baron beside her. They *all* liked her. All the men, that is. He'd seen it before they'd come into dinner. Maura had circulated the drawing room discreetly with Aunt Sophie, talking to the guests.

Where Sophie fussed over each gentleman in a fashion that hovered between obvious and annoying, Maura had been more subtle; a little smile here deployed at crucial times to show interest, a quizzing furrow of her brow there to encourage further elaboration on a topic, a light touch on a sleeve to help a nervous guest feel at home. She had a little trick for each of them to make them welcome, to make them feel important.

Riordan signalled for another glass of wine,

his eyes narrowing as he watched Baron Hesperly watch Maura. More precisely, as Hesperly watched Maura's bosom. The gown revealed far too much of her, Riordan decided. The aquamarine confection was cut fashionably, no lower than the other ladies' gowns at the table. Yet Maura's clung to her curves and nipped at the waist in all the right places with impeccable detail, leaving everything and nothing to the imagination.

A gentleman couldn't help but notice, and since the moment of her arrival in the drawing room, several gentlemen present had noticed. *He'd* noticed them noticing her. Lucifer's stones, he was getting foxed at his own party. What was this? His fifth glass of wine? Not counting the fortifying brandy he'd taken privately while dressing.

To be fair, the gentlemen in question might have been noticing Maura's fine conversation, or the way she gave them all of her attention when she listened to their stories—all of them boring, no doubt. But maybe, because he knew how gentlemen thought, they were thinking as he was. If so, only a few of those thoughts were about her elegant table manners and scintillating conversation.

Most of his thoughts were about the way the simple strand of pearls lay at the base of her neck right where her pulse beat, or the way her hair resembled spun cinnamon in the light of the chandelier, or, most wickedly, how he'd like to push the delicate sleeves of that gown down off her shoulders and see for himself how those high, firm breasts of hers fit into his palms. Great. Now he was aroused and drunk.

In an effort to sober up, Riordan took another serving of venison *à la jardinière* and studied the table. Aunt Sophie had assured him the four young ladies in attendance were highly sought after, veritable toasts of the Season.

On his left was Lady Helena Bostwick, daughter of the Marquis of Southdowne. She'd come with her brother, the heir. A pretty, well-spoken blonde, Lady Helena seemed quite aware of her own consequence and eager to help others achieve that same level of awareness.

Further down the table was Miss Ann Sussington, Hesperly's daughter. She had luminous grey eyes and a sharp wit that apparently sparkled at her end of the table, or whenever the marquis's son turned his attentions her way. But she'd been rather reserved when Riordan had spoken with her before dinner. There was Lady Audrey, whose best feature was her money, which accounted for all the attention she'd drawn early in the Season, and finally, at the far end, next to his aunt, Lady Marianne, who might have brilliant conversation if she could ever get a word in edgewise.

All accounted for, his aunt had chosen well for his first foray into the marriage mart. Riordan recognised, too, it was something of a coup that he'd been able to gather such a fine collection all under one roof. He had no illusions as to why they'd all deigned to come. Pure curiosity had brought them to his table: curiosity about his brother's death, curiosity about the legendary Riordan Barrett himself. 'Legendary' might not be quite the right word there. 'Nefarious' or 'notorious' would be more apropos. When else could an upstanding girl see the notorious rake up close in a decent setting without risking her reputation? And, of course, there was the timing. The first throes of mourning were barely passed and he was giving a party. *That* had to spark a curiosity of its own.

He knew from the rumours circulating in London's ballrooms the party had confirmed to everyone that he meant to marry this Season and that created the subsequent dilemma. The Chatham earldom was generally held to be a prize. Parents of aspiring candidates hoping to be Chatham's next countess had to weigh the pros and cons of marrying their daughters to it; the gem now came with the notorious Riordan Barrett attached as husband and the scandal of Elliott's death. He could imagine the conversations whispered between mothers and fathers as they debated the merits of sending their girls tonight.

'How do you enjoy spending your leisure time, my lord?' Lady Helena enquired, dragging his attentions back to his end of the table.

'I haven't had much free time lately,' Riordan said tersely. It wasn't the most helpful of replies since it gave Lady Helena very few places to move the discussion, but at the moment he was more interested in catching the snippets of Maura's conversation. She was laughing at something the widowed Hesperly had said and Hesperly was far too fixated on what that laughter did to the rise and fall of Maura's bodice.

'When you do have time, though, how do you like to spend it? Surely you must have hobbies?' Lady Helena pressed.

'I paint.' Maura was still laughing. Dammit all, he wasn't holding this dinner party for *her* to find a husband. A mean and surprisingly jealous thought took hold. Did Maura want a husband? Surely she must, all women did, even governesses. Why hadn't he thought of that before?

He was starting to see Baron Hesperly through her eyes. A governess might think him a bit of a catch: titled, with two grown children who didn't need mothering, one of them his heir. The baron was in his late forties with hair that hadn't entirely gone over to grey and a belly that hadn't become a paunch. He was likely considered attractive for an older man. He had grey eyes like his daughter, and those eyes were thoughtful and kind. He seemed a gentle soul. He was what women would call a 'comfortable lover'. Maura would need more than that in a man.

'What do you paint?' Lady Helena was still trying to have a conversation. Riordan thought about saying 'nudes', just to put her in her place.

'Hard to say, I haven't painted much recently.'

'Do you have a favourite painter? I admire Turner's work myself.'

'Titian,' Riordan said with sudden energy. He was trying to give the illusion of looking at Lady Helena while actually looking past her. 'His paintings play with colour in the most extraordinary of ways. I spent hours studying them in Venice.' He knew Titian's works by heart. 'Hours' was no exaggeration. He'd spent days, in fact, staring up at *The Assumption of the Virgin* over the high altar of Santa Maria Gloriosa dei Frari.

Riordan's hand began to itch. He wanted to clear the room and whisk Maura upstairs. He wanted to work on his painting. Thoughts of Maura in his studio took hold: images of her with her hair down, images of her positioned just so on his sofa. He spent the remainder of the meal arranging and re-arranging Maura mentally in his head, sometimes with clothes, sometimes without, while congratulating himself on making adequate conversation with Lady Helena.

'You've travelled, then?' Lady Helena seemed impressed or thankful that he'd finally given her something to talk about. At the moment, Riordan didn't care. He was too busy staring at Maura.

* * *

It wasn't until Aunt Sophie rose and gathered the ladies for tea in the drawing room that Riordan realised he hadn't been entirely successfully in capturing Lady Helena in his web of charm. What she said next was meant to be overheard by those nearest them.

'This has been most enlightening, Lord Chatham,' Lady Helena said coolly, rising to her feet as Maura passed. 'It's always interesting to see what a man will do when left to his own devices. I hope you find time to enjoy your, um, painting.'

The dinner party wrapped up quickly after that. Many of the guests would move on to the balls getting underway at other mansions in Mayfair that evening, Riordan included. He was expected at the Dalforths' rout, although the entertainment held less appeal than it had before. He wondered briefly if Maura would go with him, but he knew she would not. He'd already pushed her far enough tonight with the party. Her reluctance to attend had been puzzling. Who wouldn't want to sit at such a fine table if given the chance? Whatever her reasons, her reluctance had been genuine and he felt a twinge of guilt for having coaxed her into it.

He wanted to talk with her. He wanted the party dismissed and the house quiet. He wanted to thank her for the evening. But there was no chance. Baron Hesperly and his daughter were also headed to the Dalforths' and had offered to take him up in their carriage, an offer he couldn't refuse under the watchful eye of Lady Helena without raising her nascent suspicions. Riordan could barely manage a discreet nod in Maura's direction before he was bundled off with the baron on one side and his daughter on the other. The daughter was already looking dejected over being separated from the Marquis's son who was headed off to another destination. Miss Sussington would be disappointed further to know that destination happened to be an apartment of rooms in Piccadilly owned by an Italian opera singer. The baron could wallow in disappointment, too, shortly, once Riordan informed him Miss Caulfield was definitely off limits. He only hoped the good baron wouldn't make him explain the reasons for that because Riordan didn't think he could.

Chapter Twelve

Goodness, the house was quiet! Maura let the odd stillness settle around her. Aunt Sophie and Uncle Hamish had been the last of the guests to leave. She'd served her purpose as a twelfth and now she'd been abandoned. What had she expected? That Lord Chatham would take her on to the balls and routs? That she could actually accept if he'd asked? There was no question of going. Risking such a thing was begging to be discovered.

Maura lifted her skirts and began the climb to her room with a wistful sigh. She'd had a wonderful evening, dressed up in a pretty gown, eating from a delicious array of foods. The chocolate ice cream at the end had been an absolute hit, sure to secure fond memories when the guests thought of the new Earl of Chatham. He'd most assuredly been the earl tonight, that wicked smile of his honed to urbane perfection as he turned his charms on each lady in turn, herself included.

He'd shown a surprising amount of tact and good manners tonight, apart from the staring, which she could only pray had not been noticed. But she could not say he'd been polite. There was nothing polite about him. He radiated a sensuality, a wickedness that went far beyond anything politeness could cage. But he'd been heart-stoppingly handsome doing it. The women had been hard pressed to keep their eyes from him. He'd been elegant in black, his evening clothes a perfect foil for the deep-crimson waistcoat he wore and the diamond-and-onyx stick pin that winked in his cravat like an expensive flirt—a veritable symbol of the man himself.

Maura closed the door to her room behind her and kicked off her slippers. She *did* wonder what he was doing now. Was he dancing with Miss Sussington? Or was he dancing with another lucky woman? It had been ages since she'd danced and, oh, how she loved to dance—

the country reels, the long quadrilles, she loved them all. It was doubtful she'd be dancing any time soon.

Maura swayed a little and hummed a tune, enjoying the feel of her skirts belling and swirling about her legs. 'Why, yes, dear sir, I would love to dance.' She curtsied to an invisible partner. There was precious little room to dance in her chamber, but she managed a few steps of a country dance, laughing with her invisible partner.

Lucifer's stones, who was up there with her? Riordan knew a moment's panic. His first thought was that Hesperly had sneaked back, too. After all, it wasn't beyond the realm of possibility that if he found the rout tedious against the comparison of Maura waiting at home, Hesperly did as well. Whoever was up there with her, she was enjoying his company.

Behind the door of her room, Maura laughed, a light sound that conjured up images of her, head thrown back, slim throat exposed. A surge of jealousy took him. How dare she! It was beyond audacity to entertain gentlemen thusly, and she accused *him* of boldness? 'I don't mind if I do,' he heard her say.

That was enough! Riordan pushed the door open with more force than necessary just to make his point. 'Well, I do. What exactly is going on here?' He scanned the room, expecting to see Hesperly's form half-hidden behind the curtains. But there was no Hesperly present. Only a flushed, pink-cheeked-with-embarrassment Maura.

'I was dancing.' She held out the edges of her skirts as if in explanation. 'It seemed too good of an opportunity to waste.'

It was his turn to feel foolish. It was what he deserved for measuring Maura by his own debauched standards. He might be the sort to sneak a companion up to his rooms—actually there was no 'might' about it, he'd done it on plenty of occasions—but Maura was above reproach in that regard. 'I'm sorry, I heard voices…'

There were no adequate words without impugning her honour with an explanation of what he'd thought she was doing up here. 'So, you were dancing? Without a partner?' He smiled, falling back on his charm as he stepped towards her. He took one hand in his and fitted his other hand at her waist. 'I think we can remedy that.' He whisked her into a brisk polka step in the hopes she'd overlook his less-than-generous misstep, and because he wanted to.

She had no choice but to follow his lead. 'What are you doing home?' she asked breathlessly, willing to let him sashay them out into the dark hallway, dancing them up and down the length of the hall.

'I didn't want to be there so I left,' he said simply. It had been a rather frightening revelation that upon arrival at the Dalforths' he had realised there wasn't a woman in the ballroom he wanted to dance with. He wanted to dance with Maura.

'The hostess will be put out.'

'She wouldn't be the first.' Riordan laughed and swirled them for a return trip down the hall.

'Shh, the children,' Maura scolded with a half-hearted protest, but Riordan only slowed as they passed the nursery door.

'More likely Baron Hesperly will be put out. He was quite taken with you.' He chose his next words carefully. 'Hesperly had all sorts of questions about you in the carriage. What do you think of that?' He brought them to a halt, but he was unwilling to relinquish her. Both of them were breathing hard from their exertions, and the banister railing was at her back. She had nowhere to look but up into his face. She would not be able to hide her entire reaction. If she fancied the baron's attentions, he would see it.

'The baron seems like a nice man,' she responded with equal care. Perhaps she sensed the irrational anger that hummed beneath his surface at the thought of the baron.

He gave a harsh laugh. 'Nice? The baron's manly pride would be wounded. No man wants to be thought of as nice.' Envy over the baron urged him on, pushing him too far. He leaned close, his mouth at her ear. 'Do you want to know why? Nice men can't pleasure a woman worth a damn.' *Not like me. I can pleasure you in ways beyond your imaginings.* He let the implicit message lie between them, potent and provocative in the darkness of the hallway.

'That is quite enough.' Maura's eyes flashed with green anger and disappointment. Disappointment in him, and it stung. 'Your language is shocking and your implications even more so. Is this what you came home to do?'

He'd succeeded in irritating her and she was right. This was *not* what he'd intended when he'd rushed home from the Dalforths'. He'd wanted to talk with her. He'd wanted to tell her about his trip, about the man who'd died with him at his bedside. But now that he was back, he wanted to do more than talk. He wanted to kiss her, wanted to stake his claim, as irrational as it was. Nothing could come of that kiss, nothing permanent at least. He had to marry to save the children. But for now, he wanted desperately to know she was his. Not Baron Hesperly's, nor any other man's who'd looked upon her tonight. *His*. He was just starting to understand that her charm was something more than the sum of her beauty.

He cupped her jaw in the cradle of his hand, his thumb stroking her cheek, the anger leaving them both. He'd known women before who drew men to them, but Maura did more than that. She improved them.

Her eyes searched his, questioning, unsure of what happened next or what *should* happen next. There was good reason they should both beat a hasty retreat to their separate chambers. But Riordan had never been one for reason. He

bent his mouth to hers. 'I came home for this.'
And, heaven help him, because there might be
an outside chance she could improve even him.

Two blond heads stared in rapt amazement
from the crack in the nursery door. Uncle Ree
was kissing Six! This was going splendidly and
they hadn't had to do a thing. 'I told you they'd
fall in love by morning,' Cecilia said smugly.
'It's just like the fairy tales.'

Ever the practical thinker, William frowned.
'Isn't that usually when something bad happens?
Like the evil witch finds the princess, or the
spell is about to end?'

Cecilia pursed her lips and thought for a moment. Her brother had a point there. 'Well, *those*
things only happen in fairy tales. *This* is real
life, Will. We don't have witches and spells.
What could possibly go wrong?'

Chapter Thirteen

R̲iordan set aside the newspaper to meet his aunt's horrified gaze the next morning. She'd come over the moment decency allowed and it took little guessing to know why. The society column had not been kind. A certain someone had wasted little time in tipping off the powers that be with regard to his dinner party. He could guess who that was.

"'Lord C— spent more time casting glances at Miss C— than he did paying attention to his higher-ranking and wealthier guests, all the more shocking given that Miss C— is none other than his latest governess. The attention was no small coincidence. Other sources report that Lord C— arrived at the Dalforths' ball only to leave conspicuously early for home. Such behaviour causes one to wonder if Lord C— is really in earnest about catching a wife or if this is a cover for another of his notorious flirtations.'" Aunt Sophie read out loud in case he hadn't already committed the passage to memory. 'We're ruined and we've only just begun.'

'Nonsense, I was ruined long before this and you're already settled. This is nothing to you.' Riordan dismissed her growing hysterics. It was ridiculous. Society columns held no sway over him and society had made its mind up about Sophie and Hamish ages ago. It was Maura he worried about. She had been slandered the most with the least avenue for redress. And, of course, he worried about the Vales. This would be more grist for their mill, another example of how unsuitable he was to act as guardian for the children.

'What we need, Aunt, is a counter-manoeuvre to dispel the rumour.'

'It's not a rumour, Chatham, it's in *print*, in the paper!' Sophie nearly screeched.

Riordan folded his napkin and set it beside his plate. 'I will invite Miss Sussington on an outing, something with the children, I think. It will look very proper and very familial. Everyone will forget what they think they saw at the dinner party.'

Aunt Sophie perked up at the idea of a plan. 'Your uncle is a member of the Royal Zoological Society. You could go to the zoo in Regent's Park.'

Riordan nodded. The zoo was only open to members. It seemed Uncle Hamish had another useful function. Who would have thought? The zoo was perfect. The children would love it. 'I'll send a note right away.' It was such a harmless venue it would surely convince the *ton* of his newfound staid ways.

Aunt Sophie paused. 'Is it to be her, then? You've decided on Miss Sussington?'

Where was his dear aunt's brain? 'This is merely a manoeuvre,' Riordan explained again patiently. 'It doesn't have to mean anything, it's just for show. Besides, how could I make my mind up so quickly? I've barely met her.'

He'd picked her because she seemed the safest choice. She'd preferred the marquis's son last night. If she'd set her cap in that direction, all the better. She'd be less likely to expect or *want* any further overtures from him. She would be a stop-gap until he found a woman he wanted to court seriously, although he couldn't stall too long, not with the Vales waiting to pounce. Maybe his aunt was right. He should marry Miss Sussington and be done with it.

Aunt Sophie's eyes narrowed in speculation. 'Just as long as you assure me there's no truth in this malicious gossip.'

'I'm shocked you'd think that.' Riordan tried to muster an appalled tone. For all her silliness, Aunt Sophie had her moments of shrewd insight, made all the more frightening because one never knew when they'd strike.

'I'm not shocked I think it at all.' Sophie pointed a finger at him. 'I saw the way you looked at her last night. You weren't fooling anyone. The paper's proof enough of that. Just remember, once the wife is in, that pretty governess is out. No decent woman would countenance her living under the same roof, not after this.' Sophie gathered up her reticule and parasol. 'I'll leave you to think on all this, Nephew. I have calls to make. I need to salvage what might be left of your matrimonial expectations. Make sure you send the invitation right away.'

Riordan distractedly scribbled out a note for

Miss Sussington and sent it on its way. Aunt Sophie was right and he hadn't seen it. How could Maura stay? He hadn't thought that far ahead. Even if the scandal hadn't broken in the paper, the issue would still have existed.

The children would be devastated if she left. They were settling into a routine with her and Maura adored them. Cecilia had stopped breaking things. William was less withdrawn. Their lives, this house, were getting back to normal. And he was about to take all that away. It was the very last thing he wanted to do. It would ruin their hard-won stability. Riordan laughed to himself. She was rubbing off on him at last. Maura would be pleased to know the thought of 'stability' had crossed his mind, finally, after all her efforts to instil in him the importance of a schedule.

Fielding brought the mail, reminding Riordan he had work to do. There were other things that needed his attention besides Maura's future. He would give her an excellent reference. She'd need one once she found out about the newspaper. He could find a nice appointment for her in the country—maybe Merrick and Alixe could use her with their darling twin girls. Then he could still see her on occasion.

Riordan winced at the direction of his thoughts. Giving up Maura sat poorly with him and it wasn't only for the children's sake. He didn't want to give her up for reasons and intentions that were still an amorphous fuzz in his mind. He only knew he wanted her with him, with *them*. But what to do? How could he save her and the children, too?

He would start with a message to the newly returned Browning. He needed a copy of Vale's financial statements, legally obtained or otherwise. Riordan flipped through the mail, looking for something suitable. He also needed to put in a decent appearance or two tonight. His hand stalled on a simple white note. Mrs Pendergast's agency had deigned to write while he'd been in Sussex. Perhaps one mystery would soon be solved.

Riordan opened the note and scanned the lines, only to be disappointed. He'd hoped Mrs Pendergast would know something more about Maura Caulfield. But all Mrs Pendergast did was reiterate Maura's skills and the date she'd registered with the agency—the very same day she'd come to work for him. The lack of information was unnerving, really. Paragons didn't appear out of nowhere. Then again, he shouldn't look a gift horse in the mouth.

She'd come to him at a time when he'd needed her. But now there was no doubt she was driving him to distraction. He'd importuned her three times with hot kisses and more. Never mind that she'd returned those kisses with equal passion. A decent employer didn't initiate those kisses to begin with. He'd never been decent in his life and it was deuced hard to start now. Last night had been the worst. He'd been possessive and angry because the baron had looked at her, because *he* had wanted to be the one sitting beside her at dinner watching the bodice of her gown. He'd seen her come down the stairs for dinner and the world had stopped for him. She had been beautiful in a way that surpassed the physical arrangement of her face with its delicate bones and angles. She was good and wholesome and pure, all the things he had stopped being years ago, and he'd wanted to lose himself in her. Oh, how he wanted.

It had been certain torture to stop at a kiss, to know he could not reach out and claim her in his own house, the one place where he was supposed to reign supreme. What would a man like him do with a prize like her? He would ruin her, sully all that purity and goodness with his fallen ways. That was exactly what he'd done. He had spoken filthy words to her and slandered a decent fellow. For what? To prove to her that she should want his poor self instead and his indecent offer? He was lucky she hadn't gone already. Which did pose a question of its own—why was she still here? She must like him at least a little?

It had been a long time since he'd wondered if a female liked him and even longer since he'd cared. Liking was good, but not essential for bed sport. His women had liked what he could do for them, but had they liked *him*? Had he liked them beyond their bodies and the pleasure? It was Maura's fault he was even thinking about such mundane things.

Fielding came in with a note from Miss Sussington, just two streets over. Riordan read it quickly. She'd be glad to accompany him this afternoon. 'Fielding, tell Miss Caulfield to have herself and the children ready at one o'clock today. We're going to the zoo.'

* * *

Maura was not looking forward to the outing. She'd played the coward this morning and done everything possible to avoid Riordan after last night. Not because she was afraid of him but because she was afraid of that kiss. Last night's kiss had been far different from their earlier kisses. This time there were no brandy-laced excuses to hide behind. It had meant something with its sweet, slow intensity and she was far too afraid to take that meaning out and look at it for fear of what might be revealed: impossibility upon impossibility.

Now she'd have to face his company all afternoon. There'd be others present, certainly— the children and Miss Sussington. She wasn't worried anything untoward would occur in such a group. With Miss Sussington along, Riordan, *Lord Chatham*, would have his attentions trained elsewhere, a thought that provoked a profound sense of disappointment, especially when she thought of him kissing Miss Sussington as he'd kissed her. Really, she had to start thinking of him again in more formal terms. She'd known this would happen. Informality bred familiarity and familiarity bred the illusion of friendship or the illusion of something more when apparently there was neither.

What sort of man kissed a woman like that while he was courting another? Lord Chatham was a rake. Mrs Pendergast had told her as much from the start and he'd proved it over the month she'd been here. Last night had just been another example. It had also been an example of how far she'd been taken into his web of debauchery, of what a consummate master of his art he was to have led her down such a well-manicured path of depravity without her knowing, without her truly seeing all the little incidents for what they were—the proverbial forest through the trees.

What had started out as a little flirting at the dinner table that first night had led to a stolen kiss at midnight, to drinking brandy, to the introduction of unspeakable, wicked pleasure between them, and to a dance on the landing and a soft kiss full of fairy-tale promises neither of them should make or keep but from which she'd none the less drawn conclusions that had kept her up half the night, wrapped in the fairy-tale aspect of the illusion, only to have it shatter at dawn.

Reality was strict and brutal in its reminders. Lord Chatham had no intention of keeping those unspoken promises. He might be jealous of Baron Hesperly's attentions, but only in the way a boy covets another boy's toy boat. Lord Chatham was most assuredly a rake, nothing more. She could no longer allow herself the luxury of questioning that. She'd given him the benefit of the doubt for too long now and it had led nowhere appropriate.

She should hate him for this: for using her, for showing her the possibilities of a passion that could not be fulfilled. Maybe after today she would. An afternoon of watching him court Ann Sussington was precisely the antidote she needed to really drive home his true nature. It would be no less than she deserved. This was what came of working in a bachelor household without other women present to act as buffers—too much contact, too much intimacy from daily interactions with a man who was already too informal. But she knew, before they even set out for the zoo, it would be easier said than done.

Maura gathered up the children, dressed in spring jackets and sturdy shoes for the outing. She tried to keep her mind on the practicalities of the outing. It had rained in the night and even though the skies were clear now, there was no telling what kind of muddy conditions they would find at the zoo.

'Uncle Ree says there's a new chimpanzee at the zoo,' William said excitedly as they went downstairs. 'He's come all the way from Africa. His name is Tommy. Maybe when I grow up, I'll be an explorer and bring back animals for everyone to see.' William's chatter eased the transition into the barouche. William rode up front with the driver, much to his great pleasure, while she and Cecilia sat with Miss Sussington and Chatham.

Miss Sussington was well turned out in a walking dress of pink-sprigged muslin and a matching pelisse that set off her dark hair and grey eyes, a fashionable mannequin of perfect style. She would look lovely gracing any man's arm. If she'd been surprised by the inclusion of the children and their governess in the outing, she didn't show it. Neither, though, did she show delight over their presence. Maura was beginning to wonder what emotions Miss Sussington *did* show. Some might call her demeanour unflappable. Maura thought it haughty.

'The children are adorable,' Miss Sussington commented as they drove. 'However did you come by them?' There was a slight chill to her tone, or did Maura imagine it? She certainly didn't imagine the stiffening of William's back at the impersonal reference.

'They were my brother's wards,' Lord Chatham said in reserved tones that matched Miss Sussington's. 'They came to me upon his death.' His voice suggested he would not be more forthcoming on the subject. Maura tried not to look at him more than courtesy allowed. If he'd spent the morning suffering misgivings over last night, there was no sign of them. In fact, there was no sign of any feeling on his usually expressive face. He was, well, in a word, stoic.

Miss Sussington offered Chatham a coy smile and dimpled delightfully, a look she must have practised for hours in the mirror to perfect. 'You must be the kindest of men to take on such a burden when there are likely other relatives who could have stepped in if you'd asked.'

'I am afraid you're wrong on all accounts.' Chatham's response bordered on harsh. 'I'm not kind and the children are not burdens in the least. I would have them with no other.' Miss Sussington had the grace to understand she'd been rebuked and tactfully changed the subject to something less personal.

At the zoo, Maura kept the children with her, one on each side, while their uncle walked ahead with Miss Sussington on his arm. Occasionally, he'd stop and turn back to talk to them about an exhibit. Beside her, Maura could feel William's anger rising along with Cecilia's tears. She did her best to keep up a steady conversation with them, as much for her sake as for theirs. Talking kept her mind off what was playing out in front of her.

'What do you think lions eat, William?' she asked as they paused by the newly relocated lion exhibit.

'Their keepers.' William smiled up at her naughtily with boyish good humour. 'I heard the lion bit someone last winter and that's why they had to be moved.'

'I wish the lion would eat Miss Sussington,' Cecilia said.

'Cecilia!' Maura scolded, but she couldn't

quite repress the smile Cecilia's comment evoked.

'Well?' Cecilia challenged. 'She's not particularly nice. She talked about us like we weren't even sitting in the carriage with her. She acts like we're stray pets Uncle Ree took in.'

'If Uncle Ree marries her, she'll probably send us away,' William said darkly. 'She'll send me away first because I'm the oldest.'

Now Cecilia's tears did spill over and she threw her arms around her brother. 'You can't leave me, you can't leave me, Will. You promised.'

Maura knelt swiftly by the children, sweeping them both into her arms. 'Hush, William, you're making your sister cry. No one is sending anyone away. Cecilia, it's all right.' She sat down on the ground, heedless of what damage the dirt would do to her dress and gathered Cecilia to her, rubbing the little girl's back.

'Everybody goes away and leaves us.' Cecilia was sobbing loudly with big gasping hiccups.

Chatham and Miss Sussington approached, the latter looking annoyed at the interruption. 'Can't you make her stop crying?' She stared directly at Maura. 'What kind of governess can't make a child stop crying?'

Maura looked over Cecilia's head and met Miss Sussington's gaze coolly. 'One who knows sometimes children need to cry. We can't always pick the time or place.'

Lord Chatham knelt beside her, taking Cecilia in his arms. He lifted the little girl up. 'What is this, Cee-Cee?' he asked gently. 'Did the lion scare you? You know nothing will ever happen to you as long as I am here.' He gave Cecilia a wink. 'You know what else? Six looks rather capable to me. I doubt she'd let anything get you.'

'Me, too!' William spoke up. 'I'll protect you, Cee-Cee.'

Chatham held out his free hand to William. 'You're a good man, Will, to look after your sister,' he said with great seriousness. 'And I'm here to look after both of you. I want you to know that.'

Maura had never seen Lord Chatham look so serious before or so sincere and it touched her most unexpectedly. How was she to reconcile this man with the rake that kissed her in the dark and danced her down hallways full of false promises or at best indecent ones? Just when she thought she could succeed in hardening her heart, he went and melted it. *Again*. He was a man impossible to hate, but she would settle for the ability to ignore him.

Her own gaze was misty at his declaration. But Miss Sussington's was sharp and calculating. In the midst of the little scene, she'd been edged to the periphery of their group. She stood there now, studying them, looking from Maura to Lord Chatham and back.

Maura stood up and brushed at her skirts, getting most but not all the dirt off. 'Oh, I'm so sorry, Miss Caulfield. Your dress is ruined,' Miss Sussington said with false concern, calling attention to the remaining spots.

'It is a small sacrifice.' Maura took up William's hand, hoping to forgo further conversation.

Miss Sussington smiled thinly, her voice low for Maura alone. 'I'm sure it is when the real prize is so much bigger. Be careful you don't overreach yourself, or you'll find yourself out of more than a dress.' She returned to Lord Chatham's side, no doubt discouraged to find his arms were no longer available. He'd lifted Cecilia on to his shoulders. Maura smiled. He seemed perfectly content to leave the child there, safely balanced by both his hands. Miss Sussington would have to walk on her own.

Chapter Fourteen

He'd made a splendid muck of it, Riordan thought, sorting through his brushes in the studio. It was too late in the day and the light was gone for any decent painting, but the activity gave him something to do, something to absorb his restlessness. Two perfectly decent wifely candidates alienated in two days. First Lady Helena and now Miss Sussington—it had to be a record. Riordan couldn't recall a time when he'd had this much trouble obtaining a woman. That left Lady Marianne and one other whose name he couldn't remember, only that she had seemed far too young to truly be a mother figure for Cecilia and William.

He could only remember Maura—Maura

kneeling with the children in her arms, comforting them. He'd felt like a family in those moments at the zoo. He could see Maura in his sitting room with her face full of wonderment as he brought her pleasure and, later, as she brought his. He rather doubted Miss Sussington would ever let herself writhe against his hand in complete abandon. But Maura had looked at him with awe. He didn't think he'd ever inspired such a reaction in a woman before. He didn't deserve it because he was going to have to tell her about the article.

Riordan spread out his brushes, laying them on a cloth and then rearranging them again. The action was nothing more than busy work, something to do to keep his hands and thoughts occupied while he waited for her. His behaviour, as unintentional as it was, had embroiled her in scandal and she had a right to know. The dinner party had landed Maura in the rumour-ridden society pages. The trip to the zoo had been an attempt to mitigate that scandal, but had done just the opposite instead. News of that outing would be through the ballrooms by tonight.

Maura would thank him for neither.

'You wanted to see me?' The object of his

thoughts stood warily in the doorway with an expression on her face that said she'd hoped he'd forgotten about the desire to paint her.

'Come in, sit down.' Riordan gestured to the curved sofa. 'We have things to discuss and Cook is happy to tuck the children in.' He picked up a pad of paper and balanced it on one knee, starting to sketch, his fingers remembering the sweep of charcoal on paper as it formed image and shape.

Maura remained skeptical. 'What are you doing?'

He looked up and smiled. 'Sketching.' *Giving my hands something to keep them busy without touching you.*

'I thought I had objected to being painted,' Maura corrected.

'You did. I'm not painting. I'm *sketching*. You never objected to that.'

'You never asked.'

This was going poorly. She was prickly, not the best of dispositions to approach with bad news. He'd hoped the sketching would keep her distracted enough to not be really angry when he told her the bad news. Maybe he'd do better starting off with the pot sweetened.

'I owe you,' he began. He owed her for the dinner party, for the outing today at the zoo, for so many things. The list was quite long. He wasn't sure where to start.

She shook her head hastily, the light catching the rich highlights of her hair: copper, burnt umber, sienna. 'No, please don't apologise.'

Riordan laughed. 'Don't worry, I wasn't.' He shaded in the angles of her cheekbones. 'I was going to say, I owe you a dress to replace the one that was damaged at the zoo.' He didn't know a woman yet, rich or poor, who turned down new dresses.

'It's not necessary. Dirt washes out.' Maura stood up. 'I think I should get back.'

'I disagree.' Riordan nodded towards the sofa. 'Now, if you'd sit back down, we could continue.'

She did sit, but her jaw was tight. There was more to this than a poorly executed outing to the zoo. 'You're displeased, Maura, please elaborate.'

'You and I both know it's improper for me to accept a gift of clothing from a gentleman. It implies exactly what we're trying to avoid.'

'What if the dress is from my aunt? I'll tell

her to send it,' Riordan pressed, although he knew what Maura's response would be.

'You and I would still know. If there's nothing else, Lord Chatham?'

He cringed at the use of his title. Riordan set aside the pad of paper. Sweetening hadn't helped. He'd have to take a straight run at it. 'There is something else.' He reached for the folded newspaper on his work table. 'It seems our dinner party has created a little gossip. Nothing that will last, I assure you. However, I have accidentally placed you in rumour's wake and I fear I might need your help to rectify the situation.' He passed Maura the newspaper and waited for the storm to break.

Might need help? Accidentally placed her? A little gossip? The pretty phrases were woefully inadequate. Maura stared at the article with growing horror. He was definitely going to need help, far more of it than she was capable of giving. More than that, *she* was going to need help. An obscure dinner party for twelve had suddenly turned lethal to her anonymity. Her presence had been broadcasted to all of London...to all of England, really.

Maura tamped down her growing panic, her rational defences in place. 'Miss C—' could be anyone. Odds were there were multiple governesses in London who could be Miss C. Her uncle would have to know that she'd used the name Caulfield in order for this to help him find her. And how could he possibly know that? She was overreacting.

'It's not as bad as all that.' Riordan smiled and kept drawing. 'You're pale as milk. It will vanish the moment another scandal comes along. As scandals go it's not that bad.'

Maura raised her eyebrows in censure. 'You're an expert on such things, I'm sure.'

He grinned. 'I'm an expert at a great many things, and honestly, this will pass.'

But not before it did her possible harm. The scandal would pass, but the proof wouldn't, it would go out to every subscriber in the country. Her uncle would read it, and, depending on how hard he was searching for her and how smart he was, he might find reason to connect 'Miss C.' with her. Discovery would depend on very few variables now, only three of them actually. Had they uncovered her alias? Had anyone recognised her at the coaching inn and looked beyond the difference in name long enough to follow up on the similarities in physical appearance? If so, had they tracked her yet to Mrs Pendergast's agency? It all came down to timing. What did they know and when did they know it?

'All I can say is I'm sorry. I didn't mean for this to happen.'

Maura followed him with her eyes, watching him stride about the room, stopping to stand in front of one covered canvas. 'Didn't mean for what to happen, Riordan? Didn't mean to kiss me the first time, or the second time or the third time? Didn't mean to overstep the boundaries between employer and employee? Didn't mean to embroil me in a scandal not of my making?' *Didn't mean to tempt me into developing feelings for you and then to play the rake?*

Her challenge made him angry. Well, good. This was one situation he couldn't charm his way out of with a wink and a smile. His gaze was dark when he looked her way, his blue eyes veiled, his usually transparent soul obscured. He shook his head. 'Any of it—I didn't mean for any of it to happen.'

By that, she knew he meant more than what had happened between them. The room went still, as if his words had sucked all the air, all the life out of it.

'Young women want a paragon, they want this.' With a fluid movement, Riordan pulled off the tarp to reveal the portrait of a young man who looked vaguely familiar: the dark hair, the blue eyes, the smile. The features were the same as Riordan's and yet not the same at all.

Maura stared. She'd never mistake the man in the portrait for Lord Chatham. His eyes weren't nearly lively enough to compete with Lord Chatham's dancing sapphires. His smile was not mischievous enough, his hair too perfect against Riordan's ruffled unruliness. This was no early version of Riordan as he'd been in his youth. All at once she knew. 'This is Elliott. This is your brother.'

He nodded, his eyes fixed on the painting. 'It was one of the last I did before I went to Italy. He would have been twenty-five.'

'Your work is good.' Maura studied the detail evident in the portrait right down to the pattern of the waistcoat peeping ever so briefly out from under the coat with its buttons. The work was excellent, in fact, and it made her wonder a thousand things about the man who stood beside her. It had always been the wonder, the intrigue about him that had drawn her. This was dangerous ground, to let herself be intrigued again. Even when she thought she knew the sum of him, there was another layer revealed.

'Elliott was the ideal earl: handsome but not audacious, immaculate without being fussy, authoritative without being tyrannical. He knew how to balance all things against each other for maximum benefit. Everyone loved him.'

She heard a wealth of meaning in those statements. 'People like you, too.'

He chuckled at that. 'Thank you for your validation. People like me well enough, but for reasons I'm ashamed to admit in a lady's company.' He paused, his jaw working as he debated something in his mind. His jaw tightened. Whatever it was, he'd decided.

'It's true, Maura. I'm awful. Do you know where I was when the news came?' It was a rhetorical question. Maura waited. 'I was at the Academy art show with the express purpose of seducing Lady Meacham. We were standing in front of Turner's latest and I was stroking her arm. I'd just closed the deal, so to speak.' He drew a breath. 'You see, I'm awful.'

The admission stunned her. It was patently false. 'Flawed, maybe, as we all are, but you're not awful,' Maura argued.

'How would you know? Have you met a truly awful man?'

She held his eyes. 'I have and you are not awful.' It was the most she'd told him about herself, her real self.

'I shouldn't have even told you these things.'

She laughed softly to ease his angst. 'Don't fear for my sensitivities. I'm not as innocent as all that. I'm well aware of the inclinations of men.' There were layers to her, too. She was tempted to let it all spill out, how she'd run out days before her wedding, how Wildeham had pawed at her every chance he got, the horrid things he'd said to her, describing what he'd do to her once they were married, how it was such a horrible life to contemplate she'd preferred running away and giving up the life of a lady for the anonymity of a governess. But she didn't dare say any more.

'That doesn't make you less of a lady, Maura.'

Maura blushed. 'That is generous of you.' He had a way of making her feel special. She wondered if he meant it.

Riordan looked back to the portrait. 'The question that haunts me is this—with all his perfections, why did Elliott die? It should have been me. I'm reckless. I've been in more dangerous races than I can count.' He couldn't look at her as he spoke. She understood what it cost him to speak the words out loud.

'Things happen, people take ill,' Maura began, groping for the familiar comforts people offered in the face of such tragedies. She knew before she began the words would be useless. The words had meant nothing to her when her parents had died.

Riordan shook his head, his tone harsh as he dismissed her platitudes. 'He took his own life. Polite society called it a self-inflicted bullet wound to the head, trying to pretty it up and make it sound like a hunting accident. The blunt truth of it is, the very proper, very perfect previous Earl of Chatham committed suicide.'

Maura stared in horrified fascination at the portrait, pieces of incomplete ideas coming together. This must be one of the reasons the governesses had left. Suicide was a grievous sin no matter who did it. Some even thought it a curse or bad luck.

'I never meant for something like that to happen, not to Elliott. I never wanted his title, never wanted to be the heir.' Riordan pushed a hand through his hair. 'You see, I was there with him just weeks before. He'd asked me to stay and delay my trip to London for a month. Usually we came up together. Since his death, I've often wondered—if I had stayed, would Elliott be alive? Could I have saved him if I hadn't gone off to London to win a ridiculous wager over Lady Meacham? I think I could have.'

His voice wavered, coming dangerously close to breaking. Layers, Maura thought again. He carried so much beneath his laugh and his merry eyes. He swallowed hard. 'When I was in Sussex, I learned something disturbing. Two days before Elliott's death, a relative, Viscount Vale, was in the area. He met with Elliott, but not at the house, which is why the servants didn't report anything out of the ordinary. The foreman for our home farm happened to spot them out riding. Vale never came to the house afterwards, it was as though he didn't want to be seen. The foreman said it all seemed very furtive and when he approached Elliott later, Elliott seemed distracted.'

Riordan took up his seat once more beside her. 'I wonder if that had something to do with it. Do you think I'm crazy? Am I seeing conspiracies where there are none?'

She wanted to reach out and give him absolution, but that was not hers to give. He had to forgive himself before any words from her would have merit.

'I think it's natural to want to look for reasons. When we have reasons we can generate solutions and that creates a kind of understanding. When my parents died, I thought much the same thing,' Maura said softly. 'They were drowned in a freak boating accident. I was sixteen and I wondered if I'd gone with them that day, if I'd seen the boat from the shore, if I could have got help fast enough to save them, or maybe if I'd been with them they wouldn't have gone out in the first place. I replayed any number of scenarios. But in the end I simply had to accept what was. I was alone except for my uncle's family.' Maura shrugged here to make light of it. 'Much like you and your Aunt Sophie and Uncle Hamish.'

Something moved in his eyes. 'Oh, my mother is very much alive and well, living at a spa in Switzerland.' He paused, waiting for the first shock to settle. She *was* a bit surprised. He'd not said either way, but she'd felt from the tone of their conversations that his mother had passed. 'It was the price for her freedom, to leave discreetly and never come back. She was all too happy to pay it. She wanted my father's title, he wanted her money and an heir or two. After they'd acquired those things the bubble was off the wine.'

Maura nodded, unsure what the appropriate response was. They were both silent. Even Riordan was unsure now that the disclosure was out. 'Forgive me, I'm surprising myself.' Riordan looked down at his hands and her eyes followed his. He had beautiful hands, long-fingered and strong, perfect painter's hands. 'I've never told anyone that. People know, certainly, but not from me.'

He reached out one of those hands and caressed her cheek. 'You do that to people, Maura. You listen to them. You inspire their confidence and in turn their confidences. You inspire me.' The charming gentleman was back, his blue eyes softening with desire. The dark earl with his family and its secrets was pushed offstage.

Maura covered his hand with hers where it lay against her cheek. She had to stop this before it started. He wanted her, she could see it in his eyes. She wanted to believe him and resist him all at once, her mind and her heart torn between logic and desire.

'Riordan, nothing can come of this.' Her defence was a façade only and the words weren't entirely true. Heartache would come of this.

He nipped gently at her earlobe, his tongue tickling the conch of her ear. 'Pleasure can come of this.'

Chapter Fifteen

'Pleasure' was too small a word, far too inadequate a word as Riordan took her in his arms, lowering her back against the sofa. Fulfilment, loneliness banished, emptiness filled, those more aptly described what could come of this. He wanted Maura, *needed* Maura to fill the void inside. The profundity of that need overwhelmed him, claimed him, becoming the centre of his universe. Every kiss, every caress designed to worship her as his mouth took her breast, as his hands caressed her legs, removing stockings and pantalettes in their wake until she was bare to him, her skirts pushed up in provocative invitation over the curve of a bent knee.

Her auburn curls were damp where he touched

her, a wave of validation sweeping him. She wanted him, too, *desired* him, too, he wasn't in this alone, swept away on a current of his own making. His hands bracketed her hips, his thumbs rested at the cradle of her pelvis as his mouth bent lower.

She arched to him, her hands in his hair, fisted and tight against the tides sweeping her, the honesty of her passion pushing his own arousal to the brink. He growled her name, primal and low in his throat, his hands working his trousers. At last he sprang free and he broke from her long enough to shove his trousers past his hips, calling on the reserves of his self-control not to rush this, not to plunge into her and seek his own relief. In this room, in this moment nothing mattered—not Vale's threats, not the burgeoning scandal, only giving Maura his all, in showing her the glorious possibilities between them.

This was magnificent and irrational. All capacity for thought had fled the moment his mouth had touched her, there was only the capacity to feel, to move with him, move *to* him. Maura shifted her hips, opening to him, revelling in the feel of him against her bare thigh, hot and hard. She was feasting on sensations and yet it wasn't enough to fill her. Something more hovered on the horizon and she was hungry for it.

The one thought that clung to her consciousness was the idea that had haunted her for days: it was not going to end well for her here. Her time was limited. The scandal had ensured no wife would tolerate her presence. Why shouldn't she take the knowledge of passion and the memory of pleasure with her? In the life she'd chosen, she'd not get such a chance again.

Riordan rose above her, the muscles of his arms straining beneath the loose cloth of his shirt, the mix of bare skin and fabric intoxicatingly masculine. Perspiration beaded his brow, a testament to his efforts, to his restraint, waiting for the right time. She thought fleetingly of the kite, of the lover who waited until the most final of moments to claim the ultimate pleasures. Then he was there, at the entrance to her core, seeking purchase. She opened to him, feeling herself stretch around him as he claimed her inch by inch until he was fully sheathed within. The newness of him brought a stab of pain. His movements halted, waiting for her to urge him on and she did. She'd come too far not to see this through, not to want to see this through, this miraculous feeling of being joined to another— not just another, of being joined with Riordan.

He began to move, picking up a gentle rhythm that rocked them back and forth, growing in its intensity as she joined him. Her hips drove up to meet him, pushing them towards some inevitable, cataclysmic end that beckoned, honing their pleasure to the sharpness of a knife's edge, each thrust taking them nearer to the completion they sought until at last they were there. Riordan gave a final thrust that catapulted her into a shattering ecstasy that left her exhausted and replete, the curiosity and the desire satisfied. He was there with her in that shattering darkness, his head resting against her neck, his breathing coming hard as the pleasure took him, and this was another source of satisfaction, to know they had journeyed to this incredible place together. The only word that came to mind was 'extraordinary'. Simply extraordinary, and it described both the man and the experience. She dared to breathe the word in the darkness.

Riordan raised his head ever so slightly and whispered, 'Of course, Maura. You inspire me.'

She laughed softly, a touch of the bitter-sweet encroaching on the moment. Extraordinary, perhaps, because of its singularity. This was a once-in-a-lifetime experience. It could not happen again. It had only served to prove they were both right; heartache lay down this road she'd embarked upon, as did pleasure, although it had been more than that. Surely there must be a better word, but she could not think of it because Riordan had begun kissing her again, and the window for rational thought was closing once more, and what happened outside the room ceased to matter.

Baron Wildeham favoured his hostess with a smile. Lady Sarah Meacham was a lovely woman, all lush curves and knowledge. Her hand had lingered on his sleeve long enough to convey her message, which had been received—well received—as they talked of other things.

'Good help is difficult to come by,' she said. 'I fully understand your dilemma. When we staffed our town house, I used Mrs Pendergast's referral agency for some of the maids. She specialises in placing well-bred young women as ladies' maids or companions, governesses, too.' She tapped him on the sleeve with her fan, trailing it down his arm and leaned in conspiratorially. 'Of course, the agency is losing its edge these days. All six of Chatham's governesses have come from there, including the latest one, the one that was at the dinner party.' She gave him a worldly look. 'Chatham's aunt says the girl was there to round out numbers after a last-minute cancellation, but Chatham couldn't take his eyes off her. It was in the papers this morning.'

He'd have to catch up on his reading, not that Chatham's scandal was of any interest to him. But what Lady Meacham said next was about to change his mind. 'There was another incident today. I just heard about it from Lady Fellowes. Chatham took Miss Sussington to the zoo with his wards and the governess. He all but snubbed poor Miss Sussington while they were there. He'll never get anyone decent to marry him now. He's gone and lost his senses over a pretty red-haired chit out of nowhere.'

'A redhead?' Lady Meacham had all of his attention now. 'Have you seen her?' Perhaps Lady

Meacham could offer a full description before he went haring off on another goose chase.

'No, I've not seen her.' Lady Meacham sounded disappointed. But it was enough, Wildeham thought. He'd see what Mrs Pendergast had to say about her latest client tomorrow. After a drought in which nothing had turned up, at last there was a possibility.

Wildeham leaned over Mrs Pendergast's desk. 'Let me ask you again, did a woman meeting my description come here? We have good reason to believe she did.' The 'we' in question was Paul Digby. He slouched in the corner of the office, his presence making it clear they were not leaving until they had answers.

Wildeham continued. 'You're not telling us anything we don't already suspect. If that doesn't clear your conscience, perhaps my sharp little friend will.' The steel of a knife glinted dangerously in one hand. The woman straightened, pressing her back as far against the chair as possible to get away from the blade.

Finally, progress, Wildeham thought. He should have started with the knife in the first place. The agency owner had been a tough bird.

One name and he'd know if Chatham's governess was his errant fiancée. He'd send Digby to check out the address. 'Well, Mrs Pendergast, a name, if you please?'

'You need to know this goes against my policy of privacy.'

'And you need to know this blade can just as easily go against your throat. Or if you prefer, I can tell everyone your agency shelters women of a criminal nature. A virtuous woman doesn't need to hide her past, does she?'

'I do not harbour criminals!' In her pricked pride, Mrs Pendergast forgot to be afraid for the moment.

'You're harbouring this one,' Wildeham said with a sneer. 'If it's the girl we're looking for, she's wanted for breach of contract. She's broken a legal agreement.' He brandished his blade close to her nose. 'A name, Mrs Pendergast. I won't ask again.'

'Her name is Maura Caulfield and I sent her to Chatham House on Portland Square.'

'Very good.' Wildeham slid the knife back up his sleeve and smiled. 'As you see, I can be reasonable. Good day, Mrs Pendergast.'

Once outside and away from the agency, Wildeham and Digby assessed their options. Portland Square was high living, just the right sort of address for an earl. It was appearing more likely that Maura and Chatham's governess were one and the same. His search was coming to a close but with one complication—how to take her without drawing attention to himself?

He would definitely have to wait, watch and plan this all very carefully. Digby could do reconnaissance. Meanwhile, Wildeham decided he needed to learn all he could about Riordan Barrett, rake and newly coroneted earl. What had Lady Meacham said—he'd been through six governesses? Whatever did Barrett need governesses for? Recently discovered bastards? A man like him surely had a couple of those tucked away. With a reputation like Barrett's there were bound to be skeletons in his closet. If he could rattle a few, he just might be able to shake Maura free without a fight.

Chapter Sixteen

'You simply must pay attention and stop acting as if these meetings are a mere inconvenience!' Browning whispered in an angry hiss at Riordan's elbow. Vale's solicitor was glaring across the polished surface of the table, briefs spread before him in testimony of the validity of his claims.

'Well?' the man repeated while the viscount sat beside him, smugly satisfied. 'You've made no progress acquiring a wife, but you *have* made quite a show continuing to live a most inappropriate lifestyle for children.' He waved a newspaper for emphasis.

Riordan didn't need to read it to know it contained the account of his dinner party and a subsequent description of his outing to the zoo. Apparently Miss Sussington had conveniently cried on Lady Helena's brother's shoulder and the brother had told Lady Helena who in turn had told the society pages. All because he, Riordan, hadn't paid attention to her. Now the Vales were seeking to pillory him with it in an attempt to secure the children and their money.

'Lord Chatham, these episodes are entirely unacceptable. You are carrying on with a woman in your employment, under your own roof, in front of the children.' Vale's solicitor waved his hand in an expansive gesture. 'We're all men here, we understand as a bachelor one wouldn't think twice about the behaviour, but you're not a bachelor, you're a guardian, and the rules change.' He tut-tutted here. 'It looks bad enough on the surface, you and a single woman alone in your home without any chaperonage. But to have those suppositions confirmed so glaringly and so often…' He didn't complete his thought, he just left it dangling there with its implicit conclusion: such evidence was damning indeed. They should settle this issue and move on.

'Look, Chatham,' Vale put in, his greying,

bushy eyebrows rising as he spoke. 'I don't want this to be messier than it has to be. We're family, after all, and Lady Vale has a desire to have the children.'

Riordan raised his own, thinner, more refined brows. He fought to keep his temper under control. 'Family? Since when have I ever been "family" with the likes of you? You were nowhere when those children needed taking in.' He wanted to be home, wanted to be with Maura and the children. She was taking them to the Egyptian Hall today to see a special exhibit. He would have liked to have gone, but he simply couldn't miss another appointment.

Vale sighed dramatically. 'I didn't want to drag your brother into all this, but you leave me no choice.' He pushed a paper forwards. 'I have scheduled a hearing to have your brother's will reviewed and my request has been approved. It seems there's a good chance he wasn't in his right mind.'

Riordan clenched his fists. 'How dare you talk of family and then betray that family in the next breath. You had no right.'

'I had every right.' Vale's smug expression turned lethal. 'I will have those children, Cha-

tham, if I have to ruin you and Elliott to do it.'
He gave a cruel smile. 'Of course, you've already ruined yourself, so my job is much easier.'
He rose. 'Five days, Chatham. The hearing is in
five days. I think we're finished here.'

Riordan waited until he and Browning were
alone to let the frustration show. Riordan pushed
a hand through his hair and slumped in his
chair. 'What do we have to fear from that will?
Has any more turned up as to why Elliott…?'
He couldn't quite speak the words. Browning
would know what he meant.

'Nothing more has come to light, but there's
been an interesting development in the financial records.' Browning busied himself looking
for papers. 'Here they are.' Browning opened a
ledger. 'Your brother has regular quarterly payments going out to an unnamed source over the
last four years. In and of itself, it's not notable.
But, look here.' Browning spread out papers
containing Vale's financial record. 'Vale is receiving the exact same amount, also unspeci-
fied. The payments begin at the same point in
time.'

'When was the last payment?' Riordan ran
his eyes over the papers, noting the pattern.

'February first. All the payments were made on the first of each month.'

Riordan scanned the list. There was nothing for the first of March that matched the amount on either end. 'The payment didn't come in March.' Then Vale had visited and Elliott had died. Riordan tapped a thoughtful finger on the ledger. 'Elliott could have paid. There was plenty of money.'

'Certainly. The earldom was in no financial straits.' Browning gathered up the papers and stuffed them back in his briefcase. 'I don't know what it means or if it means anything,' Browning hedged.

Riordan nodded. He thought so, too. When singular instances aligned, they became more than coincidences. He had two events; the terse, furtive visit meant to be secret, and now this— a missed payment when there was no reason for it. 'The question now is why, Browning? Why would my brother be paying Vale? Why would these payments start within months of him taking custody of Ishmael's children?' The obvious answer was blackmail of some sort. But what secret would Vale have over Elliott? Riordan wasn't even aware Elliott and Vale knew each other beyond a passing acquaintance on the family tree. Vale was only connected to them by marriage through Ishamel.

'Keep at it, Browning,' Riordan said. 'We're close.' They had to be. He was running out of time. Did he dare risk letting Vale expose Elliott's will to scrutiny and hope it held, that there were no damaging secrets and the Vales would look like the grasping petty relatives they were? Or did he simply marry, prove himself a worthy guardian and render a probe into the will as unnecessary? Marriage was the only option that provided any stability. Without a wife, even if Elliott's will held, the Vales could still argue a bachelor of his repute was an inappropriate guardian. No, it would have to be marriage. He would not escape this particular noose.

Five days to find a bride. He wanted more time. More time with Maura, more time with things just the way they were. He was not blind to the outcome heading his way. If he secured a bride, Maura would leave. The scandal had ensured there was no room for her in the home of a newlywed Earl of Chatham and his wife. Even if scandal had not ensured it, Maura's sense of rightness would demand it. It would be far too difficult to live in the same home with her, plus a wife by his side.

The alternative was no less bleak. If he failed to secure a bride, he'd lose the children, it was a surety. Without the children, he'd lose Maura, too. It wasn't fair, either way, he'd lose her. There was no choice. He had to give her up in order to save the children. His past had come back to haunt him.

Surely there was one woman in London who would marry him. But what would happen to Maura? He would go on with the children and an indifferent wife—he could live with that for William and Cecilia's sake. But Maura? When this was over, where would she go? In all his liaisons there'd been a sense of fairness. His women had known the rules.

Maura wasn't those women. He'd slept with her, taken her virtue, he'd ruined her chances with Hesperly, and what did she get in return?

A thought struck. He'd get her another, a replacement for Hesperly, someone who wasn't picky about virtue, who had a more realistic sense of the world, someone who would see only her goodness and beauty. Why shouldn't she have a happy ending, too? Well, 'happy ending' was a bit exaggerated. Riordan tried to run through a list of possibilities much like he was picking out a pet. It was the only way he could get through it. Otherwise it hurt too much.

But Ashe, Merrick and even Jamie were all married now. He came up blank. Perhaps he could get Hesperly back. He could tell the baron he'd been mistaken about her circumstances. The baron would believe the rumours, though. He'd have to offset those somehow, give the baron a carrot he couldn't refuse.

It was useless. Trying to match Maura with a husband was impossible. He'd not expected to be quite so affected by her. He'd needed her. What they'd shared had been far more than a rake's pleasure, the pleasure he was used to. Now that he'd tasted such fulfilment, he was loath to give it up or turn it over to another. But time was running out and he had no choices left. He would not, could not, disappoint Elliott in the last thing he had ever asked him to do.

'Six, do you like Uncle Ree?' Cecilia asked quite unexpectedly while they stood looking at a case of Egyptian jewellery on display at the aptly named Egyptian Hall, a fashionable ex-hibition venue on Piccadilly.

'Your uncle is a nice man,' Maura offered neutrally. She'd brought the children to see Bel-zoni's Valley of the Kings display as a way of coaxing William's ambition to be an explorer and to teach them a little history. She'd also thought to get out of the house in the hopes some distance would clear her thoughts. She'd succeeded only on the first account. The Af-rica room with its life-size models of elephants and cheetahs had inspired all nature of excite-ment in William. But on the second account, her thoughts needed very little encouragement from Cecilia.

'He is nice,' Cecilia agreed. 'And you're nice.' Her face lit in a bright smile as if she were try-ing to appear spontaneous. 'I know, Six, you should marry him. Would you?'

Maura blushed. 'Ladies don't go around pro-posing to gentlemen.' She tried to laugh it off, but Cecilia was persistent.

'What if *he* asked, though?' Cecilia peered up at her with eyes nearly as blue as Riordan's. Someday, she'd break plenty of English hearts with those eyes and that smile. Regret tugged at Maura's own heart. She would not be around for those days.

'Your uncle will find a nice wife,' Maura reassured her, doing her best to hide the sadness that accompanied those thoughts. Since the dinner party, it had become clear layer by layer that her time at Chatham House would end, sooner rather than later. All she could do was hold on to her position and her heart as long as she could, although she feared it was too late for the latter. Perhaps it was the knowing, the sensing all this had become temporary, that had fuelled her wild plunge into reckless passion. If it could not last, why not take a piece of him with her? It wasn't as if there would be other suitors in the life she had chosen.

'Did you see the toys over here, Cecilia?' Maura steered the little girl towards a case full of ancient dolls and away from more awkward questions. It would be hard enough to leave when the time came without raising Cecilia's hopes.

William stood by a sarcophagus, studying the inlaid gems. The exhibit wasn't crowded in the early afternoon and she'd let him wander about the room with the admonition that he stay close, no more than a display or two away. But now a thick-set man had come up to look at the sarcophagus, too, and he was talking with William. It was time to retrieve the boy.

'William,' Maura called out as she approached, Cecilia in hand. 'We need to move on. We want to see the South Seas room before we go.'

The big man with William turned towards her, his gaze unnervingly sharp. 'He's a nice boy, ma'am.' He was roughly dressed, resembling a dock worker more than a museum patron. 'He's not yours, though, is he?' The stranger asked as an afterthought. 'You're far too young to have such a grown-up young man for a son.'

It was an inappropriate question, the frankness of it taking Maura back for a moment. But William puffed up under the compliment. 'She's our governess.'

That piqued the man's interest. 'Is that so?' He smiled at William, but Maura grabbed William by the hand, eager to be away before the boy could spill any more pieces of information—not that this stranger was the sort to know her uncle. She didn't want to be paranoid and think everyone posed a danger, but this man's eyes made her uneasy. There was no sense in courting danger after she'd worked so hard to be cautious. 'Come along, Will. Good day, sir.' She gave the man a stern look to discourage any further interaction in case he was inclined to follow them.

The rest of their trip was uneventful. Cecilia kept her questions about Uncle Ree to herself and William talked to no more strangers. It might have been her imagination, but Maura could have sworn she glimpsed the stranger one more time as they climbed into the carriage and headed for home, and the children were uncharacteristically quiet.

'We have to do something, Cee-Cee,' William complained in a hushed whisper. They were in the nursery playing while Six worked on lessons for tomorrow at the round table. 'They kissed a few days ago. Everything should be fine now, but it's not. Nothing's happened.' He was getting worried. If Uncle Ree hadn't asked Six, it meant he was still considering others. It was time for more direct measures.

Cecilia furrowed her brow. 'Six likes him, she told me so today. I don't understand it.' She thought for a moment. 'Maybe they just haven't had enough time to be together. He can't ask her if they aren't together.'

William thought about it. 'Maybe. Uncle Ree has been busy. He's been going to meetings since the party.' What his fun-loving Uncle Ree did at those meetings was a mystery to him.

Cecilia played with her doll's hair, plaiting it into two braids. 'We need a chance for them to be together.'

'Another dinner?' William suggested.

Cecilia smiled. 'With invitations for tomorrow evening.' Then she frowned. 'A dinner is a good idea, but how are we going to plan it? We're just children.'

'Do you still have those invitations Six saved for us from Uncle Ree's party?' William smiled a mischievous grin that would have raised Six's suspicions if she'd seen it.

'They're under my bed.' It was the usual place for most of Cecilia's treasures. 'What are you going to do with them?'

William winked and tapped his head with his forefinger. 'Don't worry, Cee-Cee. I've got a plan. We're not just children, we're *smart* children.'

* * *

'It's her, sir,' Digby confirmed. 'I followed them to the exhibition hall and back. She looked just like that picture you showed me.' He leaned back in one of Grillon's leather lobby chairs.

Wildeham grinned triumphantly. Like a spider, he'd waited patiently, slowly gathering his information, methodically spinning his web, eliminating options until everything had narrowed down to this final manoeuvre. He knew most of it now; she'd assumed the name Maura Caulfield, her mother's maiden name, and cleverly a different one than the one that crafty vixen had signed in the coaching ledger. Even if someone had remembered her arrival, it would have done little good. 'Ellen Treywick' had simply vanished. Now he just had to pounce.

The question to settle before that long-anticipated moment happened was what role did Riordan Barrett play in all this? As a dissolute rake with problems aplenty of his own, would he let Maura go, happy to wash his hands of the little traitor? Acton didn't think Barrett would like knowing a fraud was working under his roof. On the other hand, if the scandal sheets were to be believed, Maura might mean something more to him. Would he try to protect her?

If he did, Acton had leverage. He'd learned all about Barrett's situation, how he was desperately trying to hang on to his brother's wards. Surely if he knew about Maura's deceit, he would understand how damaging it would be if that information found its way to Vale. Acton rubbed his hands together. It was just like a chess game. There was no way out for Maura now.

'What next, sir?' Digby asked.

Acton grinned. 'Checkmate, Digby.'

Chapter Seventeen

Riordan set down the note from Baron Hesperly and pushed back from his desk. He'd much rather be upstairs in his studio, working on his painting of Maura. Much of it was being done from sketches and memory since she refused to sit for him, and had in fact done a good job of avoiding him since…since the night they'd made love. He'd seen her, of course, but always with the children. There'd been no time to be alone.

There. He'd said it. Not 'had sex' but 'made love'. Maura had become precious to him and now he was about to give her to another. Was that what people did with precious things? Give them away? Was he giving Maura away or was he keeping her safe? He had no reason to believe she'd fail to charm Hesperly, and Hesperly would be good to her.

Hesperly was willing to call on her, willing to be charmed. The baron had written to say he was thankful for Riordan's 'clarification' of Maura's situation. He'd been enchanted by her at dinner and a million other poetic adjectives. His note had run over with them. Riordan would have laughed at the man's excessive sentiment if he hadn't agreed with it wholeheartedly.

Riordan reached for another letter. His hand stalled on a carefully penned square of heavy paper. He *did* recognise it: a left-over invitation from the dinner party. He'd know Maura's writing anywhere, firm but loopy and definitely feminine. It was an odd item to find in his mail given the party had passed. Then he noticed the scratched-out date and time replaced with an awkwardly scrawled single word: tonight.

It didn't look like Maura's precise penmanship, but the word was tiny and that might account for its less-than-perfect nature. A knock at the study door interrupted his scrutiny. Riordan answered, 'Come', and slid the note beneath his blotter.

'Uncle Ree?' William poked his head in.

Riordan smiled. 'Come in. What are you doing out of the nursery?'

'I stole away for just a moment.' William looked over his shoulder guiltily. Riordan laughed. 'I wanted to talk to you.'

'Well then, you had better come over here and tell me what's on your mind.'

'Your marriage, sir.'

Of all the things Riordan thought William would want to discuss, this had not been one of them. Perhaps it should have been considering Cecilia's outburst at the zoo. He needed to give the children more credit. 'I'm not married, not even engaged, Will.' Riordan frowned. It wasn't for lack of trying.

'Yet. Not yet. But you'd like to be,' William continued, standing in front of the big desk and trying to look so very grown up with his jaw set in a most serious expression.

'I'd like you to have a mother, William,' Riordan answered with equal seriousness. 'Wouldn't that be nice?' He hoped William wouldn't hear the missing pieces in that statement.

William nodded. 'If she were the right person that would be very nice, Uncle. But she'd have to be someone *all* of us liked.'

'That would be best,' Riordan acceded. *Probably not possible given the looming deadline.* He studied William's face, watching the boy gather his thoughts. There clearly was something more the boy wanted to say. 'Of course, I haven't found anyone,' Riordan offered encouragingly. Perhaps William was worried he'd settled on someone.

William's features shifted into hesitant brightness. 'May I make a suggestion?'

'A suggestion?' Riordan covertly scanned the room with his eyes, half-expecting to see a woman emerge from the panelling dressed in a wedding gown. What kind of a woman would an eight-year-old boy know?

'Six,' William said simply and Riordan knew he didn't mean to make six suggestions. In their house, there was only one Six.

'Six?' Riordan repeated as coolly as he could. *Maura.* The children were definitely smarter than he realised.

'Well? Why not?' William warmed to his argument. 'She's a lot of fun, she actually likes us and she likes you. Cecilia asked her at the exhibit yesterday and she said she did.' William paused and looked at his feet before going on. 'You like her, too. That makes her perfect.'

Riordan raised his brows at this last. 'Why do you think I like her?' Heavens knew what else William had picked up on. It was a novelty getting love advice from an eight-year-old.

'We saw you kissing her the night of the party,' William confessed with a blush, as well he should blush. It had been a hell of a kiss. 'So? Why not marry Six and make all of us happy?'

Riordan shook his head. 'It's not as simple as all that.' How did he explain this tangle to the boy without being alarming? Without looking like a terrible example to William? Even rogues had rules and he'd broken most of them since meeting Maura.

'Yes, it is,' William replied. 'You just have to ask her. What's so hard about that?'

Riordan laughed. 'Spoken like a man who's never yet had to propose. You can tell me the answer to that in about twenty years.'

His humour was lost on William, who was absorbed in his single-minded mission. 'So? Will you do it?' William pressed.

Riordan didn't have an answer. 'Why don't you get back to the nursery before Six comes looking for you?' Then, before William could ask him again, Riordan said, 'I'll think about it, Will.'

Good lord, how the mighty had fallen. The man who could make a woman climax at fifteen feet was getting advice from a child. It was quite the new experience, especially when he had no answer for Will. Why not Maura? The longer he thought about it, the more he liked the idea.

Riordan fished out the invitation from beneath his blotter. He had a better suspicion now who *and* what was behind this. He pulled out his watch. Five o'clock. Just enough time to make himself presentable or was it 'proposable'?

Maura hesitated on the stairs, nervously fingering the folds of her second-best dress, a shimmery silver-grey satin with brilliantes sewn into the hem to add to the starry effect. Maura couldn't believe she'd let Cecilia talk her into this; the dress *and* accepting the dinner invitation, whose source was somewhat indeterminate, although she had her suspicions. She had not faced Riordan since, well, just since. She'd leave it at that. She wasn't even sure he *wanted* to face her. True, she hadn't sought him out.

She'd kept herself busy with the children and field trips. But neither had he seemed to make an effort to seek her out. Maybe he'd realised, too, just how impractical anything more than one night was. But now this invitation threw those suppositions into question.

She supposed the answer depended, too, on what kind of dinner this was meant to be. A seduction by candlelight? A farewell? Perhaps a mix of both? Would he casually tell her over wine he'd decided on a bride?

'Miss Caulfield, your dinner awaits.' Riordan strode forwards, his hand outstretched. Her breath caught at the sight of him. He'd taken extra care with his appearance. Everything about him was immaculate, his unruly hair brushed to perfection, his jaw shaven and smooth, his dark evening clothes pressed. He wore a dark-emerald waistcoat beneath with an onyx stick pin in his cravat.

If a man could look ravishing, Riordan did. Ravishing and masculine. The gaze he cast her said he would devour her if she let him. It was to be seduction, then.

Would she let him? She slipped her hand into his. He raised it to his lips, his message clear.

He would endeavour to persuade her, but the decision would be hers. The game had begun.

By the time the beef course was served, Maura realised she'd mistaken the game. There was something more than seduction and another night of pleasure at stake. What that could possibly be, Maura could not guess. She'd been so certain of her earlier interpretation. Now, she was starting to see it in a different light. Riordan's sartorial splendour, even his flirtation tonight, was a notch above the usual.

His flirtation was not in his innuendo-laced words, or blatant touch. It was in his eyes, in his gestures. Dinner was served *à la français* and she honoured the tradition, letting him serve her, letting him pick the best pieces of meat for her, reminiscent of chivalrous knights of old choosing for their ladies. From another man, the gesture would look over-solicitous, ridiculous, even patronising. But Riordan carried it off with a subtle aplomb that managed to ratchet her desire to dizzying heights. Who would have thought the act of putting roasted beef on one's plate or pouring a small glass of wine could create, could *inflame* desire?

She chewed, she swallowed, but her attentions were all claimed by him, by the motion of his mouth as he ate, the caress of his fingers around the stem of his wine glass, from which he drank sparingly, the curve of his lips as he made conversation, laughing with her over the visit to the Egyptian Hall. All the while she feared she'd clutch her glass so tightly it would shatter.

'There is something I'd like to discuss with you, Maura,' he said finally over a plate of strawberries dipped in chocolate. He held one up and offered it to her. She took a tiny, sweet bite. Was this how farewell started?

'We have not talked since the other night. I regret that.' His eyes were holding hers, a light smile on his lips that did nothing to help her relax. It was a seductive smile that said 'I know what you're feeling and you're safe with me. You don't need to fight it.' So much for nonchalance. It was unnerving how transparent she was to him.

'You've been busy.' She offered the polite excuse.

'I have. That's no excuse. When a gentleman takes a woman's virtue there should be words afterwards.' His blue eyes were serious, sparking a knot of dread in her stomach right next to the roast beef. Surely he didn't feel he owed her anything. She recalled how he had offered her a new gown and the pocket of dread grew. Maura swallowed hard. It would positively demean their one night, their one indiscretion if he offered her recompense for it. *Please don't*, she silently pleaded.

'I meant it when I said you inspired me, Maura.' He reached for her hand, gripping her fingers. 'Since I've met you my other entertainments have lost their allure. I've come to believe the reason I can't settle on a wifely candidate is you, which leads me to the conclusion that I should marry you. Would you do me the honour of being my wife?'

Dread and disbelief warred with the beef. Marry her? It was impossible for so many reasons. 'You hardly know me.' She tried to pull back her hand. If he touched her any longer she'd capitulate. It was a fairy tale she had no right to. It would cost him in ways he couldn't guess. 'You've only known me a little over a month.'

'I know enough.' Riordan's eyes fairly seared

her as if they could burn compliance from her. 'I know you're good, and kind, and the children adore you.'

'And you? Do you adore me?' She was starting to see that other agenda she'd suspected over the beef. This dinner was about something far bigger than a one-night seduction. It wasn't even about his personal desire to marry. It was something larger.

'I do believe I am falling in love with you,' Riordan whispered softly, letting his lips skim the knuckles of her hand before he turned her hand over and covered her palm with gentle kisses.

'Marriage is not an institution lightly undertaken,' Maura replied, wishing she could see as much in his face as he usually saw in hers. 'Why do you wish to marry so precipitously?' What was it he'd said the day he'd asked her to plan the party? *I find myself compelled to marry? I cannot wait until next Season.* There was something more afoot.

'Now you sound like the vicar.' Riordan chuckled against her hand. 'And you haven't answered my question. Will you marry me?'

Maura met his gaze with seriousness. 'You

haven't answered mine. What's really going on that an earl with a reputation suddenly wants to marry and then suddenly wants to marry the governess? You have to agree it looks somewhat suspect.' When Riordan said nothing, she said, 'I will not commit to a marriage where we cannot have complete honesty between us. This would be an ominous beginning indeed.'

He let go of her hand. He drew a deep breath and she braced herself. Perhaps she should have settled for the romantic half-truths he'd spun. Whatever he had to say was going to hurt.

'The Vales will take the children if I don't marry or produce at the very least a likely wife in the next four days.' Oh heavens, she hated being right. If it wasn't for the children's involvement, she might have felt like a consolation prize. As it was, all she could manage was, 'The Vales? The same who visited Elliott?'

'The viscountess is the children's cousin on their mother's side. She declined to take them the first time around,' Riordan offered briefly.

'How long have you known?' Longer than she'd been here, she was sure of that. This drama had been going on before she'd arrived. She was starting to see the whole sordid mess he was coping with: the precipitous suicide of his brother, the battle for the children. There'd been so much more occurring beneath the surface than simply settling children into a new life with a new guardian, so much more than what she'd seen or guessed at and Riordan had taken it all upon his shoulders.

'Since the funeral. It hardly matters. She's after their trust funds, which are significant.' Riordan lowered his voice. 'They were penniless orphans when their father died. Elliott changed that. There's money and an estate for William and a respectable dowry for Cecilia. There's a trust for raising them, William's school, Cecilia's début. The children are wealthy in their own right.'

'But Elliott left them to you.' Maura tried to assemble all the pieces in to a coherent whole. It would break him to lose those children.

'They mean to contest the will if they have to. They mean to suggest Elliott was mentally imbalanced and didn't know what he was doing when he bequeathed the children to me.' Riordan stretched his hands wide on the table. 'I am an unfit guardian, you see. Only a crazy man would think otherwise.'

'And marriage? Where does that fit in with all this?'

'With a wife I can prove there's a motherly presence in the home and that I've redressed my wicked ways.' Riordan gave a harsh laugh. 'Apparently, a man is considered upstanding if he has a wife by his side.'

Maura wished she could erase the pain from his face. 'These meetings you've been at, they've been about the children?'

'Yes, and about the will. We've been trying to determine what we might have to fear from the exposure of Elliott's will.' He shook his head. 'There's been a development in the ledgers that gives us hope we might discover the reason, but also concern over what that reason might be. We don't want it used against us.'

Something crossed his face that hadn't been there before. Fear. That rocked her more than the sight of his personal pain. She'd not thought the Earl of Chatham, Riordan Barrett, lived in fear of anything. But she saw now there was fear over losing the children, over his brother's memory, his legacy, and maybe fear, too, that he wasn't up to the challenge of preserving both, that his father had been right all those years ago.

'It's not the most elegant of proposals, Maura. But I do care for you, that's not a lie, and I can make a good life for you.' He picked up her hand again, caressing it in circles, the beginnings of a seduction. 'I can give you—'

She would not let him do this. She would not let him beg. 'Stop.' The firmness of the command made him look up. 'Don't you dare sell yourself like this.' How many times had he done this before? she wondered. Promising the one thing he felt he could give in exchange for what? For a few moments where he succeeded in driving back the pain of the past? How had she not guessed? Not seen the layers of him? The vulnerability he was a master at hiding?

'If you won't believe in my ability to love you, Maura, believe in my ability to give you pleasure. You know I am not promising it idly.' The grip on her hand tightened to almost painful. 'I would sell my very soul for those children. I have nothing else to bargain with. The Vales have no interest in them beyond the money. They'll be packed off to boarding schools and who knows what will happen to the funds. Vale's pockets are nearly to let, he's not as solvent as he appears. Please, help me. Help William and Cecilia.'

Tears brimmed in her eyes. Riordan needed the one thing she couldn't give him. 'I can't marry you.' She breathed the words in a whisper. She could not give him the decency he needed. Marriage to her would solidify his wicked reputation—the man who married a woman promised to another. It was only a hair's breadth away from bigamy and her uncle had the papers to prove it.

His face became a mask of stoicism and she knew he didn't understand. He thought she was rejecting *him*, that he was unsuitable when in reality it was she who was the unsuitable one. He reached into his evening coat. 'Then perhaps you'll want this. It's a note from Baron Hesperly indicating his intentions. He'd like to call on you, and I think you can safely assume his attentions will lead to a certain outcome.'

Maura covered her mouth with a hand, stricken. She didn't bother to pick up the note. 'It's not that I can't marry you. I can't marry anyone.' She pushed back from the table. What a horrible mess this had become. She had to get away from here, get away from him before her secrets tumbled out. She'd been right to keep them from him. He would take on her burdens as he had the others.

She was too late. Riordan had her by the arm, his grip hard, his eyes blazing, his voice angry as he growled one word. 'Why?'

Chapter Eighteen

'That's my business.' Maura tugged at her arm, but Riordan held fast. She was his last chance, his *best* chance. He would not let her go.

'You've refused my proposal. I have a right to know on what grounds.' He raked her with a searing glance. 'Especially when I am certain there have been no others.' This last was said meanly. He hoped to prompt an angry response, something other than her defiant resistance. 'I am uncertain, however, that we haven't made a child between us. Have you thought of that?' His argument gained purchase with her. She paled a little at the possibility. 'Nature does not care if it's your first time or your hundredth.

That child could be the next Earl of Chatham. All you have to do is say yes.'

His tactics were completely unfair. He knew Maura would put consideration of a child above her own. But this was now a zero-sum game and he would win. He had to win. He had children of his own now to consider. Whether they knew it or not, their futures hinged on his victory with Maura. He bent his lips to her ear. 'Tell me your secret, Maura. It is safe with me, you are safe with me.' And she was, he realised with a shocking intensity. These were not the idle words of a desperate swain. Whatever dreadful secret she carried, he would protect her.

Maura turned her head away and gave a final tug. This time he let her arm drop. 'Telling you won't change anything. Knowing won't magically make me able to marry you.' There was regret mixed with her defiance. He was encouraged. She *would* marry him if she felt free to do so. He just had to convince her she could. That meant ferreting out her secret and convincing her it wasn't nearly as insurmountable as she believed.

Riordan strode towards the wide double doors to the dining room and pulled them shut. With a resolute flick of his fingers he locked them. 'Why don't you sit? If my powers of deduction aren't up to snuff, it may be a long night.'

Maura hesitated. 'What are you doing?'

Riordan grabbed a small chair from against the wall and swivelled it backwards, straddling it. 'I am settling in for a game of Rumpelstiltskin. I will guess your secret.'

Maura sat confidently. 'You can't make me tell you.'

'You won't have to. I will guess all night and in the end I will have the truth whether you tell me or not.'

'Very well, I won't *admit* to it.'

Riordan smiled wolfishly. Let her be slightly alarmed, he thought. He needed this secret, he needed *her*. 'You won't have to.' He should have learned more about her from the beginning when his initial suspicions had been raised: the fine manners, the well-made clothes, the ability to host a dinner party, the oblique reply from Mrs Pendergast's agency. But he hadn't looked further than the surface, just as he hadn't looked beyond Elliott's suicide for the same reasons. What lay behind the surface explanations threatened to be too painful or too dangerous and so he'd chosen not to, hoping there would be no need. Now there was every need and he might have left it too late.

'Let's begin with the obvious. There is no secret lover in the shadows waiting to carry you away.'

'So this is to be twenty questions?' The little minx was confident she could resist giving anything away.

'Of a sort,' Riordan replied, a smile flitting across his lips. Verbal responses were only one way truths were revealed.

'No, there is no secret lover,' Maura confirmed. He knew there wasn't, but he watched her face anyway for tells that suggested she might be mincing words, that there was some small grain of truth down that path. Not a lover in the most literal of terms, but a hidden sweetheart. He doubted it. Maura was not the sort of woman who would engage in casual sex. A secret sweetheart made no sense when her attraction to him was very real.

If there was no one to run to, perhaps there was something to run from. What had she said? She'd lived with her uncle's family since she was sixteen. Her parents were dead, leaving her alone in the world. She was twenty or even twenty-one, and lovely. Perhaps it was a scandal she fled. She'd been horrified when he'd told her about the society column.

'Not a sweetheart. What about a scandal, Maura? Was there some unpleasant business?' A scandal didn't quite ring true. She'd been a virgin when he'd taken her. Whatever scandal there might have been, it was smoke only, a rumour, hardly enough in all likelihood to make a young woman flee the security of her home and family, especially a family of some means if her clothes were to be believed.

Maura shook her head, her auburn hair catching the candlelight. He wanted to be through with this deduction and move on to seduction. Her stubbornness was denying them both.

Option two, then—not running from something, but perhaps someone. Riordan thought again about the uncle, a man of means with a marriageable niece. Maura was bound to have attracted plenty of attention, not all of it good, not all of it the right sort of attention.

'Not a sweetheart. How about an unwanted suitor?'

'No,' Maura said, but her eyes had darted

ever so slightly to the right, indicating a hint of truth. Semantics, Riordan thought. Not a suitor in the strictest sense, but a pursuer who was not being thwarted by her uncle, the man who should have been her first and best line of defence.

Riordan elaborated. 'There's a man your uncle wants you to marry.' He suspected 'want' was too weak of a word. 'Force' might be more appropriate. 'It's the awful man you mentioned in the studio.'

'You are conjuring up plots worthy of the stage,' Maura said tightly, but she'd made her last mistake. She rose and began to pace, her movements obscuring her face from him, her hands fisted at her sides. Riordan grinned in triumph. He had her.

He stood and moved towards her, his sense of victory fleeting in the wake of his discovery. He could only begin to imagine the depths of the situation for her to need to escape in such a drastic way, to disappear into service, into anonymity. He'd fled once, too. If he could not relate precisely to what had driven her, he could understand the philosophic grounds behind it. She paused by a long window overlooking the street, lifting back the curtain to gaze out at the carriages passing by on their way to parties and balls.

Riordan came up behind her, his arms sliding about her waist and drawing her against him, his voice tempting and soft. 'Tell me, Maura. Tell me what your uncle did—who is the man he meant for you to marry?' Maura sighed against him, a sigh full of weary capitulation. She was going to give in, having no doubt come to this point where she realised keeping her secret was no longer protecting anyone.

She spoke barely above a whisper. 'Acton Humphries, Baron Wildeham.' Maura's head lolled back against his chest and he savoured the trust, the compliance of the action. She was *with* him. 'How did you know?'

'Simple deduction. A young lady of means does not throw away all she has on a fancy. Tell me, Maura, how bad was it that you were willing to do so?'

'I was payment for a lost horse race.'

'Your uncle bet you?' Riordan was appalled.

'Not initially. It was more genteel than that. My uncle had wagered money, but when he lost, something he thought an unlikely possibility, he didn't have the money to pay. Wildeham offered to take the house in exchange for the funds. But that was unacceptable and then Wildeham offered for me and that was much more acceptable than losing the house.' There was bitterness in those words, a sense of betrayal. Riordan's anger grew. He'd like to call out the ungrateful uncle, but there was more.

'There had already been an incident involving myself and Wildeham.' She was holding back, sugar-coating the previous 'incident', but Riordan understood the gist of it. Now he wanted to call out Wildeham for putting Maura in an untenable position.

'Wildeham thought a marriage would tie up the, shall we say, loose ends into a nice package. My uncle thought so, too.'

'But you disagreed?'

'Wildeham is a man with dark proclivities,' Maura said quietly. 'There are rumours about him in the district and his home goes through a rather large number of maids.' She tensed in his arms as she spoke. It was more than rumours, she was remembering something distasteful.

'What is it, Maura? Something he did? Something he said?'

'He had some rather graphic details about how we'd spend our wedding night that he felt compelled to disclose. I'm grateful he did, however, otherwise I might not have had the courage to run.'

And she had run straight to him. Some might think she had merely traded one rake for another, but he'd never use coercion or guilt or force to bring a woman to his bed.

She turned in his arms, her face uptilted, her hair falling back, all beauty and loveliness. 'I'm a bad person, Riordan. You think I'm good, but I'm not. I'm selfish. My uncle will be turned out of his home, but I can't marry to save them.'

Riordan stole a kiss and then another. The secret was out and he could manage it. 'I was wrong about you, Maura. All this time I thought you were a defiant little minx. You're not. You're brave. Very brave.' He knew only a few women with that rare courage, who were brave enough to stand up for the life they wanted even if it meant splitting with family. Merrick's wife, Alixe, was one of them.

Maura wasn't convinced. 'If I was brave, maybe I would have stayed and seen it through.'

Riordan scoffed at the notion. 'It's his own

fault. Your uncle shouldn't squander your future for his foolishness.' He was feeling confident now. 'Is that why you won't marry me?'

She shook her pretty head. 'I'm dangerous to you. My uncle will be looking for me. If I marry you, he will find me. An earl's marriage can't stay hidden. He will come for me and he'll expose everything. That won't help you. The Vales will use it to wrest the children away. You will have proven to them, to everyone, you're just as bad as your reputation suggests.'

'I have money, piles of it now that I'm the earl. We can pay your uncle's bill if we have to.' Solutions were becoming easier now that he knew the parameters. She was in his arms and she was willing if he could strip away the last obstacles. All he wanted, all he needed, was so very close. 'You know the children set this dinner up?' He bent to kiss her again, a longer, lingering kiss this time, a prelude to love-making. The dining table beckoned.

'Stop, Riordan.' She stiffened, the panic in her eyes giving him a moment's pause. 'You cannot simply buy my uncle's debt. There are papers, papers that promise me to the baron.'

'Did you sign them?'

'No, but…'

He pressed a finger to her lips. Maura was far too honourable by half. Papers could be contested, if and when they were brought to light. 'No more worries, Maura.' He kissed her hard now. It was time to remind her why she was going to say yes before the night was through.

The air about them changed, the kiss left her breathless and his intentions obvious. Riordan's eyes sparked with passion and desire, a clear declaration that the time for negotiating and discussion was done. He lifted her hand to his shoulder, his hand dropping to her waist. He moved in to her, she stepped back intuitively, once, twice, and they were dancing. Not a fast polka like they had upstairs, but a slow waltz that was anything but sedate.

It was charged and sensual, bodies touching in ways that would not be condoned in London's ballrooms, his hips pressed to her skirts, his hand warm at her back until they were flying, soaring in their silent dance about the dining room. Everything was possible—in his arms there were no limits, no papers, no uncles, no realities beyond his. She laughed up at him from the exhilaration, the freedom of it. He took her mouth in a kiss. Desire flamed to life, a hungry fire needing to be fed.

Her back was to the wall and he was lifting her, her skirts falling back, her legs wrapping around his waist, his kisses hot at her neck, his breath coming as hard and as fast as hers as desire swamped them both. She would never know quite how he managed it, but he was there, his body supporting hers, the wall their only point of stability, his voice a harsh warning at her ear. 'I don't think I can be gentle.' Her acquiescence was nearly as incoherent as he took her in a swift thrust. She cried out, hands anchored in his dark hair, her legs clutching him to her, urging him onwards. He had her hands shackled to the wall beneath his own, his mouth devouring until she thought she'd weep from the rough sensations of the coupling. She nipped at his ear, his wildness claiming her, driving her forwards with him to the ultimate release, more potent than ever because now she knew, she knew what waited at the peak of their climb.

She could feel her own body gathering for the final ascent, she was crying out loudly and without inhibition now, Riordan hot and sweating against her, all vestiges of the well-groomed gentleman gone, replaced by a man driven by passion and desire. They soared, fast and hard, and she was defying gravity, like Icarus rising to the sun in an explosion of speed and exhilaration, and then she melted oh so slowly until at last she fell to earth, irrevocably changed. This new Maura was loved. This Maura would not flee. This Maura would fight.

Riordan gently disengaged from her and set her on her feet, her arms still wrapped about his neck, keeping him close. His lips parted and it was her turn to silence him with a finger to the lips. She didn't want him to say it, to bargain with what they'd done. 'Yes, Riordan. The answer is yes.'

Riordan gave her a lopsided grin. 'Good. You've made me the happiest of men.'

'Why is that?'

'Because soon I'll have you naked in a bed as is only proper,' he whispered wickedly and Maura laughed, believing for the first time since she'd left Exeter that tomorrow would take care of itself.

Chapter Nineteen

Acton took a last bite of the excellent steak. He was pleased with the results of this lunch. Across from him, Viscount Vale was fairly salivating over the piece of information he'd just revealed. 'As you can see, your concerns over Chatham are well placed.' Acton tucked the papers back into his breast pocket. 'His latest governess is an absolute fraud and he's allowing her to work with the children.'

They both knew Vale didn't care who was watching the children, but it would make a good argument tomorrow at the hearing. 'Will you swear to it?' Vale enquired, still sceptical of this stranger bearing gifts.

'Better than that, I'll come in person.' Acton

leaned back in his chair, certain they had nearly reached a satisfactory conclusion. He would be at the hearing with witnesses to his presence and while he was there, promoting justice, Digby would make his move on the town house.

Vale studied his plate. 'I have to ask—why would you do this for me? You don't know me.'

Acton leaned forwards. 'You and I are men of the world. We understand no one does anything for nothing. In this case, helping you serves my purposes while you serve yours. You want the children and I want her. The governess belongs to me.'

'Are you sure I can't come?' Maura fussed with Riordan's cravat in the hall of Chatham House. It didn't need adjusting, but it gave her something to do with her hands. The hearing over the children was this morning at eleven and Riordan had elected to go alone no matter how hard she argued.

Riordan captured her hands, a smile belying his seriousness. 'It won't be pleasant. I wouldn't have you be a party to it. They're going to trot out all my past sins in an attempt to discredit my ability to act as a decent guardian. If that doesn't work, they're going to go after Elliott's will. There's nothing you can do by being there. The children need you here.' He winked. 'Besides, I don't want you changing your mind. My past is not exactly a bedtime story.'

Maura looked down to where their hands were joined at his cravat. 'Are you sure this is what you want?' By *this* she meant marriage. After a day of wandering about in a daze, it was still something of a shock to realise what she, what *they*, had committed to. She'd more than half-expected Riordan to change his mind, to realise this was folly.

'You are what I want.'

'Earls don't marry governesses,' Maura reminded him softly. Even if it was to merely plug a hole in the dyke, he was marrying her for the children's sake.

'You're not really a governess,' Riordan answered. 'You're a gentleman's daughter, niece of a baronet.' He smiled. 'I have an answer for everything. Kiss me once for luck; I'll see you when I get home.'

Maura let him go and went to work with the children on their morning lessons, but that didn't stop the foreboding. This was wrong, mixed up and awkward, ultimately flawed. He wouldn't be marrying her if it wasn't for the children. She wouldn't have accepted either. But the children were counting on Riordan's bridal gambit to succeed. She had no illusions about this being a love match, no matter how great his passion, no matter how flattering his love words. Both were designed to secure compliance. And they had.

In those heady moments last night, she'd believed anything was possible: that he could offer protection against her uncle, that she'd be accepted into his world, that he might carry genuine affection for her. She'd wanted to believe all that, had looked for any excuse to believe it because somewhere between being knocked over on his front step and dancing silent waltzes in the dining room, she'd fallen in love with him and she wanted to believe he'd done the same.

She did not want a loveless marriage or one riddled by infidelity. She was not sure Riordan could give her that. Maura knew she would be devastated if he continued to play the rake. But it was too late to call off her promise. By now, he'd be arriving at the offices of Vale's solicitors in Lincoln's Inn. Shortly, he'd be smugly announcing he had secured a bride, that his wards would have a motherly presence in the home and that he'd become 'decent' by *ton*ish standards.

'Miss Caulfield.' A maid appeared at the open nursery door out of breath. 'There's a man downstairs asking to speak with you.' The maid looked nervous. 'He doesn't look like a gentleman to me, though,' she added.

Maura rose. She hoped it wasn't bad news already from Riordan's meeting. 'He might be a Runner from Lord Chatham.' That would explain the man's appearance. She was worried none the less and it took a large amount of self-control not to run down the stairs, the children following behind her.

'Look, it's the man from the museum,' William said halfway down the stairs.

Maura halted, frozen. She'd been too lost in thoughts of 'what if' over Riordan that she'd not paid attention to the man in the hall. Her instincts screamed danger. What was he doing here? All of the sudden she knew. He wasn't here because of Riordan. He was here because of *her* and it was too late. There was no place to run.

'Miss Maura Caulfield?' He grinned, showing a mouth missing a few teeth. 'Or should I call you Miss Harding, your legal name? Caulfield is your mother's name, I believe?'

Beside her the children were frightened. She could feel Cecilia edging closer to her skirts. William stood stoically on the stair beside her. She took Cecilia's hand in hers and reached for William's. If she could hold him, he wouldn't try anything gallant and stupid.

'What do you want? I don't believe we've been introduced,' Maura said in her haughtiest best.

'I think that should be obvious, Miss Caulfield.' The stocky man grinned again, producing a pistol from his belt beneath his coat. 'I'm here for you.'

Cecilia squealed in fright. Anger fired Maura, overriding fear. 'Put that gun away. How dare you come in here and threaten children?' In hindsight, it was a ridiculous outburst. He wasn't going to put the gun away. It was the one thing holding everyone at bay. Fielding and a footman had hurried into the hall, only to be brought up short by the sight of the weapon.

Two rough-looking men crowded through the door behind him. 'We need to hurry, Miss

Caulfield, to ensure no one gets hurt. You and the children are to come with us.' He waved the gun for emphasis. 'Now.'

The men advanced and Maura thrust the children behind her and bargained, 'Leave them out of this and I'll come with you.'

The man with the gun gave a guttural laugh. 'I am under orders to take all three of you and to shoot whomever I must to accomplish that.' The gun swivelled and fired, eliciting a scream of shock from Maura as the footman went down clutching his leg.

'He'll live.' The man scowled. 'Next time, you might not be so lucky, Miss Caulfield. It might be the children, heaven forbid. Take them, men.'

A man moved to grab Cecilia. Maura shoved him, hitting at him with her fists, earning a ringing slap across the face. She stumbled, Digby grabbing her up and tossing her over his shoulder in a most undignified manner. The children were seized and dragged out, screaming and kicking. There was a scramble behind them, Fielding galvanising the servants into action, but Digby turned and fired once more as she and the children were stuffed into a waiting carriage, stifling any hopes of a rescue.

Maura drew the children to her in the lurching carriage, thankful not to be bound and unable to console them. Cecilia was sobbing uncontrollably.

'Shut her up,' the man growled, shoving the second pistol back into the waistband of his pants. He snarled at Will, 'Don't even think it, boyo. You're no match for me. You try any funny business and you'll end up in that sarcophagus you were admiring so much.'

Maura put an arm about Will in comfort and stared down their captor. 'Who are you and where are you taking us?'

He smiled meanly. 'My name is Digby. You know where we're going—back where you belong.' It was no answer. Did that mean all the way to Exeter? Was her uncle here in the city?

This was all her fault, Maura thought with a sinking feeling, and now others were going to pay for her rashness. She'd managed to get Riordan's wards kidnapped. If word of this got out, it would ruin his chances to keep them. He couldn't possibly marry her now. Nor would he want to. She was nothing but trouble and he needed stability above all else.

'And the children? There's no need for them to be involved.'

Digby's words were cold. 'They're collateral, to make sure you don't do anything stupid. You don't think the earl will come racing after you, do you? Once he finds out how you've deceived him and endangered his wards, he'll be all too glad to let you go in exchange for their return.' He added nastily, 'Then you can go ahead and marry Wildeham and all the loose ends will be tied up, just like you. I hear Wildeham likes a bit of rope.' He glanced at the children. 'This is what happens, mateys, when you tell lies. Someone always finds out.'

This was what falling in love did to a man, Riordan thought with a light heart as he approached the offices of Vale's solicitors. It made a man feel invincible. Or maybe it was Maura. She made him feel invincible. He didn't fear what lay beyond these doors. He and Browning would listen patiently to Vale's formal accusations and then he'd squash Vale's hopes with his announcement. Riordan chuckled to himself, Browning falling into step beside him from where he'd stood waiting. It would feel good to put Vale in his place.

Riordan pushed open the door to the assigned room. He and Browning were the last to arrive. A long polished table dominated the centre of the panelled room, chairs lined on either side. At the head of the table sat the Honourable Franklin DeWitt, bewigged and robed, arbiter of his fate. DeWitt had a reputation for tradition. He wasn't likely to go against a standing order from a peer without extraordinary compunction.

On the far side of the room, Viscount Vale and his team, his rather *extensive* team, were already gathered behind their chairs. Riordan recognised the weasel and his assistant from earlier meetings, but the other face was unknown.

'I see introductions are in order.' Vale stepped forwards, gesturing to the stranger with the grey-streaked dark hair and hard eyes. The man looked positively menacing. 'This is Baron Wildeham. He has information relevant to our discussion today.'

Riordan's fists clenched silently at his sides, his stomach cold with apprehension. The awful man, the man Maura had run from.

'You might know him better as a relation of your current governess, Miss Harding.' Vale paused for effect. 'I'm sorry; you would know her as Miss Caulfield.'

Riordan's blood started to heat. He opted not to play the polite aristocrat. 'You're the scheming bastard who claimed her for a gambling debt.'

Wildeham didn't flinch. A small, icy smile flitted on his lips. 'Is that what she told you?' He turned towards DeWitt, shaking his head in disbelief. 'As you can see, we are just in time.'

'In time for what?' Riordan gauged the width of the table, wondering if he could leap it and get a punch in before someone dragged him off the baron.

Vale tossed him a sympathetic look. Riordan decided he'd plant Vale a facer next, then they'd see who needed sympathy. 'Why, to keep you from committing a most atrocious crime, unintentional as it is, dear cousin.'

'And what might that be?' Riordan ground out.

'Bigamy.' Vale fired off the word with the force of a cannon ball. 'Even you haven't tried that one on yet.'

Riordan crossed his arms in a defiant stance. 'Rubbish. There is no bigamy here. She is not married to him.'

'Gentlemen, please,' Franklin DeWitt counselled swiftly to abort a brawl. 'Remember your stations. This is clearly a complicated matter. If everyone would take their seats, we could sort through this from the beginning.'

Riordan sat reluctantly, his gaze fixed between Wildeham and Vale. He'd been right when he'd told Maura this was going to be messy. But he'd been wrong about the reasons. This hearing wasn't going to be about dredging up his disreputable past. It was going to be about Maura's.

Vale's solicitor began, all earnestness and sympathy. 'We would like to acknowledge Lord Chatham's attempts to take a bride and put a maternal presence in his home. However, it is unfortunate that he has chosen poorly. The woman he intends to wed is not a suitable candidate. She is contracted to wed another. She is in no position to contract such an agreement with you, Lord Chatham, while that agreement stands. We regret you have fallen victim to her wiles.'

Riordan watched Vale's posture change as the sympathy fell away from his solicitor's tone. Something was coming, something Vale felt certain would be a blow. 'However, your honour, this latest escapade of Lord Chatham's is further illustration of his rather erratic behaviour and bad judgement.'

Riordan stiffened. DeWitt raised his brows. 'Please explain.'

'He intends to marry his governess. He's engaged in flirtatious behaviour with her, if not more. It's not seemly conduct for a gentleman.'

'This is ridiculous!' Riordan broke in. 'Either I seduced her or she seduced me, you can't have it both ways. Don't stand there defending her honour and then in the next breath malign her lack of it.'

Wildeham gave a sad look. 'This is typical of Maura. She sucks a gentleman in so deeply one cannot really know how one arrived at this place where one wants only to defend her. She plays the innocent so well.'

'I've had enough of this.' Riordan turned towards DeWitt. 'Miss Caulfield is an upstanding young woman of perfectly marriageable background for a fellow of my standing. If she fled, it was because her uncle meant to use her as payment against her will. If anyone is of questionable character at this table, it's Wildeham. No gentleman encourages such a dishonourable arrangement.'

Riordan cast a glance at Browning and mouthed, *Do something.* Maura had warned him this would happen, that her past would catch up with her. He hadn't thought it would happen so soon. He was regretting not marrying her yesterday. A special licence would have done the trick, but for once in his life, he'd opted to do the right thing. To offset rumour, to shut the mouths of gossipmongers, he'd wanted to wait a decent interval for the wedding so no one could say he'd married in haste. He'd wanted it for Maura's sake and the children's. He didn't care what society said about him. Now, he wished he'd bound her to him legally no matter what the rumours.

'I'd like a word with the baron, if you please.' Riordan stood and motioned they should adjourn to a private antechamber. Riordan shut the door behind him and faced Wildeham squarely. It took all his restraint to pretend a modicum of neutrality.

'The gloves are off now. You are owed money. Fine. I'll pay her uncle's debt. In return, you rip up the marital agreement and drop your slander against Maura. How much is the bill?' It was a dangerous road to go down with a man like Wildeham. If he could get money this way, what would stop him from extracting more in the future?

Wildeham snorted. 'You've been bitten hard by that strawberry tart of Harding's. What a man in love won't do. She's really got her hooks into you.' He sneered. 'Have you had her already? How is that strawberry pie?'

Riordan snapped. He topped Wildeham by a head. He grabbed the shorter man by the lapels and hauled him up against the wall. 'You will not speak that way about her again without risking pistols at dawn. Now, about that bill?'

'It's not that simple, Chatham.' Wildeham grunted, sagging a bit against the relief of being let go. 'I don't want money. I want her. I have papers. She's mine. A court will side with me—the intent of the papers are clear.'

'Maura didn't sign them,' Riordan said tersely.

'Harding signed on her behalf, as her guardian until she's twenty-three. It's as good as her signature.' Wildeham's eyes narrowed. 'Your little marriage gambit has cost you everything. You picked the wrong wife and now you'll lose the children and the girl.'

Riordan stared at the man. He could imagine quite well the agreement Wildeham had with Vale. If the two of them could bring the Earl of Chatham down, that's exactly what would happen. Vale would have the children and Wildeham would have Maura. Cold fingers of fear clamped about his stomach. What else did this man have in motion?

Riordan shook his head. 'No.'

'No?' Wildeham looked at him incredulously. *'No?'*

'Did I stutter?' He would plant the man a facer, DeWitt's code of gentlemanly conduct be damned. 'I will not accept that outcome.'

Wildeham gave an oily smile. 'You don't have to accept it, it's already a *fait accompli*. I thought you might not agree with my position. With luck, I've already got her.'

'You don't scare me.'

'Maybe I should. Let me know after you get home.'

Chapter Twenty

It was all bravado on his part, Riordan thought, listening to the talks going on about him. Browning was doing his job and the discussions had dwindled to nothing conclusive. Wildeham had been quiet since they'd returned from the antechamber, but his words still haunted Riordan, gaining power in his mind as he replayed the threat over again.

Riordan told himself it was nothing. Wildeham had meant to scare him. If he hadn't been convinced Wildeham wanted him to go running out of the chamber and race home, he would have done just that. He wanted to assure himself Maura and the children were safe. If he gave in, Wildeham would know just how deeply his feelings ran and then use that in some new perverse deal. He checked his watch. Four o'clock. The afternoon was gone and nothing had been decided. 'Settle this up,' he whispered to Browning. DeWitt could decide nothing today. As long as things remained at a stalemate, Riordan hadn't lost. There was still a chance to win, but he was going to need reinforcements.

'I will need time to consider the contract between Miss Harding and Baron Wildeham,' De-Witt said in tones that signalled the discussions were at an end for now.

'I trust this won't take a long time?' Vale put in. 'My wife and I are eager to see the children in a stable home as soon as possible. The longer this takes…' His voice trailed off.

DeWitt fixed him with a stern look. 'It will take as long as it needs to, my lord. Justice does not run on a clock. There were many accusations made today that need substantiation if you want them to be considered. A peer of the realm has left a legitimate will. You risk much by seeking to tamper with its provisions.'

Riordan hid a smile. It was a small scrap from the table of the British legal system, but he'd feast on it. Once outside, he turned to Browning. 'You've got Vale's financial statements? We'll need to roll those out to prove he's after the trust funds. Once DeWitt sees how indebted Vale is, Vale will lose momentum.'

'And Miss Caulfield? Is there anything I can do there?'

'I'll talk to her when I get home.' Riordan leapt up on to the step of his carriage, eager to be off, wanting to see Maura and talk it all over with her. She would be horrified to know Wildeham was here.

Riordan took the stairs to his town house two at a time. Traffic home had been slow and crowded. There'd been a dray overturned and it had taken what had seemed like for ever to negotiate around it. He opened the door, surprised to have beaten Fielding to the task. Fielding was a great stickler for the little things.

Something was wrong. The hall felt wrong. Wildeham's threat came back. *What's waiting for you at home...* 'Maura!' Riordan raced up the stairs. 'Maura!' Where was everyone? He began throwing open doors, looking in little-used rooms—his method knew only madness as he tore through the hall.

'Milord!' Fielding's sharp tone stopped him. Riordan had the impression Fielding had been calling him for some time. Fielding never raised his voice. 'Milord, I didn't hear you come in.' Fielding was pale, his steady hands shaking. 'We've had an accident, milord.'

'Maura? The children?' Riordan heard the crack in his own voice.

'They're gone, milord. Men came and took them away. Walter was shot.'

'What men?' *Guns*. There'd been guns in his home.

'We don't know, milord.'

But Riordan knew. He didn't know their names, but he knew who'd sent them. He sank to an upholstered bench in the hall, his head in his hands, his mind a jumble of tasks. He had to go see Walter, had to listen to Fielding, had to go after Maura. But for a moment he would wallow in his grief, regret raw and searing in his throat. He should have married her when he had the chance. It would have offered her some protection even when he wasn't with her. 'Fielding, do something for me.' He was remembering something in his latest pile of mail.

'Anything, milord.'

'Ashe Bedevere and Merrick St Magnus have just arrived in town. Send for them immediately.'

Within the hour, Ashe and Merrick arrived, wives in tow. It had been too long since the trio had seen each other. Ashe embraced him. Unable to come to Elliott's funeral because of duties at home, Ashe had sent a sincere letter. Ashe's own brother had died not long before and Riordan knew Ashe had felt his own loss just as keenly. Merrick and Alixe hugged him, Alixe offering regrets that her brother, Jamie, was out of town, away on an extended honeymoon on the Continent. Then Ashe's wife, Genevra, the American heiress Riordan had yet to meet, stepped forwards, concern in her grey eyes as she took his hands in hers. 'Tell us what has happened and we'll make it right.'

Riordan thought those words might be his undoing. He'd been fighting all day and feeling very much alone. He'd told Maura once that he hadn't much family left, no one of use anyway. One couldn't really count Sophie and Hamish and a mother exiled to Switzerland. But he'd been wrong. He had a family right here in his friends.

'They've taken Maura and the children,' Riordan blurted out. Merrick and Ashe looked at him patiently, expectantly, as if there was more to say.

Ashe's mouth quirked in a half-smile. 'I think we're going to need a little more information than that.'

'Let's adjourn to the drawing room, Riordan,' Alixe put in, slipping a comforting arm through his. 'I'll ring for tea and you can tell us everything.'

'Tea, yes,' Riordan muttered. 'I'm always forgetting the tea. I forgot tea the first day I met Maura.' Just over a month ago she'd rung his bell and he'd landed on her on his front step. It seemed a lifetime ago. Impossible to think so much had changed in just a handful of weeks.

He did not miss the look that passed between Ashe and Merrick. 'What?'

'I was just thinking,' Merrick drawled, 'that you've got it bad.'

Riordan grimaced. He wanted to shout at Merrick that Merrick had no idea what he was going through, that the woman he loved had been placed in grave danger. But that wasn't true. Merrick did know. Merrick had hovered on the brink of death from a knife wound after saving Alixe from an avaricious imposter. Ashe had faced even worse treachery, losing his home, his brother and very nearly Genevra in a fire engineered by his cousin. They knew exactly what he felt at this moment: impotence, fear and regret that perhaps he'd waited too long to claim the one woman who made him feel whole.

In the drawing room, Alixe settled everyone and poured tea. The tea tray was immense, filled with sandwiches and cold meats along with cakes. Alixe smiled at the big tray. 'One always calls for tea in a crisis, Riordan, because servants need to feel useful, too. None of us is good at merely sitting around waiting.'

Riordan smiled and took a sandwich. 'I'll make a note of it, Alixe, although I hope I won't have another chance to make use of the information.' He gestured towards the decanter on the side table. 'There's brandy, Ashe, if you and Merrick want something stronger.'

Ashe rose and went to pour a small glass for each of them. He raised an empty tumbler. 'Riordan, anything for you?'

Riordan shook his head. 'No.' He wanted to be clear-headed for Maura, for the children. It was something of a surprise to realise he hadn't touched the stuff lately. He took wine at dinner, but he'd been too busy painting, too busy with Maura. His silver flask had taken a holiday in the top drawer of his bureau.

Ashe grinned. 'It's far worse than I thought, Merrick.' They laughed at his expense, but not unkindly. 'All right, we're all settled, let's hear it. Don't spare the details.'

Riordan told them everything: the hunt for a governess which had landed Maura on his doorstep, the dinner party which had started the scandal, the Vales' threat to wrest away custody of the children unless he married.

'At which point, it made sense to marry Maura,' Merrick summarised.

'It made more than sense.' Riordan spread his hands on his thighs. 'By then, I knew I was falling in love with her. No one else held my interest, I was jealous of any man that looked at her. I saw off a nice baron who would have courted her. All the signs were there. But then she refused me and there seemed to be no legitimate grounds for that refusal.' Riordan chuckled. 'After all, what is there not to like? I'm an earl, I have money and estates, I'm handsome, so the ladies tell me.'

'And he can make a woman…' Merrick began, but Alixe swatted at him.

'That's when she told me about her uncle using her marriage as a means of settling a gambling debt. She told me none too soon. The unwanted suitor, Wildeham, showed up four days later at the hearing with the Vales. He's done his research. He knows exactly what the situation is and he's used it as leverage to fulfil his own needs by throwing his lot in with Vale.'

'Exactly how has he done that?' Ashe leaned forwards, green eyes narrowed in thought, a shrewd look on his face Riordan didn't like. Ashe saw something here that he'd overlooked. But that was why he'd called for his friends. He needed more viewpoints than his own.

'He's told the Vales he'll help block my marriage to Maura by proving her unsuitable. They will get custody of the children and he'll get Maura. To hedge his bets, he sent men here and seized them.'

'Now he doesn't have to comply with anyone's demands. He doesn't have to wait for the judge to decide about the contract. This Wildeham can simply walk away now and not testify any further if he chooses. He has what he wants.' Genevra set down her tea cup and surveyed the group with solemn eyes. 'Possession is nine-tenths of the law, we like to say in America.' Genevra's voice was quiet and firm. 'There's nothing stopping him from marrying her now.'

Genevra's words had awakened his fears again. On her own, Maura would resist. But Wildeham had the children and Maura would do anything to keep them safe. The three people he loved most in this world had simply disappeared while he'd wasted his afternoon trying to make deals with a man who had already decided he wouldn't deal with anyone. 'I don't know where to look or even where to start.'

'We'll start backwards,' Merrick put in. 'How did Wildeham discover she was here? What led him to you?'

'The newspaper reports?' Riordan said weakly. He didn't really believe that answer. Only people who knew him would understand the references and there had to be more governesses in

London besides Maura whose last name started with a 'C'.

Merrick shook his head. 'I doubt it. It's likely not even something you did tipped Wildeham's hand, but instead something she did, something she left behind on her trail.'

'The agency,' Riordan said simply. 'Mrs Pendergast's Referral Service for Well-Bred Ladies, or something like that.'

Merrick nodded and checked his watch. 'It's nearly six o'clock now, but if I hurry, perhaps we can talk to someone before it closes.' He rose and Alixe did, too. 'No, Alixe, you stay here. Mrs Pendergast, is it? I'll need to work alone.'

Alixe laughed up at her handsome husband, one of London's most notorious rakes before he'd settled to marriage. 'Absolutely, my dear. I'd certainly hate to cramp your style.'

'Perhaps it would help if Alixe and I interviewed the servants again about what happened here while we wait for Merrick,' Genevra suggested. 'There might be a fact or detail that has been overlooked. Now that the initial excitement of the incident has passed, people's memories might be calmer.'

He was left with Ashe as the others moved

off to their tasks. Riordan had no doubt Merrick's efforts with Mrs Pendergast would bear fruit but that didn't make the waiting any easier. 'What do we do now?'

Ashe fixed him with a solemn stare and said very seriously, 'Now, you and I talk. I can't promise you'll like what I have to say.'

'You've always been honest with me, Ashe.'

'Does she love you?'

'Does she love me? What hell of a question is that?'

'Is it one you can answer?' Ashe looked at him meaningfully. 'The one thing I've heard running through all you've told us is the plot to save the children. You would not have chosen to marry if not forced to it. Obviously she would not have chosen to marry either. She came here looking for anonymity, for escape.'

'Maura would do anything for the children. She adores them.' Even as he said the words, Riordan saw the truth of Ashe's question. Maura had called him extraordinary. She'd desired him. But never once had she said she loved him.

'Anything for the children?' Ashe repeated.

'Even marry me, apparently.' Riordan swallowed hard.

'And you? You would do anything for those children, even marry a woman you've only known for a month.'

'Six weeks,' Riordan corrected in desultory tones.

'Are you sure you're in love with her and not in love with the solution she provides? Be honest, Riordan, you didn't even know her real name until today.'

'That doesn't mean we're just going to let her rot.' Riordan jumped to his feet, pacing the room.

'Of course not. But it does mean you should think about what you do afterwards,' Ashe said. 'If you can prove Vale is after the trust funds, you don't need to worry about marriage. Vale will have no more grounds to contest the will. Everything he does in that regard will look suspect and, frankly, English justice doesn't like to tamper with peers.'

Riordan knew he spoke with authority on that point. Ashe's own father had left a potentially troublesome will naming regents to oversee the estate as long as his eldest son lived. Ashe's brother had been mentally incompetent, a victim of a nervous breakdown. As odd as the request had been, it had been upheld with ironclad backing.

'I can tell you're upset with me,' Ashe cajoled. 'You always pace when you're angry. I just want you to have a good marriage. When it happens, it's for ever, Riordan. You don't want to look across the dinner table some night and ask yourself what you're doing with her, how did you end up here? If you were free to choose, would your choice be the same?'

'Milord.' Fielding bowed at the door, a salver in his hand. 'This arrived for you at the back door.'

Riordan picked up the note. It was folded and written on heavy paper. Wildeham then, he guessed. A hired man would have set a note on thin, cheap paper, assuming he could write at all. The message was hardly surprising. He passed the short note to Ashe.

'Leave Maura to me and the children will be home before midnight,' Ashe read out loud.

Very simple, very easy, except he couldn't do it. He couldn't leave Maura to the fate her uncle had designed. He loved her, and while Ashe had a point it seemed to matter less. Did Maura love him? Maybe. But he wouldn't have his answer until he found her.

'If the boy is waiting to take a reply, tell him no.'

'Is that all, milord?'

'Yes. Simply no.'

In the hour before Ashe and Merrick's arrival, he'd walked every inch of the house, trying to organise his thoughts. He supposed he'd succeeded. All his thoughts had organised around one thing: Maura. She was there in each room; the house was full of memories of her. In the time she'd been at Chatham House she'd left her mark. There was the sitting room where he'd made her laugh until brandy had come out her nose. The dining room where they'd made love against the wall, where he'd first flirted with her, where she'd hosted a dinner party for *him*, the drawing room where she'd dazzled his guests, the staircase where he'd watched her descend, the study where he'd kissed her the first time, the library...the list went on. There were other places, too, that would be irrevocably changed for him. He would never go to Gunter's again without remembering the way her eyes had lit up over the chocolate ice. He would not fly a kite again without thinking of that day in the park.

'I wish you'd say something.' Ashe shoved his hands in his pockets and balanced on the balls of his feet.

Riordan smiled. 'Come with me, Ashe. While we wait for Merrick, I want to give you a tour of my house and show you my etchings.'

Ashe looked at him as if he were headed for Bedlam. 'I've seen Chatham House before, and I don't really think I need to see your, um, etchings.'

'Yes, you do.' He would show Ashe Chatham House and all the ways that Maura had changed it. There would be no doubt of his feelings then.

Chapter Twenty-One

'You should know we've made the earl an offer. I do not expect it to be refused.' The familiar snide tones made Maura jump.

Her stomach plummeted. Wildeham was here! She swivelled her head around to find the voice in the dim light of the room, careful not to wake the children. They'd fallen asleep against her, exhausted by the ordeal and the fright. She gently dislodged them from her arms and rose, trying to mask her own fear. This was so much worse. She'd been wrong all along. Her uncle hadn't been hunting her. It had been Wildeham.

'How can you do this? The children are innocent,' she challenged, arms crossed and defiant.

'I'm sure it's been explained already.' He

feigned patience. 'They're insurance. You won't run. I know you, Maura, and you'd never leave them. It did surprise me that you played me false in that regard. I didn't imagine you'd leave your family and refuse to honour the debt. It disappointed me as well.' He circled her, a sneer on his lips. 'I had such plans for you, for us. Your aunt Mary is beside herself with worry. She's taken to her bed. Here she thought she had a wedding to plan for her dear niece who was going to make a spectacular match, only to discover you'd run off with no regard for her and your young cousins.'

Maura stood her ground. 'I will not be guilted into returning. I will not marry you.'

'You may have no choice.'

'You can't kidnap me.'

Wildeham laughed at that. 'You call this kidnapping?' He made a wide gesture to encompass the elegant suite. 'First of all, I have papers which clearly define the nature of our relationship. You can't kidnap wives. Second of all, kidnappers don't whisk people off to expensive hotels with first-rate trappings. They take you to dark cottages in the wilds where no one would ever find you.' He shook his head, mocking her claims. 'I think you would find your version of the story very hard to sell.'

'You sent men with guns to my home. We were forcibly removed. There were witnesses. A servant was shot.'

'At least one.' The glib remark put fear into Maura. If he was this callous about the shooting, what else would he dare without so much as a blink? Wildeham's violence knew no bounds. 'Your earl was most impressive today.' He trailed a lazy finger down the bodice of her gown, chuckling when she stiffened. 'You'll come to like a little petting, my dear.' Maura fought the bile rising in her throat. If Riordan had been hurt, she would not forgive herself.

'Don't worry, my dear,' Wildeham crooned. 'Chatham's fine, for now. I did tell him what a tease you were, how you entice men all the time, how you had no business entering into any commitment with him when you were promised to another.' He stopped here to pick at a spot of lint on his sleeve. 'I think he was rather hurt to know Caulfield wasn't your real name. He didn't know.' He tsked. 'Secrets are always bad business, Maura. Anyway, I made him a deal. He should be receiving it right about now. The children will be going home shortly, I should think. But maybe not. It depends on you.'

'What deal?' Maura asked, trepidation ratcheting up her nerves. Wildeham positively made her skin crawl.

'The deal where he leaves off any claim to you in return for getting the children back. And, of course, you agree to marry me. They could be asleep in their beds tonight, all of this nothing more than a bad memory, an incident that could have been avoided if their governess had been truthful and done what she was told.' He shook his head. 'All of this could have been avoided, Maura, if you'd followed directions. If you're worried about the children, you have only yourself to blame. This is your fault; don't think the earl won't understand that.'

He leaned forwards as if imparting a secret. She could feel his breath against her cheek. 'Don't think he'll spare you a second thought, Maura. You made him look the fool today at that hearing; you and your little lies solidified the Vales' claims that the earl is no better than his reputation. If he loses the children, it will be your fault, too.'

'And if I don't comply?'

'Then I'll send the children to the workhouse or an orphanage. I'm sure Chatham would eventually find them, but he won't thank you for your hand in it.'

'I hate you.' Maura spat the words with vehemence.

'You really hate yourself. I am just a convenient target,' he whispered silkily, drawing a clammy hand the length of her jaw. He paused, feigned concern in his eyes when she flinched at the contact. 'Oh dear, you didn't think the earl actually loved you? You didn't think he saw you as anything more than an easy solution to his problem, did you? Well, it will be over soon enough. I'll leave you to your thoughts.'

The children for her. Maura waited until Wildeham left the room before swiping at the tears smarting in her eyes. He was wrong, he had to be wrong! Riordan would come. Riordan would never accept such a deal. Riordan loved her, he'd said nearly as much. *But not exactly.*

Wildeham's words haunted her. Maybe Riordan would say anything to get what he wanted. Maybe she'd been blind, had wanted to be blind to realities. Riordan was an experienced flirt, after all. She'd known his measure from the first, warned herself from the beginning about his nature. But she'd been too willing to ignore those signs, and look where it had landed her—kidnapped and on the brink of marriage to an absolute reprobate of a man who meant to make her life a complete misery. Her only hope of rescue lay with a man who would be debating right now whether or not he could trust her, whether or not she was worth it, a man who had asked her to marry him, but had not told her he loved her.

That was when the fight went out of her. The only thing she could be sure of, was herself. She had to finish this adventure as she'd begun it, alone. The only bargain she could trust was a bargain she made. If selling herself to Wildeham was the only way to see the children safe, then that was what she'd do.

'I have news!' Merrick sailed into the drawing room, waving a sheet of paper in his hand. 'Mrs Pendergast was *very* generous.'

Everyone looked up expectantly. It seemed he'd been gone an age. Merrick passed the slip of paper to Riordan. 'A man came to the agency making enquiries. It was Wildeham. She regretted telling him anything, but he had a knife.'

'Did you console her?' Alixe teased.

'I did my absolute best,' Merrick answered before continuing. 'This explains how he found her.'

'But it doesn't explain where she's been taken.' Riordan didn't want to squash his friend's excitement, but he wasn't sure this information constituted headway.

'It tells us who is helping him,' Ashe clarified. 'It might be important. We can start asking around in certain places where men of his ilk are for hire. Chances are someone's heard of him.'

Merrick shook his head. 'I doubt it. Mrs Pendergast said he had an accent like he was from up north.' He nodded in Riordan's direction. 'Exeter. That means Wildeham is working privately. He's not as certain of his claim. He'd have Bow Street on it if he thought he was entirely legitimate. I would bet Maura is not tucked away in any hidden location. Wildeham doesn't know of any place to stash her.'

'Hiding in plain sight?' Riordan supplied.

'Could be. Less likely to look like a kidnapping then at least,' Ashe said. 'Do we have any idea where Wildeham might be staying? Does he have a town house?'

'That could be like hunting a needle in a haystack.' Alixe sighed. 'He could rent a town house, or rent rooms, or stay at an inn, he could be on the city limits or in any one of the neighborhoods.'

'The possibilities are never endless if you know the person,' Ashe said slowly, turning towards Riordan. 'What do your powers of deduction tell you? You're the only one of us who has actually seen the man. Is he the type to stay in a cheap inn on the outskirts of London?'

It was usually so easy to play the fortune-telling game, to amaze a lady with the ability to guess certain things about her: her hobbies, whether or not she rode and rode well. But this was different. Tonight, his mind was cluttered with worry and doubt. What if he guessed wrong? It would cost them wasted time chasing a red herring. 'I don't know if that's a good idea,' he stalled. 'Ashe, that's just a thing I do, a parlour trick, really.' He wouldn't stake Maura's future on a game.

'It's more than that and you know it,' Ashe

pressed. 'And it's all we've got right now, so you might as well try.' Ashe rose and asked a footman to bring writing materials. 'Just start talking, tell us everything you know and I'll write it down. We can make sense of it together.'

Riordan began. He started with the man's clothes: the well-tailored cut of them, the closely clipped moustache, the straight teeth, the buffed nails—all signs of a man who took his personal grooming seriously. He moved on to the accessories the man had carried on his person: the Malacca wood walking stick, the multi-fobbed watch chain draped across his waistcoat adorned with tasteful gold fobs, the high polish of his boots, the ruby stick pin in his cravat, the very slight paunch starting to swell beneath the waistcoat. Even the most discerning of eyes would not catch it, hidden as it was beneath the layers of waistcoat and jacket, but Riordan had noticed. He'd noticed everything about the man who had threatened Maura.

'Wildeham does not strike me as a man who parts with his comforts easily or willingly,' Riordan said at last, his repertoire of remembrances exhausted. 'He did not strike me as a man who'd travel without luxuries.'

'Unless it is an act, a front to convince others he is of some standing. We must consider that,' Ashe interjected.

'Not this time.' Riordan had warmed to the subject. 'Everything was perfect about him. Men who posture towards greatness don't carry off the nuances. They forget about things like the fingernails and the shoes.'

'Like Abernathy,' Alixe offered softly. It was a name not spoken among the group; the man who had pretended to be a gentleman to lure Alixe into marriage. 'It seems so clear now that he was never what he pretended to be, but we were all swept up in the obvious: his house, his wardrobe on the whole—we didn't look at the little things about him and we should have.'

Riordan nodded. 'Wildeham is not a fraud when it comes to creature comforts. He knows what he likes.'

'Then we can rule out inns and places on the outskirts.' Genevra made a strike on her list. 'That leaves town houses, rented rooms and hotels.'

'Not rented rooms or a rented town house,' Merrick suggested. 'He didn't have time to make those arrangements and it would have been impossible to find a town house on short notice at this time of the Season.'

'That leaves hotels.'

'Berner's or Grillon's comes to mind as the most obvious watering holes for his type,' Merrick offered. 'Alixe and I have stayed at Berner's the few times we've come up.'

Riordan nodded. He could trust their judgement. Merrick and Alixe were perfectly happy on their manor in Hever with no desire to keep a place in town. They would know about hotels.

'We can go tonight.' Ashe stood. 'Ladies, I would ask you to wait. When we come back there will be plenty to do, children to comfort and all that, unless you want to return home and see to your own children?' He shot a quizzical glance at Genevra. 'We brought the baby with us and it's been a few hours,' he offered by way of explanation.

'Of course,' Riordan said vaguely, not wanting to embarrass Genevra with a direct comment. In his opinion it was rather liberated of her to want to nurse her own child.

'I'll be all right,' Genevra assured Ashe. 'It won't take you long. We'll wait.'

Riordan smothered a smile at Genevra's

veiled warning. They were to come straight home and be gone not a moment longer than necessary to retrieve Riordan's wards and governess.

Berner's drew a blank. No one under the name Acton Humphries was listed in the guest register. Riordan knew a moment's disappointment at the thought Wildeham could have used an assumed name. Not likely. People would need to communicate with him. An alias would complicate that. Merrick clapped him on the shoulder encouragingly. 'There are other hotels. We'll find him.'

Grillon's was busy. At half past eight, the lobby bustled with well-dressed people going out to evening entertainments. Riordan waited impatiently for help at the front desk. 'I'm looking for a Baron Wildeham,' he asked a bespectacled clerk who looked frazzled by the night's activity.

'May I enquire why? We're not in the policy of giving out information about guests.' It was meant to be a discouraging statement but Riordan saw only the hope. Wildeham was here!

'I have business with him,' Riordan answered smoothly.

'At half past eight?' the clerk queried in disbelief.

Riordan felt a hand come around his shoulder, a sparkling guinea flashing on the counter. 'It's a gentleman's business.' Ashe's soft tones carried a hint of menace.

'Yes, sir.' The clerk swallowed hard and pocketed the guinea, the privacy of Baron Wildeham's room failing to weigh in as much as the sum of three weeks' wages. The clerk consulted a ledger. 'Here he is—he's in the suite on the third floor, room three-twenty-nine.'

A certain manly exhilaration raced in Riordan's veins as they took the stairs. 'Remember, Wildeham is mine,' he told Ashe and Merrick. 'Remember, too, if there's any danger you're to keep yourselves safe. Your wives would never forgive me.'

The last was said jokingly, but underneath it, Riordan wasn't sure what they might encounter in the hotel room. If Wildeham had hired thugs who shot at servants simply to make a point, and if he was willing to force a woman into marriage, there was no telling how far he'd go to protect his interests. The only surety was that Wildeham would not go quietly.

They reached the door of the suite. Riordan raised his walking stick to knock.

'Who's there?' came the gruff masculine reply.

'Room service,' Riordan answered.

The door opened ever so slightly. A man's face peered out. 'What's this about? We didn't order anything from the kitchens.' He tried to shut the door, but Riordan's boot was already there.

Riordan grinned. 'I know.' Then he pushed his way in, the man at the door no match for an earl in love.

Chapter Twenty-Two

'Ah, more guests for my party, how good of you to come.' A man strode forwards, reeking of false affability as if three well-dressed men forced their way into his hotel suite with nightly regularity. Riordan took in the sight of him, focused not so much on the clothing but on his physical appearance. Ah, there it was: the telltale signs of dissipation and perhaps something more that looked an awful lot like smug satisfaction. His next thought was: *I am too late.* Riordan clenched his hand around his walking stick, fighting the urge to unsheathe the sword inside and skewer the devil. He might have done just that if Vale hadn't chosen that moment to rise from his corner and make his presence known.

'My cousin has come. I thought he might. Too bad we didn't wager, Wildeham.'

'What are you doing here?' Riordan growled. He'd not expected Vale and Wildeham to be as thick as this.

'Celebrating, same as Wildeham.'

'I'm to be married tomorrow,' Wildeham said expansively, not quite hiding the edge in his voice. 'You're just in time. I'd have been married tonight, I'm that eager, except no one will perform a ceremony until nine in the morning. Deuced silly law if you ask me.'

That was where the supposed affability ended. He stopped in front of them, he and his men arranged themselves defensively, making a wall. The man who'd answered the door stood at their backs, blocking any escape, not that Riordan was inclined to take it. He'd not come here to escape. He'd come to fight. He gave the suite a quick quarter with his eyes, searching for Maura and the children, but there was no sign of them.

'Now, who might these gentlemen be?'

'We're friends of the bride,' Ashe ground out, he and Merrick stepping up to flank Riordan.

'Ah, the exquisite Maura.' Wildeham sighed.

'She seems to collect "friends" wherever she goes.' Wildeham narrowed his pale eyes. 'Perhaps you'd like to see her? Digby, bring her out.'

Digby returned shortly, a hard hand on Maura's arm. Maura was frozen, a walking mannequin. Her hair was dressed formally with a sparkling tiara on top of her red-gold curls. She wore a gown of deep silver, full of flash and sequins almost gaudy in detail.

'Maura!' At the sight of her, Riordan took an involuntary step forwards and met with Wildeham's hand on his chest. 'What have you done to her?'

'I've done nothing.' Wildeham tossed a look at Maura. 'You told me he would come, my dear. It seems you've picked quite the gallant.'

'Where are the children?'

'Ask Maura.' Wildeham smiled evilly. 'Maura, dear, tell the earl the good news.'

Maura's eyes moved, looking at him directly for the first time. She betrayed no other emotion. 'I've sent them home. They should be there by now. I've given my consent and they're safe now.'

So that was the bargain Wildeham had forced while she'd waited for him. It was hard to breathe.

He felt as he had the one time he'd fought with Elliott. Elliott had hit him in the stomach so hard he'd lost his breath. In a way, he *was* too late. The children might be home now, but that didn't change any of Vale's charges. That particular issue would still be awaiting resolution depending on the outcome of this evening's attempt to rescue Maura.

'I have papers, Chatham,' Wildeham gloated, picking up a sheaf of documents from a nearby table and flourishing them. 'With her name on them, I might add.'

A thousand thoughts pulsed through Riordan's mind. Maura must have been frightened beyond words to have signed those papers. She must have thought there'd been no hope, no other way. Worst of all, she must have thought he wouldn't come, wouldn't save her. The last nearly destroyed him. How could she not know?

Riordan drew a deep breath, determined to hide the anguish ripping through him. He rubbed his hands together in a wiping motion in a common gesture to indicate all was finished. 'Well, that's settled, then. I assume your debt with Harding has been cleared?'

Wildeham nodded and Riordan thought,

Good, one less player in the game. Now this could be between the two of them, no third parties. The children were on their way home to Alixe and Genevra's arms. He would settle later with Vale. First things first—he had to get Maura back. He eyed Wildeham with a sly gaze. 'I find myself reluctant to let her go. Since you won her in a wager, perhaps you'd consent to another wager.'

He saw interest flicker to life in the depths of Wildeham's pale eyes, eyes that had been hardened by dissipation and fast living. This man was a gambler to his core. The only thrill that remained to him was the next dare and the next and they had to be extraordinary in order to appeal. The bigger the risk, the more intense the excitement. For a man of Wildeham's ilk, there was not much left unexplored in his world of depravity.

Wildeham turned an assessing gaze on Maura, a cruel grin taking his face. 'Would you like that, my dear? Would you like me to play for you? Perhaps it would convince you of your worth.' A little flame of hatred kindled in Maura's eyes, the first signs of true life Riordan had seen.

'I think I will play,' Wildeham said. 'But I'll need something in return. It's not fair if I'm the only one putting anything up.' He gave a dramatic pause and thought. 'I have it—if you lose, you come to the wedding tomorrow and sign as one of our witnesses.'

There would be no contesting the legality of the marriage then. How could he contest a proceeding he'd witnessed and approved? Well, he'd worry about that if he lost. 'Cards or dice?' Riordan said calmly.

'I'm a card man.' Wildeham opened a drawer on a side table and pulled out a pack. 'Brand new.' He grinned, certain he had Riordan on the run. Good. Be cocky. It would be that much easier to force a mistake.

Riordan merely nodded. 'Let's play.' It took a man of vice to recognise a fellow spirit. It was time Wildeham was beaten at his own game.

They were going to play for her! Of all the horrible things that had happened today, this was arguably the worst. It promised hope after she'd thought there was none, after she'd given up any ounce of hope for herself and yet, if Riordan won, she had no idea what that might

mean. Had he come solely for the children? Out
of a sense of duty? Her heart had leapt at the
sight of him, pressing into the room, challeng-
ing Wildeham. But his eyes had gone cold at the
sight of her. Of course, the gown was hideous,
something a demi-monde might wear, an imi-
tation of something a lady would put on. And
then he'd bet Wildeham. Did she mean so little
to him that he could afford to lose her?

Yet she wanted him to win so very much.
Whatever disappointments lay at Riordan's
hand, they would be far better than life with
Wildeham. Just two hours in his presence had
assured her that her judgement was correct on
that account. Once she'd made up her mind,
Wildeham had been willing to bargain. If she
signed her name on the betrothal documents
and put on the hideous dress—after all, he'd so
longed to see her in it—he would send the children home post-haste. If not, he'd go ahead and
sell them to a certain establishment with a certain reputation. His men and carriage were waiting. There had been no time to think. No time to
question whether or not Wildeham would keep
his end of the bargain. She'd signed and then
she'd kissed the children goodbye, fighting her

own tears as they were bundled into a carriage and given Chatham's address.

Now Riordan was here and blithely sitting down to cards with the devil's own spawn, her future once more in someone else's hands instead of her own. Riordan's friends stood vigilant on either side of him, sharp eyes no doubt watching for cheating.

She didn't want to be drawn to the game. She wanted to watch dispassionately at a distance. But she couldn't. Riordan drew people like flames drew moths. He could no more be in a room than she could ignore his presence. Maura moved quietly towards the table. There was no question of escape. Digby stood at the door. Riordan might have pushed his way in, but no one was going to push their way out.

They'd settled on the particulars—the best of seven hands of écarté. Riordan was shuffling the deck, removing the two through six of all suits. He handed it to Wildeham to deal out the five cards. Wildeham flipped up the eleventh card to determine the trump suit. Seven of hearts. Riordan made his first proposal. He wanted to exchange two cards. As the dealer, Wildeham could refuse, but the refusal risked costing him a point. Wildeham opted to play it safe and accepted, sliding two cards towards Riordan. Riordan discarded his two other cards and added the new ones to his hand.

Maura held her breath, wondering if he'd make another proposal. The object of the game was to put together the best hand possible to take as many of the five tricks as one could. The possessor of the elder hand, the player not dealing, could make as many proposals as he liked to garner the cards he wanted. The dealer could refuse at any time.

Then they would battle for tricks, highest card taking all. The game itself was fairly straightforward: one point given at the end of each hand to the person winning the most tricks. There were bonus points, too, that made it more of a gamble. It wasn't enough to win the tricks. Players could earn a point for having the king of trump, for taking all five tricks or for defeating a vulnerable player.

'Will you propose again?' Wildeham asked, watching Riordan sort his hand and growing impatient.

'No.' Riordan smiled. 'Don't need to.' Over his shoulder, Maura hazarded a peek into his hand to see if his bravado was earned and then thought better of it. If she was going to look, she'd better be sure her features were schooled. It would do no good to give anything away.

'Maura, pet, you can come look in my hand, if you'd like,' Wildeham crooned. 'You'll bring me good luck, I'm sure.'

She saw Wildeham's intent immediately in the tightened grip of Riordan's hand about his cards. Riordan's deductive skills were beginning to wear off on her. Wildeham's hopes were obvious. He would use his claim on her to distract Riordan. She could already feel his vile hands on her. He would not hesitate to kiss or fondle in the hopes Riordan would play rashly or stupidly. 'I'll just sit here,' she replied sweetly, strategically taking a chair between the two gentlemen.

The first hand, Riordan scored the point, taking three of the five tricks. The second hand, Riordan won the advantage in tricks again, but Wildeham had the devil's own luck, declaring the king of trump for a point, making the score two to one. That was a turning point for Wildeham. The third hand, Riordan elected not to propose an exchange, feeling that his hand was strong enough on his own. The choice made him vulnerable. He started off well enough, taking the first two tricks, but Wildeham held club trumps and took the next three, winning not only a point for the hand but a bonus for defeating a vulnerable player. Wildeham led three to two. For the first time in the game, Riordan was behind.

There were four hands left. The playing shifted, becoming more intense. Both Wildeham and Riordan opted to attempt more exchanges when they had the elder hand, the better to 'see' the deck, to have a sense of what might be in their opponent's hand. In the fourth hand, Riordan lost again. In the fifth, Wildeham, acting as dealer, denied Riordan his first proposal, making himself vulnerable. It was a sign of confidence in his own hand to meet anything Riordan might throw down. The hand was played slowly and with great intent. Maura's knuckles were white where they lay fisted in her lap beneath the table. Her nerves would only serve to fuel Wildeham and to worry Riordan. She breathed more easily after Riordan claimed three, the simple majority to win the hand. She nearly cheered when he went on to win all five tricks, claiming the *vole* and an extra point for the bonus, along with another extra point for defeating a vulnerable player. Wildeham swore colourfully and looked daggers across the table.

Five points to four in Riordan's favour as the sixth hand was dealt. Riordan was now dealer. He flipped the eleventh card trump. Clubs. Wildeham let out a whoop, arms raised. He tossed the king of clubs on the table. 'I've got the king of trumps this time, gentlemen. One point towards me.'

Vale congratulated him. His other men gathered around in excitement. The game was tied. He leered at Maura. 'Remember this night the rest of your life, my dear. It's the night two men of vice gambled for your virtue.' He winked at Vale. 'Such as it is. I do know when a pretty girl has been plucked, not that I'm picky when the girl is as pretty as you, darling.' Maura's cheeks burned with mortification. She kept her eyes down, not daring to look at Riordan. He won the hand.

'This is it.' Wildeham dealt the cards and sorted his hand with the assumed arrogance of a victor despite Riordan being in the lead. They both knew there were too many other ways for

Wildeham to score. With only a deficit of one point, the hand was not a foregone conclusion.

'I'd hate to be you,' Riordan drawled, sorting his own hand. 'You have the harder job. You have to decide how many proposals to accept. You have to take at least one if you want to keep me to a tie. If I'm vulnerable and I win, you'll lose it all.' He was far too relaxed for Maura's tastes. 'On that note, I'll exchange one card.'

'And I'll refuse it,' Wildeham said smugly. 'You're already ahead. A tie won't help me, so what do I care if I win the hand and you're not vulnerable?'

The battle began. Riordan played the ten of hearts, capturing Wildeham's seven. Riordan led again with the jack of spades. Wildeham triumphed with the queen. Their hands seemed to be evenly matched. Riordan won the next trick, lost the following. Wildeham led the king of clubs. Maura's heart sank. Only the ace was higher and it might still be in the deck, unclaimed. The last of her hope slipped away. Riordan flipped his card on to the table. Red flashed. The eight of diamonds lay there. 'That's trump. Trick to me.' Riordan scooped it up and added it to his pile. 'Looks like I have won.'

Maura started to breathe again.

Riordan reached for the papers in the centre of the table. He wasn't fast enough. A knife blade came down, skewering the papers to the table top, just missing his own digits. There was a collective rustling and Maura stifled a gasp. Pistols and knives appeared in nearly every hand. A small gun flashed in Riordan's. He waved it dangerously close to Wildeham's face, undaunted by the weaponry surrounding him. 'Play fair. Those papers are mine. Merrick, grab the papers. If anyone gives him trouble, I shoot the baron where he stands.'

'Get behind me, Maura.' Riordan's voice was deadly cold once Merrick retrieved the papers and tucked them in his coat. Riordan's eyes held Wildeham's without wavering, his free hand behind him, on her arm. 'I'm sorry to have to win and run.' They backed towards the door, Ashe and Merrick covering their retreat against Wildeham's men, most proving to be cowards or mercenaries, unwilling to risk being shot for the sake of another.

But at the door Vale waited, blade in hand. 'You forgot about me, cousin. You're becoming much more trouble than Elliott ever was.' He sneered. 'First a suicide and now a murder—what bad luck your family has.'

Riordan didn't hesitate. 'Looks like we'll have to take you with us.' He fired into Vale's arm, disabling the viscount's knife hand. The viscount crumpled, only to be caught up between Ashe and Merrick. They were out the door, but not nearly free. Riordan pushed her ahead of him as they lumbered down the hall. 'Run! The carriage is outside. We'll catch up.'

Maura ran. The stairs seemed endless, the lobby burgeoning with people whose only purpose was to get in her way. She pushed and she shoved, stumbling and picking herself up until at last she was there at the entrance to Grillon's, the Chatham carriage at the kerb. She flung herself towards it, calling instructions to get the door open. She hurtled inside and squeezed herself into a corner to make room for the others, Merrick climbing on top with the driver, yelling, 'Go, Go!' The carriage lurched into rapid motion, Riordan falling against her at the sudden motion.

'We made it. Vale's passed out. It'll make him more co-operative for the Watch,' someone, Ashe perhaps, said in the darkness. She could hardly make out what arms went with what legs in the tangle of the interior.

'Maura, are you all right?' That was Riordan.

'Yes, are you?' She pushed at the body closest to her, certain it was Riordan's. She could smell him, familiar and warm.

'Maybe. Ouch. Stop pushing at me, I think I may be shot. That bastard, Digby, clipped me.'

Her hands came away in sticky confirmation. 'Oh, my goodness!' Maura gasped. He was bleeding everywhere.

'Somebody tell her, I'll be fine. It's just a scratch.' Riordan laughed, then he collapsed against her, out cold.

Chapter Twenty-Three

The bloody man was lucky he'd passed out. Otherwise she would have slapped him for laughing at such an inappropriate moment. Bullets were no laughing matter, neither were bullet *wounds*, although the doctor assured her Riordan was correct. It was just a scratch and sometimes scratches bled more than they had a right to.

Broken hearts did, too, Maura was discovering. It had taken a night and a day for things to return to normal at Chatham House. Ashe and Merrick had taken themselves and their families off to their residences with promises to return to check on Riordan later. The children had finally settled back into their routine, assured

that Uncle Ree was fine and the world was restored to its right order. Merrick had given her
the baron's papers. She was free. Best of all,
Browning had come that afternoon from De-
Witt's chambers with the news that after the
report of the activities at Grillon's and a closer
look at Vale's personal finances, he'd set aside
any consideration of the Vales as guardians for
the children. Everything had worked out. All
that was left to do was set Riordan free.

Maura approached his bedroom with slow
feet. She dreaded this. He didn't need her any
more. He'd been shot because of her. He deserved to be free. He'd more than paid for it.

She opened the door quietly. Maybe he'd be
asleep. No luck. He was awake, propped up by
pillows, his colour good. It was a scratch, after
all. He wouldn't be moping about like an in-
valid. If it was up to him, he'd be downstairs or
up in the nursery playing with the children. 'Ah,
you're awake.' She pretended surprise.

'Awake and bored, come entertain me with
news.' He patted the bed beside him. How could
a wounded man make a sickbed seem seductive?
'How are you, Maura? No ill effects?' They'd

not spoken since Grillon's, since he'd wagered everything on the turn of a card.

'I'm all right.' She remained standing.

'No, you're not. Now, sit down,' he insisted, tugging at her with his good arm. 'I won't break.'

I might. 'I wanted to tell you I was leaving as soon as Mrs Pendergast can send a new governess.'

He said nothing, his blue eyes staring hard at her, trying to divine answers. She pressed on, unnerved by the silence. 'What I am trying to tell you is that you're free. You don't need to marry me. You've seen Browning's report?'

'I saw it.'

There was more in the report than just the financial records. Frightened at the prospect of facing trial, Vale had confessed to four years of blackmailing Elliott Barrett, easily proven by the payments Browning had discovered in the ledgers. What hadn't shown up in the report was the reason for it. DeWitt had judiciously left out the cause—a seven-year affair with a naval officer currently up for promotion. Maura knew it would take Riordan time to come to grips with his brother's secret, not because he disapproved but because Elliott had not confided in him.

'The children are yours. You can build the life you want,' Maura went on. He should be leaping out of bed. He could have all the un-scheduled outings he wanted, drag the children to White's whenever he desired.

'You're free, too. Is that what you're really telling me?' he quizzed. 'You don't have to marry me? And you don't have to work for me. Merrick and Alixe have offered to take you to Hever with them.' She was free, but her situation was precarious. She couldn't go home. Her uncle had sided with Wildeham. There was no family there for her any longer.

'You were only marrying me for the children. We both understood that. You don't have to pretend otherwise.'

His face grew thunderous. 'I am marrying you because I love you. How many ways can I show you that?'

She took a step backwards under the weight of his declaration. 'You love me?'

'I don't get shot for just anyone.' A ghost of a smile whispered on his lips, his anger fading. 'Ashe asked me if I loved you, if I would have chosen you if I'd been free to choose. My answer is yes, so the bigger question is yours. How about you, Maura? Would you choose me?'

Maura stood in the alcove of St. Martin-in-the-Fields, smoothing the pale-green folds of her wedding gown. She was going to marry Riordan Barrett, Earl of Chatham. More than that, she was going to marry the man she loved and who loved her in return. She'd come a long way since the day she'd disembarked from the Exeter coach. Dreams of family and a home of her own had come true even after she'd given them up for her freedom.

The journey to this day had not been without cost. She'd lost her family. There would be no returning to her uncle's home. There'd been fear and uncertainty and there had been betrayal. But she'd found a family of her own now with Riordan, and Cecilia and William, all of whom waited for her at the end of the aisle.

Uncle Hamish stood with her, ready for the walk to her future. If the church was not quite full, she didn't notice. There were still the lingering remnants of scandal surrounding Riordan's marriage to his governess, even if they had waited a respectful amount of time to marry. But she had eyes only for the handsome man at the end of the aisle and the children standing with him. They'd gone from calling him Uncle Ree to Papa Ree and she liked the sound of it. They still called her Six and that was all right, too. They were putting a good life together and the promise of a future was all the happiness they could wish.

Uncle Hamish placed her hand in Riordan's and her husband-to-be smiled at her, a most wicked smile for a church. But that's what she loved about him—that and a hundred other things. The priest intoned the opening prayer and she took the opportunity to whisper in Riordan's ear the surprise she'd been keeping for just the right moment. 'You're going to be a father in about seven months.'

It wasn't every day she succeeded in shocking Riordan. But this did it. He raised his dark brow and recovered his aplomb. 'Now, that's what I call sinning successfully.'

May 1836—the Royal Academy art exhibition

'I feel ungainly.' Maura put her hand over her belly. It *was* huge, but he loved it. It was late afternoon on a weekday, fashionable society hadn't come out to play and Riordan had Somerset House to himself, free to escort his pregnant wife without society's censure over a woman about to give birth being out in public.

'It will be worth it,' Riordan promised. 'Close your eyes, you can't look until we get there.' He put a hand at her back and another at her arm and whispered, 'You're beautiful to me, that's all that matters.'

'Oh!' Her hand went back to her stomach. 'The baby kicked again.'

'I thought the doctor said babies quietened down before they were born.' Riordan steered her to the right towards the far wall.

'This one isn't.' Maura laughed. 'The kick has been different today, though. Maybe it's a sign.'

'All right, we're here. You can open your eyes.' He brought them to a halt in front of a large canvas featuring an auburn-haired woman, draped on a couch.

Maura's eyes flew open. Riordan took great pleasure in that moment. His wife was speechless. 'It's me,' she said, finding her tongue. He could see her eyes start to well with tears, not an uncommon experience these past months. 'You painted me. It's amazing. How did you do it? I didn't sit for you.'

Riordan squeezed her hand. 'I can paint you by heart.' All those nights he'd lain awake contemplating his luck, watching her sleep, her face had been etched in his mind, from the way her eyes crinkled when she smiled, to the tilt of her nose. Not a contour of her face had escaped him. He was a man in love, a man truly besotted.

She glanced to the side of the painting. 'What's this?' She waddled towards the rosette hanging from a peg and read the trailing ribbons. '"Best new artist." Riordan, I am so proud of you.' He basked in her adulation.

'Oh!' Maura grabbed at her stomach suddenly, a strange look on her face. 'Oh dear, Riordan, I think your baby wants to celebrate.'

They stared at each other for a long moment, both of them grasping what was about to happen. Riordan swept her up into his arms and laughed. 'The last time I was here, this happened, too.' The gallery wasn't crowded, but there were a few people to shoulder past with his wife in his arms. 'Coming through, coming through, I'm going to be a father.' Again. For the second time in a year. In two years, he'd become a father to three children. What were the odds of that? If anyone had told him last year he'd be happily married and the father of three, he'd have laughed and taken that bet. He would have lost and it was a bet he was happy to lose. He leaned down and kissed Maura. 'I'm thinking Six is my lucky number.'

* * * * *

A sneaky peek at next month...

HISTORICAL

IGNITE YOUR IMAGINATION, STEP INTO THE PAST...

My wish list for next month's titles...

In stores from 7th December 2012:

☐ Some Like It Wicked — Carole Mortimer

☐ Born to Scandal — Diane Gaston

☐ Beneath the Major's Scars — Sarah Mallory

☐ Warriors in Winter — Michelle Willingham

☐ A Stranger's Touch — Anne Herries

☐ Oklahoma Wedding Bells — Carol Finch

Available at WHSmith, Tesco, Asda, Eason, Amazon and Apple

Just can't wait?

Special Offers

ery month we put together collections and
ger reads written by your favourite authors.

re are some of next month's highlights—
d don't miss our fabulous discount online!

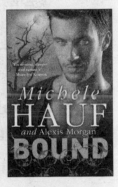

sale 16th November   On sale 16th November   On sale 7th December

Save 20%
on all Special Releases

MILLS & BOON® Book Club

2 Free Books!

Get your free books now at
www.millsandboon.co.uk/freebookoffer

---

fill in the form below and post it back to us

MILLS & BOON® BOOK CLUB™—HERE'S HOW IT WORKS: Accepting your books places you under no obligation to buy anything. You may keep the books return the despatch note marked 'Cancel'. If we do not hear from you, about a th later we'll send you 4 brand-new stories from the Historical series priced at 0* each. There is no extra charge for post and packaging. You may cancel at any otherwise we will send you 4 stories a month which you may purchase or return s – the choice is yours. *Terms and prices subject to change without notice. Offer in UK only. Applicants must be 18 or over. Offer expires 31st January 2013. **For terms and conditions, please go to www.millsandboon.co.uk/freebookoffer**

/Miss/Ms/Mr (please circle)

Name

name

dress

Postcode

hail

d this completed page to: **Mills & Boon Book Club, Free Book er, FREEPOST NAT 10298, Richmond, Surrey, TW9 1BR**

Find out more at
www.millsandboon.co.uk/freebookoffer

Visit us Online

0712/H2YEA

Have Your Say

You've just finished your book.
So what did you think?

We'd love to hear your thoughts on our
'Have your say' online panel
www.millsandboon.co.uk/haveyoursay

* Easy to use
* Short questionnaire
* Chance to win Mills & Boon® goodies